# DESERT

*a novel of terror*

# PLACES

## Blake Crouch

THOMAS DUNNE BOOKS
ST. MARTIN'S MINOTAUR
NEW YORK

for my parents, Clay and Susan Crouch

THOMAS DUNNE BOOKS.
An imprint of St. Martin's Press.

Design by Kathryn Parise

ISBN 0-312-28644-9

Printed in the U.S.A.

*They cannot scare me with their empty spaces*
*Between stars—on stars where no human race is*
*I have it in me so much nearer home*
*To scare myself with my own desert places.*

—Robert Frost, "Desert Places"

# Acknowledgments

I'VE been in good hands from the start. Linda Allen came along with her faith and encouragement and found a home for this story. She's an extraordinary agent and a wonderful friend. Marcia Markland made my first editing experience everything I'd hoped it would be, with grace, humor, and unfailing insight. Bland Simpson, greatest creative writing professor of all time, was the first to believe. His brilliance as a writer is matched only by the generosity he extends to his students. Mary Alice Kier and Anna Cottle have been amazing, and I'm grateful to have them in my corner. And Diana Szu is a superhero. Sam Stout, M.D., Ted Vance, M.D., Michael James, and Marianne Fuierer shared their medical and pharmacological acumen in answering a handful of creepy questions. Paul Lowry was my encyclopedia on firearms. Myrna Woirhaye told me all about ranching in Pinedale, and Sandra L. Mitchell, Ph.D., graciously lent her expertise on the high desert flora and fauna of Sublette County,

Wyoming. Ritchie Kendall, Ph.D., another UNC great, helped me out with a Shakespeare question. All mistakes, exaggerations, and impossibilities are mine. In this moment of completion, the love and sacrifice of my parents, Clay and Susan Crouch, overwhelm me. My brother, Jordan, lets me bounce titles off him even though he never likes any of them. He's a great guy, and he's going to be a writer. In the wife department, I'm blessed beyond belief. Rebecca, your friendship and love guide me through. And finally, a nod to Pamela Bumgarner, who stoked the coals at a delicate time.

PART I

# 1

O N a lovely May evening, I sat on my deck, watching the sun descend upon Lake Norman. So far, it had been a perfect day. I'd risen at 5:00 A.M. as I always do, put on a pot of French roast, and prepared my usual breakfast of scrambled eggs and a bowl of fresh pineapple. By six o'clock, I was writing, and I didn't stop until noon. I fried two white crappies I'd caught the night before, and the moment I sat down for lunch, my agent called. Cynthia fields my messages when I'm close to finishing a book, and she had several for me, the only one of real importance being that the movie deal for my latest novel, *Blue Murder,* had closed. It was good news of course, but two other movies had been made from my books, so I was used to it by now.

I worked in my study for the remainder of the afternoon and quit at 6:30. My final edits of the new as yet untitled manuscript would be finished tomorrow. I was tired, but my new thriller, *The Scorcher,* would be on bookshelves within the week. I savored the exhaustion that followed a full day of work. My hands sore from typing, eyes dry and strained, I shut down the computer and rolled back from the desk in my swivel chair.

I went outside and walked up the long gravel drive toward the mailbox. It was the first time I'd been out all day, and the sharp sunlight burned my eyes as it squeezed through the tall rows of loblollies that bordered both sides of the drive. It was so quiet here. Fifteen miles south, Charlotte was still gridlocked in rush-hour traffic, and I was grateful not to be a part of that madness. As the tiny rocks crunched beneath my feet, I pictured my best friend, Walter Lancing, fuming in his Cadillac. He'd be cursing the drone of horns and the profusion of taillights as he inched away from his suite in uptown Charlotte, leaving the quarterly nature magazine *Hiker* to return home to his wife and children. *Not me,* I thought, *the solitary one.*

For once, my mailbox wasn't overflowing. Two envelopes lay inside, one a bill, the other blank except for my address typed on the outside. *Fan mail.*

Back inside, I mixed myself a Jack Daniel's and Sun-Drop and took my mail and a book on criminal pathology out onto the deck. Settling into a rocking chair, I set everything but my drink on a small glass table and gazed down to the water. My backyard is narrow, and the woods flourish a quarter mile on either side, keeping my home of ten years in isolation from my closest neighbors. Spring had not come this year until mid-April, so the last of the pink and white dogwood blossoms still specked the variably green interior of the surrounding forest. Bright grass ran down to a weathered gray pier at the water's edge, where an ancient weeping willow sagged over the bank, the tips of its branches dabbling in the surface of the water.

The lake is more than a mile wide where it touches my property, making houses on the opposite shore visible only in winter, when the blanket of leaves has been stripped from the trees. So now, in the thick of spring, branches thriving with baby greens and yellows, the lake was mine alone, and I felt like the only living soul for miles around.

I put my glass down half-empty and opened the first envelope. As expected, I found a bill from the phone company, and I scrutinized the lengthy list of calls. When I'd finished, I set it down and lifted the lighter envelope. There was no stamp, which I thought strange, and upon slicing it open, I extracted a single piece of white paper and unfolded it. In the center of the page, one paragraph had been typed in black ink:

> **Greetings. There is a body buried on your property, covered in your blood. The unfortunate young lady's name is Rita Jones. You've seen this missing school-teacher's face on the news, I'm sure. In her jeans pocket you'll find a slip of paper with a phone number on it. You have one day to call that number. If I have not heard from you by 8:00 P.M. tomorrow (5/17), the Charlotte Police Department will receive an anony-mous phone call. I'll tell them where Rita Jones is buried on Andrew Thomas's lakefront property, how he killed her, and where the murder weapon can be found in his house. (I do believe a paring knife is miss-ing from your kitchen.) I hope for your sake I don't have to make that call. I've placed a property marker on the grave site. Just walk along the shoreline toward the southern boundary of your property and you'll find it. I strongly advise against going to the police, as I am always watching you.**

A smile edged across my lips. I even chuckled to myself. Because my novels treat crime and violence, my fans often have a demented sense of humor. I've received death threats, graphic artwork, even notes from people claiming to have murdered in the same fashion as the serial killers in my books. *But I'll save this,* I thought. I couldn't remember one so original.

I read it again, but a premonitory twinge struck me the second time, particularly because the author had some knowledge regarding the layout of my property. And a paring knife was, in fact, missing from my cutlery block. Carefully refolding the letter, I slipped it into the pocket of my khakis and walked down the steps toward the lake.

■

As the sun cascaded through the hazy sky, beams of light drained like spilled paint across the western horizon. Looking at the lacquered lake suffused with deep orange, garnet, and magenta, I stood by the shore for several moments, watching two sunsets collide.

Against my better judgment, I followed the shoreline south and was soon tramping through a noisy bed of leaves. I'd gone an eighth of a mile when I stopped. At my feet, amid a coppice of pink flowering mountain laurel, I saw a miniature red flag attached to a strip of rusted metal thrust into the ground. The flag fluttered in a breeze that curled off the water. *This has to be a joke,* I thought, *and if so, it's a damn good one.*

As I brushed away the dead leaves that surrounded the marker, my heart began to pound. The dirt beneath the flag was packed, not crumbly like undisturbed soil. I even saw half a footprint when I'd swept all the leaves away.

I ran back to the house and returned with a shovel. Because the soil had previously been unearthed, I dug easily through the first foot and a half, directly below where the marker had been placed. At two feet, the head of the shovel stabbed into something soft. My heart stopped. Throwing the shovel aside, I dropped to my hands and knees and clawed through the dirt. A rotten stench enveloped me, and as the hole deepened, the smell grew more pungent.

My fingers touched flesh. I drew my hand back in horror and scrambled away from the hole. Rising to my feet, I stared down at a coffee brown ankle, barely showing through the dirt. The odor of rot overwhelmed me, so I breathed only through my mouth as I took up the shovel again.

When the corpse was completely exposed, and I saw what a month of putrefaction could do to a human face, I vomited into the leaves. I kept thinking that I should have the stomach for this because I write about it. Researching the grisly handiwork of serial killers, I'd studied countless mutilated cadavers. But I had never smelled a human being decomposing in the ground, or seen how insects teem in the moist cavities.

I composed myself, held my hand over my mouth and nose, and peered again into the hole. The face was unrecognizable, but the body was undoubtedly that of a short black female, thick in the legs, plump through the torso. She wore a formerly white shirt, now marred with blood and dirt, the fabric rent over much of the chest, primarily in the vicinity of her heart. Jean shorts covered her legs down to the knees. I got back down on all fours, held my breath, and reached for one of her pockets. Her legs were mushy and turgid, and I had great difficulty forcing my hand into the tight jeans. Finding nothing in the first pocket, I stepped across the hole and tried the other. Sticking my hand inside it, I withdrew a slip of paper from a fortune cookie and fell back into the leaves, gasping for clean lungfuls of air. On one side, I saw the phone number; on the other: "YOU ARE THE ONLY FLOWER OF MEDITATION IN THE WILDERNESS."

In five minutes, I'd reburied the body and the marker. I took a small chunk of granite from the shore and placed it on the thicketed grave site. Then I returned to the house. It was quarter to eight, and there was hardly any light left in the sky.

■

Two hours later, sitting on the sofa in my living room, I dialed the number on the slip of paper. Every door to the house was locked, most of the lights turned on, and in my lap, a cold satin stainless .357 revolver.

I had not called the police for a very good reason. The claim that it was my blood on the woman was probably a lie, but the paring knife had been missing from my kitchen for weeks. Also, with the Charlotte Police Department's search for Rita Jones dominating local news headlines, her body on my property, murdered with my knife, possibly with my fingerprints on it, would be more than sufficient evidence to indict me. I'd researched enough murder trials to know that.

As the phone rang, I stared up at the vaulted ceiling of my living room, glanced at the black baby grand piano I'd never learned to play, the marble fireplace, the odd artwork that adorned the walls. A woman named Karen, whom I'd dated for nearly two years, had convinced me to buy half a dozen pieces of art from a recently deceased minimalist from New York, a man who signed his work "Loman." I hadn't initially taken to Loman, but Karen had promised me I'd eventually "get" him. Now, $27,000 and one fiancée lighter, I stared at the ten-by-twelve-foot abomination that hung above the mantel: shit brown on canvas, with a basketball-size yellow sphere in the upper right-hand corner. Aside from *Brown No. 2,* four similar marvels of artistic genius pockmarked other walls of my home, but these I could suffer. Mounted on the wall at the foot of the staircase, it was *Playtime,* the twelve-thousand-dollar glass-encased heap of stuffed animals, sewn together in an orgiastic conglomeration, which reddened my face even now. But I smiled, and the knot that had been absent since late winter shot a needle of pain through my gut. My Karen ulcer. *You're still there. Still hurting me. At least it's you.*

The second ring.

I peered up the staircase that ascended to the exposed second-floor hallway, and closing my eyes, I recalled the party I'd thrown just a week ago—guests laughing, talking politics and books, filling up my silence. I saw a man and a woman upstairs, elbows resting against the oak banister, overlooking the living room, the wet bar, and the kitchen. Holding their wineglasses, they waved down to me, smiling at their host.

The third ring.

My eyes fell on a photograph of my mother—a five-by-seven in a stained-glass frame, sitting atop the obsidian piano. She was the only family member with whom I maintained regular contact. Though I had relatives in the Pacific Northwest, Florida, and a handful in the Carolinas, I saw them rarely—at reunions, weddings, or funerals that my mother shamed me into attending with her. But with my father having passed away and a brother I hadn't seen in thirteen years, family meant little to me. My friends sustained me, and contrary to popular belief, I didn't have the true reclusive spirit imputed to me. I did need them.

In the photograph, my mother is squatting down at my father's grave, pruning a tuft of carmine canna lilies in the shadow of the headstone. But you can only see her strong, kind face among the blossoms, intent on tidying up her husband's plot of earth under that magnolia he'd taught me to climb, the blur of its waxy green leaves behind her.

The fourth ring.

"Did you see the body?"

It sounded as if the man were speaking through a towel. There was no emotion or hesitation in his staccato voice.

"Yes."

"I gutted her with your paring knife and hid the knife in your house. It has your fingerprints all over it." He cleared his throat. "Four months ago, you had blood work done by Dr. Xu. They misplaced a vial. You remember having to go back and give more?"

"Yes."

"I stole that vial. Some is on Rita Jones's white T-shirt. The rest is on the others."

"What others?"

"I make a phone call, and you spend the rest of your life in prison, possibly death row. . . ."

"I just want you—"

"Shut your mouth. You'll receive a plane ticket in the mail. Take the flight. Pack clothes, toiletries, nothing else. You spent last summer in Aruba. Tell your friends you're going again."

"How did you know that?"

"I know many things, Andrew."

"I have a book coming out," I pleaded. "I've got readings scheduled. My agent—"

"Lie to her."

"She won't understand me just leaving like this."

"Fuck Cynthia Mathis. You lie to her for your safety, because if I even suspect you've brought someone along or that someone knows, you'll go to jail or you'll die. One or the other, guaranteed. And I hope you aren't stupid enough to trace this number. I promise you it's stolen."

"How do I know I won't be hurt?"

"You don't. But if I get off the phone with you and I'm not convinced you'll be on that flight, I'll call the police tonight. Or I may visit you while you're sleeping. You've got to put that Smith and Wesson away sometime."

I stood up and spun around, the gun clenched in my sweaty hands. The house was silent, though chimes on the deck were clanging in a zephyr. I looked through the large living room windows at the black lake, its wind-rippled surface reflecting the pier lights. The blue light at the end of Walter's pier shone out across the water from a distant inlet. His "Gatsby light," we called it. My eyes scanned the grass and the edge of the trees, but it was far too dark to see anything in the woods.

"I'm not in the house," he said. "Sit down."

I felt something well up inside of me—anger at the fear, rage at this injustice.

"Change of plan," I said. "I'm going to hang up, dial nine one one, and take my chances. You can go—"

"If you aren't motivated by self-preservation, there's an old woman named Jeanette I could—"

"I'll kill you."

"Sixty-five, lives alone, I think she'd love the company. What do you think? Do I have to visit your mother to show you I'm serious? What is there to consider? Tell me you'll be on that plane, Andrew. Tell me so I don't have to visit your mother tonight."

"I'll be on that plane."

The phone clicked, and he was gone.

# 2

O N the muggy morning of May 21, as raindrops splattered onto the sidewalk, I locked the door to my lake house and carried an enormous black duffel bag toward a white Cadillac DeVille. Walter Lancing opened the trunk from the driver's seat, and I tossed the bag inside.

"Where the hell are you going?" he asked cheerfully as we rolled slowly down my drive. I'd called him three hours ago, told him I needed a ride to the airport, and to pick me up by 10:30, hanging up before he could question me.

"Going away for a while," I said.

"Where? That's a big piece of luggage you got back there." He was smiling. I could hear it in his voice as I watched my house dwindle away in the side mirror.

"Just away," I said.

"Are you being intentionally vague?" Beads of sweat had formed on his unshaven face, and he ran his fingers through his short gray hair. He glanced at me, awaiting my reply as rain fell in sheets from the charcoal sky, followed by a growl of thunder. "Andy, what's wrong?"

"Nothing. I finished my book. I'm tired. I need a break—you know how it goes." Walter sighed, and I stared out the window as trees rushed by, listening to rain patter on the windshield. Walter's wife, Beth, had ridden in this car recently. I could smell her body wash—sweet, icy juniper. Her pink emery board lay on the floor mat at my feet.

"You going back to Aruba?" he asked.

"No." I wasn't going to lie outright to him.

"So I guess you aren't telling Cynthia, either." I shook my head. "With *The Scorcher* coming out, she's gonna go apeshit."

"That's why I didn't tell her. She's a drill sergeant. Call her tonight at home for me, would you? Tell her I said I'm tired of writing, I need a vacation, and not to worry."

"And when she asks me where you went?"

"Tell her all you know is it's some tiny island in the South Pacific."

"She'll think I'm lying."

"That's her problem. She's not your agent."

"Please tell me what's going—"

"Don't ask, Walter."

The rain was still pouring when we turned southbound onto I-77. I closed my eyes and took a careful breath, my heart dancing like I'd thrown down two shots of espresso. I wanted to turn back. The book tour, and relaxing in the comfort of my home while summer burgeoned around the lake, was how I'd envisioned spending the coming months.

"Call me," Walter said. "Or write. Just let me know you're okay."

"If it's possible, I will."

"Need me to get your mail and take care of your bills?"

"Yeah. I meant to ask you before."

"You're scaring me, Andy," he said.

The scurry of windshield wipers swinging back and forth and the groan of the engine became deafening. I fiddled with the automatic window, flicking the tiny button with my middle finger, though nothing happened. The child-safety lock was on.

The minuscule skyline of Charlotte rose out of the green piedmont distance, the buildings decapitated, their pinnacles cloaked in the low ceiling of storm clouds. Walter looked over at me, attempting a smile. "I'm sure you'll be fine."

"I really don't know. That's the thing."

At eleven o'clock, we arrived at the main entrance of Douglas International Airport. We got out of the car, and I lifted my bag from the trunk and hoisted it up onto my shoulder.

"I'll come in with you if you want," Walter said.

"You can't." I glanced around at the crowd of travelers moving through the automatic doors. No one seemed to be paying us any attention, so I pulled out a manila envelope from a pocket on my bag and discreetly tossed it into the trunk.

"If I'm not back by the first of September, you can open it."

"September?"

"Walter. Listen to me. Don't show it to anyone. If the time comes and I'm not back, you'll know what to do with what's inside. I wrote instructions." He slammed the trunk shut.

Our eyes locked. His searched mine, confused, apprehensive. I took him in whole so I could carry his image with me—him standing there in that granite gray suit, no tie, a white oxford shirt with the top two buttons undone. My best friend. Walter. *Will I look back on this moment and regret not letting you help me? My God.*

"See you around," I said. Then I slapped him on the shoulder and walked into the airport.

•

I peered out the circular window and guessed that the jet was cruising somewhere over the plains. Even at six miles above the earth, I could only see a tawny ocean extending from horizon to horizon. In first class, I reclined, unbuckled, in a plush seat. Through the curtain that separated me from coach, I registered the discontented murmur of a hundred miserable passengers. I couldn't remember the last time I'd flown coach, and amid the fear that accompanied me to Denver, I found this smallest degree of luxury a comfort.

•

I stepped into the terminal. As I stared down the long corridor bustling with impatient travelers, I saw an old white man in a black chauffeur's suit staring at me. He held a piece of cardboard displaying my last name printed in tall, thin letters. I approached him.

"I'm Andrew Thomas," I said. The brim of the man's hat came only to my shoulders. He looked me up and down with wide, uneven eyes.

"Welcome to Denver. Name's Hiram," he rasped, and a smile spread suddenly across his gaunt, sinking face. "I have a limousine waiting for you outside. Shall we get your luggage?"

I followed him through the concourse, and for an old man, his stride was fast and steady. In no time, we reached the baggage claim.

As we waited for my duffel bag, I asked him, "So you know where to take me?"

"Yes sir," he said.

"Where?"

He frowned reproachfully. "Now, I was told to keep that a surprise, Mr. Thomas. I got a pretty penny for keeping this a secret, so I can't go spoiling it for you."

"You won't spoil it for me," I said, forcing myself to laugh good-naturedly, attempting to put him at ease. "Really. I'll double what he's paying you." Hiram laughed and shook his head.

"He said you'd probably try something like this. Told me to tell him if you did and he'd pay me twice what you offered."

"Fine," I said. "Forget it. Let it be a secret, then. Don't tell him I asked."

I saw my bag gliding toward us, but when I reached for it, Hiram grabbed my arm.

"Now, that's my job, Mr. Thomas."

"No, really, it's okay. That's a heavy bag."

"I get paid well for what I do, Mr. Thomas. Let me do my job." He stepped in front of me and heaved my bag awkwardly off the conveyor belt.

"I have breakable items in there," I said. "I'd prefer to carry it."

"No," he said flatly, and began walking away.

"Stop!" I yelled, drawing glances from the other passengers waiting for their luggage. He stopped, and I ran up to him and jerked the bag off his shoulder. "I'd prefer to carry it," I said. Hiram's sagging eyes narrowed. "I have to use the bathroom," I said. "I'll be back."

I found a rest room and squeezed into the last stall. Sitting down on the toilet, I opened the bag and could immediately tell it had been sifted, for my clothes were in shambles. Reaching down, I retrieved the black gun case I'd declared at the ticket counter.

I unlocked and opened the case, took out the .357, and set it on top of the clothes. I found the box of rounds buried under my socks, and I tore it open and loaded five semijacketed hollow-points into the cylinder. Then, with the .357 stuffed into the waistband of my khakis, and my oversized green polo shirt pulled down over my waist, I put the empty gun case and the box of rounds back into the duffel bag, zipped it up, and exited the stall.

Three men stood at the urinals, and I strode nervously past them. *If you get caught, this is prison,* I thought, moving through the swarm of people back toward Hiram. The gun felt so heavy, like it might fall out of my pants onto the floor.

We reached the entrance of the airport, and Hiram led me outside to a black limousine. I let him load my bag into the trunk, and then he opened the door for me and I climbed inside, half-expecting to find someone waiting for me. But there was no one—just the immaculate gray interior of the limousine.

When Hiram had settled into the driver's seat and started the car, he looked back and said, "There's a minibar and a TV if you're interested. Just let me know if you need anything else, Mr. Thomas."

Hiram pulled out of the parking space and drove away from the airport. Staring out the deeply tinted windows, beyond the glare of the tarmac, I saw a brown throng of mountains in the western distance. I wanted to lose myself in them and escape whatever hell awaited me.

# 3

**A N** hour later, I stood watching Hiram's black limousine roll down the exit ramp and speed away on the interstate, heading back toward Denver. Lifting my bag, I carried it into the shade of an aspen near the Motel 6 office. In the heat of the sun, it seemed impossible that snow glistened on the mountaintops. Across the interstate, thirty miles west, the front range of the Rocky Mountains swept up out of the plain without the warning of foothills, and though the sky shone blue directly above, thunderclouds clustered around the highest peaks. Lightning flickered farther back in the mountains, but I never heard the thunder that followed.

Sitting in the cool grass, I opened the envelope Hiram had left with me. The note inside, identical in form to its predecessor, put knots in my craw as I read the black type:

You should be reading this around two in the afternoon at the Motel 6 on I-25 north of Denver. Get a
room and pay cash for it so you can check in under
the name Randy Snider. Be packed and ready to go at
6:00 A.M. tomorrow.

•

Room 112 was on the ground level. My nerves were frayed, so I
checked the closet, the shower, even under the bed—anyplace large
enough for a man to hide. When I felt confident I was alone, I closed
the blinds and locked the door. Then I lay down on the bed with the
gun and a book and read all afternoon.

•

Sometime after nine o'clock, the sky slipped from navy into black.
Unable to keep my eyes open, I noticed the words on the page
beginning to blur. Fatigue wore me down, though I fought to stay
awake. A line of storms was rolling in from Rocky Mountain
National Park, and every few seconds, thunder cracked and lightning flashed through the blinds.

Starving, I ran outside to the vending machines and bought a
pack of crackers and two cans of soda. By the time I returned to my
door, a drenching rain was falling from the sky, and the wind gusted,
flinging dust in my eyes. As I opened the door and stepped across
the threshold, I glanced back at the parking lot. There were only
three cars, briefly visible when lightning stoked the sky with a yel-
lowish blue explosion of electricity.

I shut the door and locked it. Storm warnings scrolled across the
bottom of the television screen in alarming red. Within minutes, I finished the sodas and devoured the crackers, and, having satisfied my

appetite, my exhaustion became complete. I cut out the lights, slipped out of my tennis shoes, and climbed into bed. Nothing could stop my eyes from closing, not even the knowledge that he was coming.

I felt constrained beneath the covers, so I lay on top of them and placed the .357 on the bedside table. *I'll only sleep for an hour,* I promised myself. *One hour, no longer.*

.

A deafening blast of thunder shattered the sky—so loud, it seemed the storm was in the room. My eyes opened, and I saw the door swinging back and forth and lightning striking a mountain peak. I glanced at the alarm clock: 3:15.

*The door is open,* I thought, and I reached for the gun on the bedside table but only palmed the smooth surface of the wood. A stabbing pain shot through my left arm, and I jerked up in bed. When I looked down at the floor, I shrieked. A dark figure crouched on all fours.

My mouth turned cottony, and I could think of nothing but running before it stabbed me again. I tried to lunge off the other side of the bed and move toward the door, but nothing happened. It felt as if boulders had been strapped to my arms and legs. Even my fingers were incapacitated, and I fell back, my head sinking into the soft pillow. My eyes began to close as the dark figure stood and moved to the foot of the bed. It spoke to me, but the words melted.

Lightning, black . . .

.

Pain and darkness. The throbbing of an interstate beneath me. Muffled jazz music . . .

.

I opened my eyes to pure darkness. My hands were cuffed behind my back, feet bound with thick rope, and an aching thirst wrenched my gut. Through chapped, splitting lips, I gave voice to a broken scream. An antique moon appeared, huge and yellow. The shadowy figure of a man reached toward me, and I felt the prick of a needle. When I groaned, he said, "This will all be over soon." Darkness again . . .

■

Sunlight flooded across my eyelids. On my back, sweating, I perceived the softness of a mattress beneath me and a pillow supporting my head. My hands and feet were no longer tied, so I pulled a blanket over my eyes to block the sun.

*Be packed and ready to go at 6:00 A.M. tomorrow.*

Sitting up, I looked for the alarm clock. I wasn't in the Motel 6.

In the small square room, my bed rested flush against the back wall, one window at the level of the bed showering brilliant sunlight into the room. Black iron bars stretched across the window, and I knew they were for me. The rough, unembellished walls were built of mud red logs, each a foot in diameter, and the floor was stone. The only other furniture consisted of a bedside table, a chair, and a tottering desk pushed against the opposite wall, beside a closed door. I moved to the window and gazed through the bars.

A vast expanse of semiarid desert stretched out before me, the land flat and ridden with low homogenous vegetation. No power lines, no pavement, no signs of civilization outside this tiny room. I felt utterly alone. The sky was turquoise, and though warm in my room, I judged from the intensity of the sun that it was torrid outside.

Turning from the window, I noticed a piece of paper on the desk across the room. I stepped onto the stone floor, cold as steel despite the intolerable heat, then crossed the room and lifted the sheet of paper off the desk.

**Before we meet, let me emphasize the futility of escape, deception, or destroying me. If you'll open the middle drawer of the desk, you'll find an envelope. Take a moment to look inside.**

When I opened the envelope, I gasped: photos of me reaching down into Rita Jones's grave, a crudely sketched map of my lake property, disclosing the location of four bodies, and three typed pages giving details of the killings and revealing in which closet of my house the paring knife could be found. There was also a newspaper clipping regarding the sentencing of a man whose name (along with all other pertinent information) had been blacked out. Across the headline, he'd scribbled "INNOCENCE TAKES THE PUNISHMENT FOR MY CRIME." I returned to the letter.

**Prayers for my health and safety are in order, because there is another envelope with a map, showing where the bodies really are and telling where the knife really is. In two months, someone will deliver that envelope to the Charlotte Police Department. If I'm not there to stop them in person, you, Andrew Thomas, will go to prison. People have been convicted with less evidence than I have against you, and I've already put two individuals on death row for my crimes. (Like the newspaper clipping?)**

**Last thing. Know that your mother's safety hinges on your conduct here. Now, you've had quite a journey. Rest as much as you like, and when you're ready to learn why I've brought you here, knock on the door.**

I returned to the bed and, leaning against the barred window, looked out again upon the desert. My eyes filled with tears as I beheld the wilderness. Aside from the windblown motion of the tumbleweeds dispersing their seed, there was no movement. It was a wasteland, a deadened landscape, which at another time might have been serene. But in my present condition, it only enhanced the foreboding. Wiping my eyes, I rose from the bed, and my heart galloped as I approached the door.

# 4

A slot six inches high and a foot wide had been cut into the center of the sturdy wooden door. I knelt down and pushed on the metal sheet, but it wouldn't budge. Standing again, I drew a deep breath. Weak and hungry, it was impossible to know how long I'd lain unconscious in this room. My arms were sore and speckled with needle pricks.

Timidly, I knocked on the door and then retreated to the bed. Footsteps soon approached, clicking softly against the stone outside. The metal panel slid up, and I glimpsed another room: bookshelves, a stack of records, a white kerosene heater, a breakfast table . . . .

In place of the panel, a flap of bubble wrap descended. Someone stood before the opening, though only a form without detail, blurred behind the sheet of quarter-size plastic bubbles.

"Come here," he said. I inched toward the door. When I was a few feet away, he said, "Stop. Turn around."

I turned and waited. The bubble wrap crinkled, and I assumed he'd lifted the plastic and was now appraising my condition. After a moment, he said, "Come to the door." The slot had been cut at waist level, and when I reached the door and knelt down to peer out, he said, "No, no, don't look at me. Sit with your back to the door."

I obeyed. Though it terrified me to be in proximity to him, I emphatically reassured myself that he hadn't brought me into a desert just to kill me in my first moments of consciousness.

"How do you feel?" he asked, and in his voice I sensed true concern. He sounded nothing like the man on the phone. His voice had a slight buzzing quality, as if he spoke with the aid of a speech enhancement device. Though his voice was familiar, I couldn't place him, and I distrusted my perception after spending an indeterminate number of hours unconscious under a slew of narcotics.

"I feel groggy," I said, my tone as demure as possible. I didn't want to excite him.

"That'll wear off."

"You wrote those letters? Killed that teacher?"

"Yes and yes."

"Where am I?"

"Suffice it to say that you're in the middle of a desert, and were you to escape, you'd die of thirst and heat exhaustion before you reached the outskirts of civilization."

"How long will I—"

"No more questions regarding your quasi-captivity. I won't tell you when or where you are."

"What will you tell me?"

"You're here to get an education." He paused. "If you only knew. The substance of your learning will become manifest, so be patient."

"Can I please have my things?"

He sighed, the first sign of frustration boiling under his breath.

"We'll talk about *that* later." Then his voice softened, shedding its edge. "Pretend you're an infant, Andrew. A tiny, helpless infant. Right now, in your room, you're in the womb. You don't understand how to use your senses, how to think, how to reason. Rely on me for everything. I'm going to teach you how to see the world again. I'll feed your mind first. Fatten it up on the most brilliant thinkers in human history." A white hand pushed through the bubble wrap and dropped a book onto the floor.

"Your first meal," he said as I lifted a hardback of *The Prince*. "Machiavelli. The man's a genius. Undisputedly. Are you familiar with Hannibal, the general from Carthage who ransacked Rome? Marched his men across the Alps with an army of war elephants."

"I know who he was."

"Well, he marched his army all over the Mediterranean coast and Eastern Europe, but what made Hannibal's army singular was that there was no dissension among his soldiers. Different nationalities, beliefs, languages, and no dissension in the ranks. You know what made that peace possible?" he asked. "In the words of Machiavelli, Hannibal's 'inhuman cruelty, which, with his boundless valor, made him revered and terrible in the sight of his soldiers, but without that cruelty, his other virtues were not sufficient to produce this effect.' " He was silent for a moment, and I could hear only the dry, scorching wind pushing against the glass panes and my captor's escalated breathing. " 'Inhuman cruelty,' " he repeated. "That gives me chills." His voice had turned passionate, as though he were speaking to his lover. "So," he said, "start reading that tonight, and we'll talk about it tomorrow. Are you hungry?"

"Yes, I'm starving."

"Good. I'm gonna make dinner now, so why don't you start on that book. I hope broiled shrimp on angel-hair pasta sounds good to you." He ripped the bubble wrap away and shoved the metal panel back over the opening. My head dropped in relief that he was gone, and I sat motionless in my white bathrobe, staring vacantly into the floor.

■

A small lamp, screwed into the wall, exuded dim, barely sufficient light onto the pages. Because he'd yet to give me the duffel bag, I didn't have the aid of my glasses, so my eyes were failing me.

I dropped *The Prince* onto the floor, having finished half of it. I hoped that would be enough for him. When I reached up and turned off the lamp, the placid light of a full moon flooded in between the bars, soft and soothing. I would've dreaded to spend my first conscious night in the perfect darkness of a new moon.

The room had grown unbearable from a day's accumulation of sunlight, and though the heat had dissipated from the desert with the onslaught of night, it had lingered in my room. So I'd opened the window when the sun set, and now the dry chill of the desert night infiltrated the room, forcing me to burrow under the fleece blankets.

Closing my eyes, I listened. Through the open window, owls screeched and coyotes or wild dogs yapped at the moon, though they seemed a great distance away. Since dinner, I hadn't heard a peep from him. No footsteps, no breathing, nothing.

For the last hour, jazz music had filled the cabin. It came quietly at first, stealing in like a whisper, so that I heard only the guttural rumblings of a bass. The volume rose, and the ride cymbal pattern and the offbeat swish of a closing hi-hat pulsed into the room. When the piano and trumpet and saxes climaxed through the wall, I suddenly recognized the song, and it took me back twenty years, to a different time, a different life. It was Miles Davis, John Coltrane, Julian "Cannonball" Adderley, Paul Chambers, Bill Evans, and

Jimmy Cobb playing "All Blues," a moody, blues form piece in ⅛, off the 1959 album *Kind of Blue*.

An acute scream soared above the music. I sat up and listened. Another scream ruptured the night. Clutching the iron bars, I turned my eyes on the desert, but saw nothing save miles of moonlit sagebrush. Again, a scream—a woman's, closer than before.

Fifty feet away, a figure stumbled through the desert, choking for breath. When it was halfway past the window frame, a second, larger figure entered on the left side. It lunged upon the smaller figure and drove it into the ground at the foot of a greasewood shrub.

I heard a female voice, crying, shriller screams, pleadings, but the words were indecipherable when they reached my ears. The larger figure kicked at the ground. Then it knelt down, thrusting.

More screams, the loudest, most piercing yet. Silence.

Now only the large figure stood, staring at the ground. In a measured pace, it walked back in the direction from which it had come, pulling by long black hair what it had chased through the desert. I heard the footsteps and what it dragged sliding through the dirt, the woman's legs still twitching.

Suddenly, it turned and looked in my direction. Moonlight, bluish and surreal, streamed across the stranger's face.

I froze. My brother, Orson, stood smiling on the desert.

# 5

**A** stiff purple dawn unfolded on the desert, ending a terrible, sleepless night. I realized from here on out, whenever I closed my eyes, I would always see a man on a moonlit desert, dragging a woman through the dirt by her hair.

At the approach of footsteps, I sat up in bed. A dead bolt turned and the door swung open, revealing a man of my proportions: same thin, muscular build, same stark blue eyes. Similar but not identical, his face looked like the ideal of mine, more handsome in its superior proportionality. He stood grinning in the doorway, and in contrast to my unkempt graying hair, his crew cut shone a perfect brown. In addition to black snakeskin boots and faded blue jeans, he wore a bloody white T-shirt with sweat marks extending down from the armpits. I wondered fleetingly why he perspired so profusely before the sun had even risen. His arms were stronger than mine, and as he leaned against the door frame, he took an aggressive bite out of a large burgundy apple.

I couldn't speak. It was like seeing not the ghost of a loved one, but the demon. Tears burned in my eyes. *This is not real. This cannot be my brother, this terrible man.*

"I have missed you so much," Orson said, still hovering in the doorway. I could only stare back into his blue eyes.

Orson had disappeared from Appalachian State University our junior year, my last image that of him standing in the doorway of our dorm room.

"You won't see me for a while," he had said. And I hadn't, from that day to this. The police had given up. He'd just vanished. My mother and I had hired detectives: nothing. We feared he was dead.

Now he apologized. "I wouldn't have had you see that last night. The consequence of using old rope, I guess." I noticed fresh scratch marks on his neck and face. Specks of glitter glinted on his cheeks, and I wondered if they'd come off the woman's fingernails when she struggled. "You want breakfast?" he asked. "Coffee's brewing."

I shuddered, repulsed. "Are you kidding me?"

"I wanted to keep you in here for several days before bringing you out and revealing myself, but after last night . . . well, there's really no use is there?"

Sweat slid down my sides.

As he bit again into the apple, Orson began to walk up a short hallway. "Come on," he said.

I climbed down off the bed and followed him out of my room, heading toward the front of the cabin. My legs felt unstable, like they might sink right down into a puddle on the floor.

"Have a seat," he said, pointing to a black leather sofa pushed against the left-hand wall. As I walked into the living room, I glanced behind me. At the terminus of a narrow hallway, two rooms, side by side, constructed the backbone of the cabin, mine on the left, a door without a dead bolt or a centered metal panel on the right. A small Monet of a skiff gliding under a stone bridge hung from a log between the two doors.

The walls of the living room were covered, floor to ceiling, with books. They stood on rustic shelves that protruded from the logs, and I was amazed at the diversity of the titles. I recognized, on the end of one shelf, the colorful jackets of the five books I'd written.

My brother walked to the other side of the room, which became a tiny kitchen. A record player sat on a stool by the front door, a three-foot stack of records beside it. Orson looked at me and, smiling, set the needle on a record. "Freddie Freeloader" sprang out from two large speakers, and I eased down on the sofa.

As the song progressed, Orson took a seat on the other end of the couch. The way he stared unnerved me. I wanted my glasses.

"Do you think I could have my things now?"

"Oh, you mean this?" Nonchalantly, he pulled my .357 out of his jeans pocket. "I did tell you to bring the Smith and Wesson, didn't I?" His voice filled with angry sarcasm as his cold eyes dilated and burned through me.

"I'm sorry," I said, shifting uncomfortably on the couch, mouth running dry. "Wouldn't you have done the same? I mean, I didn't know—"

"Trying to put me in your shoes won't work." He walked to the record player and lifted the needle. The cabin now in absolute silence, he moved to the center of the living room.

"You fucked up, Andy. I told you just bring clothes and toiletries, and you brought a gun and a box of bullets." He spoke casually, as though we lounged on a back porch, smoking cigars.

"When you don't follow my instructions, that hurts both of us, and the only thing I can think of to do is show you that not following them isn't in your best interest." He opened the cylinder of the .357 and showed me five empty chambers. "You fucked up once, so we'll load one bullet." He took a round from his pocket and slipped it into a chamber.

I grew sick with fear. "Orson, you can't."

"Andy-Andy-Andy. You never tell a man with a loaded weapon what to do." He spun the cylinder, flipped it back into the gun, and cocked the hammer. "Let me explain how this punishes me also, because I don't want you to think I'm doing this just for kicks.

"I've gone to a great deal of trouble to bring you out here, and if your luck suddenly runs out and the twenty percent chance of this bullet being in the hot chamber bites your ass, I've done a lot of work for nothing. But I'm willing to take that chance to teach you a lesson about following my instructions."

When he pointed the gun at my chest, I uselessly held out my hands. He squeezed the trigger—*click*—and took a bite of his apple. I could hardly breathe, and as I buried my face in my hands, Orson put the record back on. The music started again, and he snapped his fingers to the offbeat, smiling warmly at me as he returned to the couch. When he'd removed the round from the chamber, he set the gun on the floor and plopped back down beside me. A wave of nausea watered my mouth, and I thought I might be sick.

*Holy fucking shit, he's out of his goddamned mind. I'm going to die. I'm alone in a desert with a psychopath who is my brother. My fucking brother.*

"Andy, you're free to roam the house now, and the desert. The shed outside is off-limits, and I'm gonna lock your door every night when you go to bed. You can quit pissing in the bowl. Shower at the well by the outhouse. It's cold, but you'll get used to it. The electricity comes from a new generator out back, but I've been too busy to put in plumbing."

"May I use the outhouse now?" I asked, scarcely able to muster my voice.

"Sure. Always let me know when you leave. I don't ever want to have to come find you."

Still shaking, I crossed the room and opened the door to sunlight ripening upon the russet wilderness. I shivered, girding the white bathrobe I'd worn for the last two days more snugly around my waist. When I reached back to shut the door, Orson stood in the threshold.

"I have missed you," he said.

I looked at him, and for a second he was vulnerable, like the brother I'd loved when we were young. His eyes pleaded for something, but I was in no condition to consider what they wanted.

"Who was she?" I asked.

He knew damn well who I meant, but he said nothing. We just stared at each other, a connection kindling that had lain dormant almost to its death. There remained combustible matter between us. I wasn't going to wait for him to close the door, so I turned away to walk down into the chilled dirt.

"Andy," he said, and I stopped on the steps, but I didn't look back. "Just a waitress."

# 6

I stood on the rickety front porch, in the shadow of a tin roof supported by rotten four-by-fours. A strong, steady breeze blew in from the desert, carrying the sweet, piquant smell of sagebrush, scorched earth, and flowers unknown to me.

Four wobbly rocking chairs, two on either side of the door, swayed imperceptibly, but I sat down on the steps and shoved my bare feet into shaded dirt, still cool where it escaped the sun. My eyes wandered along the northern horizon, a mass of foothills and mountains. At least thirty miles away, there was no texture to their slopes. Only hunter green at the lower elevations, denoting evergreen forests, then shattered gray rock, then cloudlike glacier fields that would never melt.

Sixty yards off the left side of the porch stood a large shed. It looked hastily built and new, its tin roof and smooth boards of yellow pine glowing in the sinking sun. A chain was wrapped snakelike around the latch that connected the double doors. Tire tracks led straight to the shed.

A mile or so beyond, the desert rose several hundred feet to a ridge of rusty bluffs that extended south, sloping gently back to the desert floor. Scraggy junipers lined the top, their jagged silhouettes blackening against the sky.

Since dawn, I'd been trying to read Machiavelli in my room. Hot and unable to concentrate on anything except how I might escape, I'd come outside looking for relief in a breeze. But even in the wind, sweat stung my eyes, moistening my skin and hair. Inside, I heard another jazz record—such an eerie sound track to this empty desert, the music so full, effecting thoughts of crowded New York City clubs and people crammed into compact spaces. Normally, I despise crowds and proximity, but now the claustrophobic confines of a raucous nightclub seemed comforting.

I sat on the steps for the better part of an hour, watching the desert turn scarlet beneath the sun. My mind blanked, and I became so engrossed in the perpetuation of mindlessness that I started when the front door squeaked open behind me. Orson's boots clunked hollowly against the wood.

"Will you be hungry soon?" he asked. The rumble of his scratchy voice caused my stomach to flutter. I couldn't accept that we were together again. His presence still horrified me.

"Yes."

"I thought I'd grill a couple of steaks," he said, and I could tell he was smiling, hoping I'd be impressed. I wondered if he were trying to make up for nearly killing me. As children, whenever we fought, he'd always try to win me back with gifts, flattery, or, as in this case, food. "You want a drink?"

*God yes.*

I turned around and looked up at him. "If you've got it, Jack Daniel's would be nice."

He walked back inside and returned with an unopened fifth of that blessed Tennessee whiskey. It was the best moment of my day, like a small piece of home, and my heart leapt. Cracking the black seal, I took a long swill, closing my eyes as the oaken fire burned down my throat. In that second, as the whiskey singed my empty stomach, I could've been on my deck, alone, getting shit-faced in the glory of a Carolina evening.

I offered the bottle to Orson, but he declined. He walked around the corner of the cabin and dragged a grill back with him. After lighting the charcoal, he walked inside and returned carrying a plate with two ridiculously thick red filets mignons, salted and peppered. As he stepped past me, he held the plate down and said, "Pour a little of that whiskey on the meat."

I drenched them in sour mash, and Orson tossed the tenderloin rounds on the grill, where they flamed for a couple of seconds. He came and sat beside me, and as the fuzziness of the whiskey set in, we listened to the steaks sizzle and watched the sunset redden, like old friends.

When the steaks were cooked, we took our plates onto the front porch, where a flimsy table stood on one side. Orson lit two candles with a silver Zippo, and we consumed our dinner in silence. I couldn't help thinking as I sat across from him, *You aren't that monster I saw on the desert last night. That is how I sit here without trembling or weeping, because somehow I know that cannot be you. You are just Orson. My brother. My blue-eyed twin. I see you as a boy, a sweet, innocuous boy. Not that thing on the desert. Not that demon.*

As the last shallow sunbeams retreated below the purple horizon, an ominous feeling took hold of me. The presence of light had

afforded me a sense of control, but now, in darkness, I felt defense-
less again. For this reason, I hadn't touched the whiskey after my
initial buzz, fearing inebriation could be dangerous here. The
silence at the table unnerved me, too. We'd been sitting for twenty
minutes without a word, but I wasn't going to speak. What would I
say to him?

Orson had been staring into his plate, but now his eyes fixed on
me. He cleared his throat.

"Andy," he said. "You remember Mr. Hamby?"

I couldn't suppress it. A smile found my lips for the first time in
days.

"Want me to tell it like you never heard it before?" Orson asked.

When I nodded, he leaned forward in his chair, blithe, wide-
eyed, a born storyteller.

"When we were kids, we'd go several times a year up into the
countryside north of Winston-Salem to stay with Grandmom.
Granddad was dead, and she liked the company. So how old were we
when this happened? Nine maybe? We'll say nine so . . ."

*You feel like Orson, and I know, I hope it won't last, but Christ, you*
*feel like my brother in this moment.*

"And Grandmom's house was next to this apple orchard. Joe
Hamby's orchard. He was a widower, so he lived by himself. It was
early autumn, and schools and church groups would come for the
day to Hamby's orchard to pick apples and pumpkins, and buy cider
and take hayrides.

"Well, since this orchard backed right up against Grandmom's
property, we couldn't resist sneaking over there. We'd steal apples,
climb on his tractors, play in the mountains of hay he stored in his
barns. But Hamby was a real bastard about trespassers, so we'd have
to go at night. We'd wait till Grandmom went to sleep, and we'd
sneak out of that creaky farmhouse.

"All right, so this one particular October night, we slip outside about nine o'clock and hop the fence into the orchard. I remember the moon's very full, and it's not cold yet, but the crickets and tree frogs are gone, so the night is very still and very quiet. It's near the peak of harvest. Some of the apples have soured, but most are perfect, and we stroll through the orchard, eating these ripened sun-warmed beauties, just having a helluva time.

"Now Hamby owned a couple hundred acres, and on the farthest corner of his land, there was this pumpkin patch we'd heard about but never had the balls to go there. Well, this night was one of those nights when we felt invincible. So we reach the end of the orchard and see these big orange pumpkins in the moonlight. Remember, Hamby had won some blue ribbons for his pumpkins at the state fair. He grew these monstrous hundred-pound freaks of nature.

"We can see his house a ways up the tractor path, and all the lights are off, so we race each other into the pumpkin patch, our eyes peeled for one of those hundred-pounders. Finally, we collapse in the middle of the patch, laughing, out of breath."

Orson smiled. I did, too. We knew what was coming. "Suddenly, just a few yards away, we hear this loud groan: 'I LOVE my orange pussy!'"

I guffawed, felt the whiskey burn my sinuses.

"Scared us shitless," he said. "We turn and see Mr. Hamby draped over this huge pumpkin the size of one of those Galápagos Island sea turtles. He's got his overalls down around his ankles, and boy he's humping this thing in the moonlight. Just talking up a storm, smacking it like he's smacking a bare ass, and stopping every now and then to take a swig from his jar of peach brandy.

"Of course we're mortified, and don't realize he's obliviously drunk. We think he'll see us and chase us if we try to run home, so we lay down in the dirt and wait for him to finish up and go home.

Well, eventually he finishes . . . with *that* pumpkin, pulls up his overalls, and goes looking for another. The next one's smaller, and after he's bored a hole in it with his auger, he drops to his knees and starts riding this one. We watch him fuck five pumpkins before he passes out dead drunk. Then we run back through the orchard toward Grandmom's, sick on apples and . . ."

*I see us on that brisk autumn night, as vividly as I see us sitting here now, climbing back over that wooden fence, both wearing overalls and matching long-sleeved turtlenecks. We wanted to be identical then. Told everyone we were, and we looked it, too. Does that bond still have a pulse?*

I had tears in my eyes when he finished. The sound of our laughter moved me, and I allowed myself to look freely into his face, surveying the space behind his eyes. But the fingernail marks across his cheek started that woman's god-awful screaming inside my head again, and I lost the comfort of the moment, and the ease with which I'd remained in his presence for the last half hour. Orson discerned the change, and his gaze left me for the black empty desert all around us.

A gust extinguished the candles, leaving us in darkness. Now the last intimation of purple was exposed against the western horizon, but it blackened the moment I saw it. The sky filled with stars—millions more than in the polluted eastern skies. Even on the clearest nights above Lake Norman, the stars appear fuzzy, as if dimmed behind diaphanous chiffon. Here they shone upon the desert like tiny moons, and many streaked across the sky.

"I'm cold," I said, rubbing my arms, now textured with gooseflesh. I could barely see Orson, only his shape visible across the table.

He stood. "If you have to use the outhouse, do it now. In fifteen minutes, I'm locking you in your room."

"Why?"

Orson made no reply. He took the plates and glasses inside, and I sat for a moment after he was gone, searching the sky for meteors. Rubbing my eyes, I came to my feet. I would be relieved to be alone in my room, with nothing to do but read and sleep. The sound of dishes in the sink made me start, and I ran across the warm dirt in bare feet to the outhouse.

# 7

DAYS passed languidly on the desert. The sun wasted no time setting the land on fire, so after ten o'clock each morning, it became dangerous to venture outside. The heat was dry and stifling, so I remained in the shaded, cooler confines of my room or the rest of the cabin when I wasn't locked away.

There was no paucity of food. In fact, I'd never eaten better. Orson kept his freezer filled with prime cuts of meat, and he prepared three exquisite meals each day. We ate steak, salmon, veal, even lobster on one occasion, and drank bottles of wine with every supper. I asked him once why he dined like royalty, and he told me, "Because I'm entitled to it, Andy. We both are."

As I finished one book, Orson would have another for me. After Machiavelli, it was Seneca, and then Democratis on the expunction of melancholy. Though I read a book each day, Orson kept constant pressure on me to read faster. What he wanted me to glean from these classic texts, I could not imagine, and he had yet to reveal.

I obsessed about potential modes of escape. Though I had the opportunity, simply walking away was out. I had neither the strength nor the resources to hike out of this desert, without even knowing a direction in which to head. But I surmised Orson's means of transportation was locked in the shed. So I'd bide my time, construct a plan, and amass the nerve and will to overcome my brother. I would not be impetuous. Only smart decisions and flawless execution would preserve my life.

Keeping a journal calmed me. Several hours after dusk, when I'd finished reading and Orson had locked me in for the night, I would sit in bed and jot down the day's events. I'd write for an hour, often longer, sometimes disgressing into thoughts of home and the lake. I'd compose elaborate descriptions of my property, summoning the smells and sounds of the lake in summer to this lonely desert. Without question, it became my favorite time of day, and I considered it a temporary oasis. It was all I could think about during the day—what I lived for. And often, by the time I'd put my pen and paper in the drawer and cut out the light, I could hear the lake lapping at the shore, its breeze stirring the trees.

With respect to time, I knew only that it was late May. Since I'd been drugged during my abduction, I couldn't be sure which day I'd come to consciousness in the desert. Several days might have passed between that stormy night at the motel and my waking in the cabin. So I labeled my journal entries "Day 1," "Day 2," "Day 3," et cetera, beginning with my first day of consciousness. I couldn't understand what drove Orson to keep the date hidden from me. It seemed like an irrelevant, useless fact in my present situation, yet it bothered me not to know.

As for the location of the cabin, I didn't have the first clue. It could've been anywhere west of the plains. I pencil-sketched views from the front porch and my barred bedroom window, including the mountain range to the north and east and the ridge of red bluffs in the west. I also sketched the local plant life: sagebrush, tumble-weed, greasewood, lupine, and several other desert flowers that I happened upon during early-evening walks.

Some nights after sunset, when just a blush of red lingered in the sky, I'd see herds of antelope and mule deer moving through the desert. Their silhouettes against the horizon pained me, for as they trudged slowly out of sight, I envied their freedom. I recorded these observations in the journal, too, along with sightings of jackrabbits and long-tailed kangaroo mice. Though I never saw one, barn owls screeched constantly through the night and turkey vultures fre-quented the sky in the heat of day. I hoped that through the observa-tions I recorded, I could one day locate this desert again. But in truth, I had no way of knowing if I would ever be allowed to leave.

■

I lay awake in bed. Having finished my journal, it was late, and Orson had disabled the generator for the night, so the cabin was silent. Outside in the dark, only the wind disrupted the oblique stillness. I could feel it pushing through cracks between the logs. Always blowing.

A memory had been haunting me for the last hour.

*Orson and I are eight years old, playing in the woods near our neighborhood in Winston-Salem, North Carolina, under a bleached August sky. Like many young boys, we're fascinated with wildlife, and Orson catches a gray lizard scampering across a rotten log.*

*Thrilled with the find, I tell him to hold the lizard down, and with a devious smile, he does. I extract a magnifying glass from my pocket. The sun is bright, and in no time a blinding dot appears on the lizard's* scaly skin. The sunlight burns through, and Orson and I look at each other and laugh with delight, enthralled as the smoking lizard squirms to escape.

"It's my turn!" he says finally. "You hold him."

We spend the entire afternoon torturing the creature. When we're finished, I throw it into the grass, but Orson insists on taking it with him.

"I own it now," he says. "It's mine."

# 8

## Day 6 (after midnight?)

*Took another shower today. The thermometer read 95°F when I scrambled naked across the blistering ground to the well. I loathe that icy water. Feels just a few degrees above freezing, and it takes my breath as it spills over me. I washed as fast as I could, but by the time I'd rinsed all the soap from my body, I was shivering.*

*At sunset, I wanted to go for a walk on the desert, but Orson locked me in my room. From my bedroom window, I saw a brown Buick heading east on a slim dirt road that runs perfectly straight into the horizon. He's been gone several hours now. It feels safer here without him.*

*The Scorcher is probably hitting the bookstores now, and I'm sure Cynthia has about nine ulcers. I don't blame her. I'm supposed to start a twelve-city book tour any day now. Signings, radio programs, and television appearances will be canceled. This is going to dampen sales; this is breaking contract with my publisher. . . . But I can't dwell on these things now. It's out of my control and only makes me crazy.*

*I'm still reading like a madman. Poe, Plato, and McCarthy in the last two days. I still don't understand what Orson wants so desperately for me to see. Hell, I'm not sure he even knows. He spends his days reading, too, and I wonder what he's searching for in the thousands of pages, if he thinks there's some character, some story or philosophy he's yet to uncover that might explain or justify what he sees in the mirror. But I imagine he only finds morsels of comfort, like that cruelty bit from* The Prince *or the psychopathic Judge Holden in* Blood Meridian.

*I hear a car approaching in the distance. This is the first time he's left me alone, and that worries me. Perhaps he just went for groceries. Good night.*

I walked from the bed to the dresser and placed the pen and paper inside the middle drawer. It would be useless to try to hide my journal from Orson. Besides, he did display a sense of decorum when it came to my writing. At least I didn't think he'd read my journal yet. He respected what he called intrinsic urges, which was writing in my case.

I crawled back into bed, reached over to the beside table, and smothered the kerosene lantern, which I'd been using the last few nights instead of the lamp. The slam of a car door echoed through the open window. I didn't want to be awake when he came inside.

∎

His voice whispered my name: "Andy. Andy. Andrew Thomas." My eyes opened, but I saw nothing. The sotto voce whisper continued. "Hey there, buddy. Got a surprise for you. Well, for us actually." The blinding beam of a flashlight illuminated Orson's face—a smile between blood-besmirched cheeks. He turned on the lamp above the bed. My eyes ached.

"Let's go. You're burning moonlight." He set the flashlight on the dresser and yanked the covers off me. Glancing out the window, I saw the moon high in the sky. Still exhausted, I didn't feel like I'd been asleep long.

Orson tossed me a pair of jeans and a blue T-shirt from my duffel bag, which lay open in a corner. Impatient, almost manic, he resembled a child in an amusement park as he paced around the room in his navy one-piece mechanic's suit and steel-tipped boots.

The waning moon spread a blue glow, bright as day, upon everything—the sagebrush, the bluffs, even Orson. My breath steamed in the cold night air. We walked toward the shed, and as we approached, I noticed the Buick parked outside, its back end facing us, the front pointed into the double doors. The license plate had been removed.

Something banged into those doors inside the shed, followed by a brief lamentation: "HELP ME!" When I stopped walking, Orson spun around.

"Tell me what we're doing," I said.

"You're coming with me into that shed."

"Who's in there?"

"Andy . . ."

"No. Who's in—" I stared down the two-and-one-eighth-inch stainless steel barrel of my .357 revolver.

"Lead the way," he said.

At gunpoint, I walked along the side of the building. The shed was bigger than I'd originally thought, the sides forty feet long, the tin roof steeply slanted, presumably to protect it from caving under the crippling winter snows, if we were, in fact, that far north. We reached the back side of the shed, and Orson stopped me at the door. He withdrew a key from his pocket, and as he inserted it into the lock, glanced back at me and grinned.

"You like buttermilk, don't you?" he asked.

"Yes," I said, though I couldn't fathom the possible relevance.

"Did you always like it?"

"No."

"That's right. You drank it 'cause Dad did, but you came to love it. Well, I think it tastes like shit, but you have an acquired taste for buttermilk. That's sort of what's gonna happen here. You're gonna hate it at first. You're gonna hate me more than you do now. But it'll grow on you. You'll acquire a taste for this, too, I promise." He unlocked the door and put the key back into his pocket. "Not one word unless I tell you." Smiling, he motioned for me to enter first. "'Inhuman cruelty,'" he whispered as I opened the door and he followed me into the shed.

A woman lay blindfolded and handcuffed in the middle of the floor, a brown leather collar around her neck, a five-foot chain running from the collar to a metal pole. The pole rose from the concrete floor to the ceiling, where it was welded to a rafter. When Orson slammed the door, the woman clambered to her feet, wobbling awkwardly around the pole, attempting to gauge our location.

She must've been about forty-five, her blond hair losing a perm. Slightly overweight, she wore a red-and-gray bowling shirt, navy pants, and one white shoe. Her perfume filled the room, and blood ran down the side of her nose from a cut beneath the blindfold.

"Where are you? Why are you doing this?"

*This isn't happening. This is pretend. We're playing a game. That is not a human being.*

"Go sit, Andy," Orson said, pointing to the front of the shed. I walked past tool-laden metal shelves and took a seat in a green lawn chair near the double doors. A white shoe rested against the doors, and I wondered why the woman had kicked it off. She looked in my direction, tears rambling down her cheeks. Orson came and stood beside me. He knelt down, inspecting the shiny tips of his boots. Suddenly, something clenched around my ankle.

"Sorry," he said, "but I just don't trust you yet." He'd cuffed my ankle with a leg iron, bolted to the floor beneath the lawn chair.

As Orson walked toward the woman, he shoved my gun into a deep pocket in his mechanic's suit.

"Why are you doing this to me?" she asked again. Orson reached out and wiped the tears from her face, moving with her as she backed away, winding the chain slowly around the pole.

"What's your name?" he asked gently.

"Sh-Shirley," she said.

"Shirley what?"

"Tanner." Orson crossed the room and picked up two stools that had been set upside down on the floor. He arranged them beside each other, within range of the woman's chain.

"Please," he said, taking hold of her arm above the elbow, "have a seat." When they were seated, facing each other, Orson stroked her face. Her entire body quaked, as though suffering from hypothermia. "Shirley, please calm down. I know you're scared, but you have to stop crying."

"I wanna go home," she said, her voice shaky and childlike. "I want—"

"You can go home, Shirley," Orson said. "I just want to talk to you. That's all. Let me preface what we're going to do by asking you a few questions. Do you know what *preface* means, Shirley?"

"Yes."

"This is just a hunch, but when I look at you, I don't see someone who spends much time in the books. Am I right?" She shrugged. "What's the last thing you read?"

"Um . . . *Heaven's Kiss*."

"Is that a romance?" he asked, and she nodded. "Oh, I'm sorry, that doesn't count. You see, romance novels are shit. You could probably write one. Go to college by chance?"

"No."

"Finish high school?"

"Yes."

"Whew. Scared me there for a minute, Shirley."

"Take me back," she begged. "I want my husband."

"Stop whining," he said, and tears trickled down her face again, but Orson let them go. "My brother's here tonight," he said, "and that's a lucky coincidence for you. He's gonna ask you five questions on anything—philosophy, history, literature, geography, whatever. You have to answer at least three correctly. Do that and I'll take you back to the bowling alley. That's why you're blindfolded. Can't see my face if I'm gonna let you go, now can you?" Timidly, she shook her head. Orson's voice dropped to a whisper, and leaning in, he spoke into her ear just loudly enough for me to hear also: "But if you answer less than three questions correctly, I'm gonna cut your heart out."

Shirley moaned. Clumsily dismounting the stool, she tried to run, but the chain jerked her to the floor.

"Get up!" Orson screamed, stepping down from his stool. "If you aren't sitting on that stool in five seconds, I'll consider it a forfeiture of the test." Shirley stood up immediately, and Orson helped her back onto the stool. "Calm down, sweetheart," he said, his voice recovering its sweetness. "Take a breath, answer the questions, and you'll be back with your husband and—do you have kids?"

"Three," she said, weeping.

"With your husband and your three beautiful children before morning."

"I can't do it," she whined.

"Then you'll experience an agonizing death. It's all up to you, Shirley."

The single bare lightbulb that illuminated the room flickered, throwing the shed into bursts of darkness. Orson sighed and stood up on his stool. He tightened the bulb, climbed down, and walked to my chair. Putting his hand on my shoulder, he said, "Fire away, Andy."

"But . . ." I swallowed. "Please, Orson. Don't do—"

Leaning down, he whispered into my ear so the woman couldn't hear: "Ask the questions or I'll do her in front of you. It won't be pleasant. You might close your eyes, but you'll hear her. The whole desert'll hear her. But if she gets them right, I will let her go. I won't rescind that promise. It's all in her hands. That's what makes this so much fun."

I looked at the woman, still quivering on the stool, felt my brother's hand gripping my shoulder. Orson was in control, so I asked the first question.

"Name three plays by William Shakespeare," I said woodenly.

"That's good," Orson said. "That's a fair question. Shirley?"

"*Romeo and Juliet,*" she blurted. "Um . . . *Hamlet.*"

"Excellent," Orson mocked. "One more, please."

She was silent for a moment and then exclaimed, "*Othello! Othello!*"

"Yes!" Orson clapped his hands. "One for one. Next question."

"Who's the president of the United States?"

Orson slapped the back of my head. "Too easy, so now I'm gonna ask one. Shirley, which philosopher's theory is encapsulated in this quote: 'Act only on that maxim through which you can at the same time will that it should become a universal law'?"

"I don't know! How the hell should I know *that*?"

"If you knew anything about philosophy, you'd know it was Kant. One for two. Andy?" Hesitating, I glanced up at Orson. "Ask the question, Andy!"

I deliberated. "On what hill was Jesus Christ crucified?" I looked up at Orson, and he nodded approvingly.

"Golgotha," she said weakly.

"Two for three," Orson said, but he didn't sound as happy this time.

"Fourth question. When—"

"I've got one," said Orson, interrupting. "You can ask the last one, Andy. Shirley, on what continent is the country of Gabon?"

She answered quickly, as if she knew. "Europe."

"Oh, no, I'm sorry. Africa. Western coast."

"Don't do this anymore," she begged. "I'll give you money. I have credit cards. I have—"

"Shut up," Orson said. "Play fair. I am." His face reddening, he gritted his teeth. When it passed, he said, "It all comes down to this. Andy, hope you've got a good one, 'cause if it isn't, I have a perfect question in mind."

"The subject is history," I said. "In what year did we sign the Declaration of Independence?" Closing my eyes, I prayed Orson would let the question fly.

"Shirley?" he said after ten seconds. "I'm gonna have to ask for your answer."

When I opened my eyes, my stomach turned. Tears had begun to glide down her cheeks. "1896?" she asked. "Oh God, *1896*?"

"EEEEEHHHHH! I'm sorry, that is incorrect. The year was 1776." She collapsed onto the concrete. "Two for five doesn't cut it," he said, walking across the floor to Shirley. He bent down and untied the blindfold. Wadding it up, he threw it at me. Shirley refused to look up.

"That's a shame, Shirley," he said, circling her as she remained balled up on the floor. "That last one was a gimme. I didn't want my brother to have to see what I'm gonna do to you."

"I'm sorry," she cried, trying to catch her breath as she lifted her bruised face from the floor. Her eyes met Orson's for the first time, and it struck me that they were exceptionally kind. "Don't hurt me, sir."

"You are sorry," he said. He walked to a row of three long metal shelves stacked piggyback against the wall beside the back door. From the middle shelf he took a leather sheath and a gray sharpening stone. Then he strolled back across the room and pulled his stool against the wall, out of my reach and Shirley's. Sitting down, he unsheathed the knife and winked at me. "Shirley," he coaxed. "Look here, honey. I want to ask you something." Again, she lifted her head to Orson, taking long, asthmatic breaths.

"Do you appreciate fine craftsmanship?" he asked. "Let me tell you about this knife."

She disintegrated into hysteria, but Orson paid her sobs and pleadings no attention. For the moment, he'd forgotten me, alone with his victim.

"I acquired this tool from a custom knife maker in Montana. His work is incredible." Orson slid the blade methodically up and down the sharpening stone. "It's a five-and-a-half-inch blade, carbon steel, three millimeters thick. Had a helluva time trying to explain to this knife maker the uses to which I'd be putting this thing. 'Cause, you know, you've got to tell them exactly what you need it for, so they'll fashion the appropriate blade. Finally, I ended up saying to the guy,

'Look, I'll be cleaning a lot of big game.' And I think that's accurate. I mean, I'm gonna clean you, Shirley. Wouldn't you consider your-self big game?"

Shirley hunched over on her knees, her face pressed into the floor, praying to God. I prayed with her, and I don't even believe.

Orson went on, "Well, I've got to say, I've been thrilled with its performance. As you can see, the blade is slightly serrated, so it can slice through that tough pectoral muscle, but it's thick enough to hack through the rib cage, too. Now that's a rare combination in a blade. It's why I paid three hundred and seventy-five dollars for it. See the hilt? Black-market ivory." He shook his head. "An utterly exquisite tool.

"Hey, I want your opinion on something, Shirley. Look up here." She obeyed him. "See the discoloration on the blade? That comes from the acids in the meat when I'm carving, and I was wondering if it's scarier for you, knowing I'm getting ready to butcher you, to see those stains on the blade and realize that your meat will soon be staining this blade, too? Or, would it be more frightening if this blade was as bright and shiny as the day I first got it? 'Cause if that's the case, I'll get a crocus cloth and polish it up right now for you."

"You don't have to do this," Shirley said, sitting up suddenly. She gazed into Orson's eyes, trying to be brave. "I'll give you whatever you want. Anything. Name it."

Orson chuckled. "Shirley," he said, perfectly serious, "I'll say it like this. I want your heart. Now if you get up and walk out that door after I've cut it out, I won't stop you." He stood up. "I've gotta piss, Andy. Keep her company." Orson walked to the door, un-locked it, and stepped outside. I could hear him spraying the side of the shed.

"Ma'am," I whispered, breathless. "I don't know what to do. I am so sorry. I want—"

"I don't want to die," she said, begging me with her stormy eyes. "Don't let him hurt me."

"I'm chained to the floor. I want to help you. Just tell me—"

"Please don't kill me!" she screamed, oblivious now to my voice. She rocked back and forth on her knees like an autistic child. "I don't want to die!"

The door opened, and Orson cruised back in. "Well, you're in the wrong place," he said, " 'cause it's that time." He held the knife by his side and moved deliberately toward her. She crawled away from him, using only her knees because her hands were still cuffed behind her back. The chain always stopped her. Orson giggled.

"No!" she screamed. "You can't do this!"

"Watch me," he said, bending down toward her, the knife cocked back.

"Stop it, Orson!" I yelled, my heart beating in my throat. With the woman cowering at his feet, a puddle spreading beneath her, Orson looked back at me.

*Think, think, think, think.* "You just . . . you can't kill her."

"Would you rather do it? We can't let her go. She knows our names. Seen our faces."

"Don't cut her," I said. The lumpiness of tears ached in my throat.

"I do it to all of them, and I don't make exceptions."

"While they're *alive*?"

"That's the fun of it."

"You're out of your mind!" Shirley screamed at Orson, but he ignored her.

"Not this time, Orson," I implored, rising to my feet. "Please."

Shirley screamed, "*Let me go!*"

"Bitch!" Orson screamed back, and he kicked her in the side of the head with the steel tip of his boot. She slumped down on the floor. "Open your mouth again, good-bye tongue."

He looked back at me, eyes blazing. "It's perfect with you here," he said. "I want to share this with you."

"No," I begged. "Don't touch her."

Orson glanced down at his victim and then back at me.

"I'll give you a choice," he said. Walking to the stool, he set down the knife and pulled out my .357. "You can shoot her right now. Save her the pain." He approached and handed me the gun. "Here. Seeing you kill her painlessly would be as good to me as killing her the way I like to." When he looked at Shirley, I glanced at the back of the cylinder. The gun was loaded.

"Shirley, get up. I told you it was a lucky coincidence for you that my brother was here."

She didn't move.

"Shirley," he said again, walking toward her, "get up." He nudged her with his boot, and when she didn't move, Orson rolled her onto her back. Her temple smashed in, blood drained out of one ear. Orson dug two fingers into the side of her neck and waited. "She's dead," he said, looking incredulously at me. "No, wait, it's there. It's weak, but it's there. I just knocked her out. Andy, now's your chance," he urged, taking several steps back from the woman. "Squeeze off a few rounds before she comes to. Aim at the head."

I pointed the gun at Orson. "Slide me the keys," I said, but he didn't move. He just stared at me, sadly shaking his head.

"This is gonna set us way back in the trust department."

I pulled the trigger, and the gun fired. I squeezed it again and again, the plangent crack of gunshots filling up the shed, the gray smoke of gunpowder ascending into the rafters, until only the clicking of the hammer remained, thumping the empty shells.

Orson hadn't flinched.

I looked down at the gun, eyes bulging.

"Blanks, Andy," he said. "I thought you might just threaten me, but you pulled that trigger without hesitation. Wow." He took the knife from the stool and walked toward me. I threw the gun at him, but it missed his head and struck the back door.

"She's dead, Andy," he said. "I wasn't going to make you watch her suffer. Not the first time. And this is how you repay me? He was close now, gripping the knife. "Part of me wants to shove this into your stomach," Orson said. "It's almost irresistible." He pushed me back down into the lawn chair. "But I'm not gonna do that," he said. "I won't do that." He went to the stool, set down the knife, and walked to the .357, which was lying against the back door. Picking it up, he took two bullets from his pocket. "I'd say your little stunt constitutes fuckup number two." He loaded the bullets and spun the cylinder. When it stopped, he aimed the gun at my chest. "These aren't blanks," he said.

*Click.*

I saw the relief on Orson's face. "Don't make me do this again," he said. "It'd be a real shame if I had to kill you." He returned the gun to his pocket, pulled out the key for the leg iron, and slid it across the floor to me. "You can use my knife," he said. "I'll be back for the heart. Don't botch it up. Put her on one of those plastic sheets in the corner over there. Otherwise, you'll be scrubbing this floor till Christmas."

I'd regained my voice, and I said, "Orson, I can't—"

"You have four hours. If the job isn't done when I return, we'll play our little game again with three bullets."

He opened the back door, and I saw the sky coming into purple. It didn't seem like dawn should be here yet. It didn't seem like it should ever come.

Orson closed the door and locked it. I felt the key in my hand, but I wanted to remain in chains. How could I touch Shirley? She stared at me, those kind eyes open but empty as she lay on the cold, hard floor. I was glad she was gone. Glad for her.

# 9

**THAT** *is a human being. She was bowling with her family a few hours ago.* I leaned down and kissed her forehead. "I am so sorry," I whispered. "You did not . . ." *Don't lose it. This won't help you now. There's nothing you could've done to save her; there's nothing you can do to bring her back.* I'd witnessed unadulterated evil—the mental torture of a woman, and I wept savagely. When my tear ducts were dry, I steeled myself, wiped my eyes, and got to the task at hand.

Years ago, when I had time to hunt in the North Carolina mountains, I'd gut the deer I shot in the woods near my hillside cabin. *This is no different. No different from an animal now. She feels nothing. Dead is dead, regardless of where it resides.*

The work was difficult. But if you've taken an organ from one large animal, you can take one from another. What made this so difficult was her face. I couldn't look at it, so I pulled her bowling shirt over her head.

The ascension of the sun quickly warmed the shed, and soon it became so unbearably hot that I could think of nothing but a cold drink from the well. My thirst hastened my work, and when I heard the door unlocking, long before the four hours had expired, I'd nearly finished my chore. Orson walked in, still sporting the mechanic's suit. Through the open door, I saw the morning sun, already blinding. It would be another glorious blue day. A breeze slipped in before Orson shut the door, and it felt spectacular.

"Smile, Andy." He snapped a Polaroid. It was strange to think that the worst moment of my life had just been captured in a photograph.

My brother looked tired—a melancholic darkness in his eyes. I stopped working and put the knife down. Because I'd done most of the work on my knees, they were terribly sore, so I sat on the red plastic. Orson circled the body, inspecting my work.

"I thought you might be getting thirsty," he said, his voice now frail, depleted. "I'll finish this up, unless you want to."

I shook my head as he peered down into the evisceration. "That's not a bad job," he said. He picked the knife up and wiped it off on his pants. "Go get cleaned up." I stood, but he stopped me from walking off the plastic. "Take your shoes off," he said. I was standing in a pool of blood. "We're gonna burn these clothes anyway, so just strip here. I'll take care of it."

I removed my clothes and left them in a pile on the plastic. Even my boxers and socks were stained. When I was naked, my arms were red up to my elbows and a smattering of blood dotted my face, though it was nothing a cold shower wouldn't rinse away.

I walked to the door and opened it. The sunlight caused me to squint while I gazed across the desert. As I stepped onto the baking dirt, Orson called my name, and I looked back.

"I don't want you to hate me," he said.

"What do you expect? After forcing me to watch this and making me . . . cut her."

"I need you to understand what I do," he said. "Can you try?" I looked at Shirley, motionless on the plastic, the bowling shirt still hiding her face. *What utter degradation.* I felt tears coming to shatter the numbness that had sustained me these last few hours. Without reply, I closed the door, and after several steps, the soles of my feet burned, so I hustled to the well. A showerhead was mounted to the side of the outhouse. I filled the bucket overhead and opened the spigot. When the ice water hit the ground, I dug my feet into the mud. The hair on my arms was matted with dried blood. For ten minutes, I scrubbed my skin raw as the silver showerhead, an oddity in this vast desert, sluiced freezing water upon my head.

I cut the water off and walked to the cabin, standing for some time on the front porch, naked, letting the parched wind evaporate the water from my skin. Guilt, massive and lethal, loitered on the outskirts of my conscience. *Still so dirty.*

I saw a jet cutting a white contrail miles above the desert. *Do you see me?* I thought, squinting to see the glint of the sun on the distant metallic tube. *Is someone looking down at me from their tiny window as I look up at them? Can you see me and what I've done?* As the jet cruised out of sight, I felt like a child—already in bed at 8:30 on a summer evening, not yet dark, other children playing freeze tag in the street, their laughter reaching me while I cry myself to sleep.

Orson emerged from the shed, bearing the woman wrapped in plastic. He walked fifty yards into the desert and threw her into a hole. It took him several minutes to bury her. Then he came toward the cabin, and as he approached, I noticed he carried a small Styro-foam cooler.

"Is it in there?" I asked when he stepped onto the porch. He nodded and walked inside. I followed him in, and he stopped at the door to his room and unlocked it.

"You can't come in here," he said. He wouldn't open the door.

"I wanna see what you do with it."

"I'm gonna put it in a freezer."

"Let me see your room," I said. "I'm curious. You want me to understand?"

"Get some clothes on first." I ran to my room and put on a clean pair of jeans and a black tank top. When I returned, Orson's door was open, and he stood inside before his freezer chest.

"May I come in now?" I asked from the doorway.

"Yeah." Orson's bedroom was larger than mine. To my immediate right, a single bed sat low to the floor, neatly made with a red fleece blanket pulled taut from end to end. Next to the bed, against the wall, Orson had constructed another bookshelf, much smaller, but crammed with books nonetheless. Against the far wall, beneath an unbarred window, stood the freezer chest. Orson was reaching down into it as I walked up behind him.

"What's in there?" I asked.

"Hearts," he said, closing the freezer.

"How many?"

"Not nearly enough."

"That a trophy?" I pointed to a newspaper clipping tacked to the wall near the freezer. Skimming the article, I found that the names, dates, and locations had been blacked out with Magic Marker. " 'Mutilated Body Found at Construction Site,' " I read aloud. "Mom would be proud."

"When you do a good job, do *you* like to be acknowledged?"

Orson locked the freezer and walked across the room. Prostrating himself on the bed, he stretched his arms into the air and yawned. Then he lay back on top of the red fleece blanket and stared into the wall.

"I get like this after they're gone," he said. "An empty place inside of me. Right here." He pointed at his heart. "You couldn't imagine it. Famous writer. I mean absolutely nothing. I'm a man in a cabin in the middle of a desert, and that's it. The extent of my existence." He kicked off his boots, and grains of sand spilled onto the stone. "But I'm more than what's in that freezer," he said. "I own what's in that freezer. They're my children now. I remember every birth." I sat down and leaned back against the splintery logs. "After a couple days, this depression will subside, and I'll feel normal again, like anyone else. But that'll pass, and I'll get a burning where the void is now. A burning to do it again. And I do. And the cycle repeats." He looked at me with dying eyes, and I tried not to pity him, but he was my brother.

"Do you hear yourself? You're sick."

"I used to think so too. A tenet of stoicism advises to live according to your nature. If you try to be something you aren't, you'll self-destruct. When I accepted my nature, violent as it is, I made peace with myself. Stopped hating myself and what I do. After a kill, I used to get much worse than this. I'd contemplate suicide. But now I anticipate the depression, and that allows me to take the despair and sense of loss in stride." His spirits improved as he analyzed himself. "I actually feel better having you here, Andy. It's quite surprising."

"Maybe your depression stems from guilt, which should be expected after murdering an innocent woman."

"Andy," he said, his voice brightening, a sign that he'd changed the subject. "I wanna tell you something that struck me when I read your first novel, which was good, by the way. They don't deserve the criticism they get. They're much deeper than slasher stories. Anyway, when I finished *The Killer and His Weapon*, I realized that we do the same thing."

"No. I write; you kill."

"We both murder people, Andy. Because you do it with words on a page, that doesn't exonerate what's in your heart."

"People happen to like the way I tell crime stories," I said. "If I had the chops to write literary fiction, I'd do that."

"No, there's something about murder, about rage, that intrigues you. You embrace that obsession through writing. I embrace it through the act itself. Which of us is living according to his true nature?"

"There's a world of difference between how our obsessions manifest themselves," I said.

"So you admit you're obsessed with murder?"

"For the sake of argument. But my books don't hurt anyone."

"I wouldn't go that far."

"How do my books kill?"

"When I read *The Killer and His Weapon,* I didn't feel alone anymore. Andy, you know how killers think. Why they kill. When it came out ten years ago, I was confused and terrified of what was happening in my mind. I was homeless then, spending my days at a library. I hadn't acted on anything, but the burning had begun."

"Where were you?"

He shook his head. "City X. I'll tell you nothing about my past. But every word in that book validated the urges I was having. Especially my anger. I mean, to write that protagonist, you had to have an intimate knowledge of the rage I lived with. And of course you did—" he smiled—"my twin. Unfortunately, I didn't have the tool of writing to channel that rage, so people had to die. But your book . . . it was inspiring. It's kind of funny when you think about it. We both have the same disease, only yours makes you rich and famous, and mine makes me a serial murderer."

"Tell me something," I said, and he sat up on one arm. "When did this start?"

He hesitated, rolling the idea around in his head. "Eight years ago. Winter of nineteen-eighty-eight. We were twenty-six, and it was the last year I was homeless. I usually slept outside, because I didn't leave the library until nine, when it closed, and by then the shelters were full.

"If you wanted to survive a cold night on the street, you had to go where the fires were—the industrial district, near these railroad tracks. It was an unloading zone, so there was plenty of scrap wood lying around. The homeless would pile the wood in oil drums and feed the fires until morning, when libraries and doughnut shops reopened.

"On this particular night, the shelters were full, so when the library closed, I headed for the tracks. It was a long walk, two miles, maybe more. Whole way there, I just degenerated. Became furious. I'd been getting this way a lot lately. Especially at night. I'd wake myself cursing and screaming. I was preoccupied with pain and torture. I'd run these little scenarios over and over in my mind. It was impossible to concentrate. Didn't know what was happening to me.

"Well, I got down to the tracks, and there were fires everywhere, people huddled in tight circles around them. I couldn't find a place near a fire, so I sat down on the outskirts of one, people sleeping all around me, under cardboard boxes, filthy blankets.

"I was getting worse inside. Got so angry, I couldn't sit still, so I got up and walked away from the fire. Came to the edge of the crowd, where the people were more spread out. It was late, near midnight. Most everyone was sleeping. The only conscious ones were by the fires, and they were too drunk and tired to care about anything. They just wanted to keep warm.

"There were these train cars close by that hadn't been used in years. I was standing near one when I saw a man passed out in the gravel. Didn't have anything to keep warm. I stared at him. He was a black man. Squalid, old, and small. It's funny. I remember exactly what he looked like, right down to his red toboggan hat and ripped leather jacket. Just like you vividly remember the first girl you're with. He smelled like a bottle of Night Train. It's how they made it through the night.

"Nobody was paying attention to anything but the fire, and since he was drunk, I grabbed his feet and dragged him behind the train car. He didn't even wake up. Just kept snoring. Adrenaline filled me. I'd never felt anything like it. I searched for a sharp piece of scrap wood, but I thought if I stabbed him, he'd have a noisy death.

"When I saw the rock, I smiled. So fitting. It was about the size of two fists. I turned the man gently over onto his stomach. Then I pulled off his hat and dashed the back of his head out. He never made a sound. I had an orgasm. Was born again. I left the body under the train car and tossed the rock into a river. Who'd give a shit about a dead homeless man? I walked the streets all night, bursting with limitless energy. Never slept a wink, and that was the beginning.

"The one thing I didn't expect was for the burning to return so soon. Two days later, it was back, stronger than it had ever been, demanding another fix."

Orson rolled onto his back and stared up at the ceiling. I felt nauseated.

"I'm gonna lock you in your room now, Andy, so I can get some sleep."

"My God. Don't you have any remorse?" I asked.

Orson turned over and looked at me. "I refuse to apologize for what I am. I learned a long time ago that guilt will never stop me. Not that I wasn't plagued by it. I mean, I had . . . I still do have a conscience. I just realize it's futile to let it torment me. The essential thing you have to understand about a true killer is that killing is their nature, and you can't change something's nature. It's what they are. Their function. I didn't ask to be me. Certain chemicals, certain events compose me. It's out of my control, Andy, so I choose not to fight it."

"No. Something is screaming inside you that this is wrong."

He shook his head sadly and muttered Shakespeare: " 'I am in blood/Stepped in so far, that should I wade no more,/Returning were as tedious as go o'er.' "

Then he looked at me strangely, as if something had just occurred to him. There was honesty in his voice, which unnerved me more than anything he'd said all morning: "I know that you've forgotten. But one day, I'll tell you something, and this will all make perfect sense."

"What?"

"Today is not that day. You aren't ready for it. Not ready to use what I tell you."

"Orson . . ."

He climbed off the bed and motioned for me to rise. "Let's get some sleep, brother."

# 10

## Day 10

I feel free again. Orson gave me the afternoon, so I'm sitting on top of that bluff I always write about, looking out over a thirsty wasteland. I'm a good four hundred feet above the desert floor, sitting on a flat rock, and I can see panoramically for seventy miles.

A golden eagle has been circling high above. I wonder if it nests in one of the scrawny ridgeline junipers.

If I look behind me, five miles east beyond the cabin, I see what appears to be a road. I've seen three silver specks speeding across the thin gray strip, and I assume they're cars. But that does me no good. It wouldn't matter if a Highway Patrol station were situated beside the cabin. Orson owns me. He took pictures of me cutting that woman. Left them on my desk this morning.

*Dreamed about Shirley again last night. Carried her through the desert, through the night, and delivered her into the arms of her family. Left her smiling with her husband and three children, in her red-and-gray bowling shirt.*

*I've seen a significant change in Orson's mood over the last day. He's no longer morose. Like he said, this is his normal time. But the burning will return, and that's what I fear more than anything.*

*I'm considering just killing him. He's beginning to trust me now. What I'd do is take one of those heavy bookends and brain him like he did that poor homeless man. But where would that leave me? I have complete faith that Orson has enough incriminating evidence to send me straight to death row, even if I killed him. Besides, something occurred to me last night that horrifies me: In one of his letters, Orson threatened that someone would deliver a package of evidence to the Charlotte Police Department, unless he stopped them in person— who's helping Orson?*

I tossed the clipboard onto the ground, hopped off the rock, and looked intently down the slope. At the foot of the bluff, on the hillside hidden from the cabin, a man on horseback stared up at me. Though nothing more than a brown speck on the desert floor, I could see him waving to me. Afraid he would shout, I waved back, put the clipboard into a small backpack, and scrambled down the bluff as quickly as I could.

It took me several minutes to negotiate the declivitous hillside, avoiding places where the slope descended too steeply. My ears popped on the way down, and I arrived spent at the foot of the bluff, out of breath, my legs burning. I leaned against a dusty boulder, panting heavily.

The horse stood ten feet away. It looked at me, whinnied, then dropped an enormous pile of shit. Dust stung my eyes, and I rubbed them until tears rinsed away the particles of windblown dirt. I looked up at the man on the horse.

He wore a cowboy hat the color of dark chocolate, an earth-tone plaid button-up jacket, and tan riding pants. His face, worn and wrinkled, held a vital quality, which suggested he wasn't as old as he seemed, that years of hard labor and riding in the wind and sun had aged him prematurely.

I thought he was going to speak, but instead, he took a long drag from a joint. Holding the smoke in his lungs, he offered the marijuana cigarette to me, but I shook my head. A moment passed, and he expelled a cloud of sweet-smelling smoke, which the wind ripped away and diffused into the sweltering air. His brown eyes disappeared when he squinted at me.

"I thought you was Dave Parker," he said, his accent thick and remote. "I'll be damned if you don't look kinda like him."

"You mean the man who owns the cabin on the other side of that hill?"

"That's him." He took another draw.

"I'm his brother," I said. "How do you know him?"

"How do I know him?" he asked in disbelief, still holding the smoke in his lungs and speaking directly from his raspy throat. "That used to be my cabin." He let the smoke out with his words. "You didn't know that?"

"Dave didn't tell me who he bought it from, and I've only been out here a few days. We haven't seen each other in awhile."

"Well hell, all this, far as you can see, is mine. I own a ranch ten miles that a way." He pointed north toward the mountains. "Got four hundred head of cattle that graze this land."

"This desert?"

"It's been dry lately, but it greens up with Indian rice grass after a good rain. Besides, we run 'em up into the Winds, too. Yeah, I'd never have sold that cabin, except your brother offered me a small fortune for it. Sits dead in the middle of my land. So I sold him the cabin and ten acres. Hell, I don't know why anybody'd wanna own a cabin out here. Ain't much to look at, and there's no use coming here in the winter. But hell, his money."

"When did he buy it from you?"

"Oh shit. The years all run together now. I guess Dr. Parker bought it back in '91."

"*Dr.* Parker?"

"He is a doctor of something, ain't he? Oh hell, history maybe? Ain't he a doctor of history? I haven't spoken to the man in two years, so I may be wrong about—"

"He made you call him Dr.?" I interrupted, forcing myself to laugh and diverting the man's attention from my barrage of questions. "That bastard thinks he's something else."

"Don't he though," the cowboy said, laughing, too. I smiled, relieved I'd put him at ease, though I'm sure it wasn't all my doing.

"He still teaching at that college up north?" the man asked. "My memory ain't worth two shits anymore. Vermont maybe. Said he taught fall and spring and liked to spend summers out here. Least he did two years ago."

"Oh. Yeah, he is. Sure is." I tried to temper the shock in my voice. Not in a thousand years had I expected to come into contact with another person in this desert. It was exhilarating, and I prayed Orson wouldn't see this cowboy riding so close to his cabin.

"Well, I best be heading on," he said. "Got a lot more ground to cover before this day's through. You tell *Dr.* Parker I said hello. And what was your name?"

"Mike. Mike Parker."

"Percy Madding."

"It's a pleasure to meet you, Percy," I said, stepping forward and shaking his gloved hand.

"Good to know you, Mike. And maybe I'll drop in on you boys sometime with a bottle of tequila and a few of these." He wiggled the joint in his hand; it had burned out for the moment.

"Actually, we're leaving in several days. Heading back east."

"Oh. That's a shame. Well, you boys have a safe trip."

"Thank you," I said, "and oh, one more thing. What's that mountain range in the north and east?"

"The Wind Rivers," he said. "Loveliest mountains in the state. They don't get all the goddamned tourists like the Tetons and Yellowstone."

Percy pulled a silver lighter from his pocket, relit the joint, and spurred his horse softly in the side. "Hit the road, Zachary," he said, then clicked his tongue, and trotted away.

# 11

**MID-AFTERNOON,** I walked in the front door of the cabin, dripping with sweat. Orson lay on the living room floor, his bare back against the cold stone, a book in his hands. I stepped carefully over him and collapsed onto the sofa.

"What are you reading?" I asked, staring at the perfect definition of his abdominal and pectoral muscles. They shuddered when he breathed.

"A poem, which you just ruined." He threw the book across the floor, and his eyes met mine. "I have to read a poem from beginning to end, without interruption. That's how poetry blossoms. You consume it as a whole, not in fractured pieces."

"Which poem?"

"'The Hollow Men,'" he said impatiently, gazing up into the open ceiling, where supportive beams upheld the roof. He sprang up suddenly from the floor, using the sheer power of his legs. Sitting down beside me on the sofa, he tapped his fingers on his knees, watching me with skittish eyes. I wondered if he'd seen the cowboy.

"Go get cleaned up," he said abruptly.

"Why?" His eyes narrowed. He didn't have to ask me a second time.

■

Looking in the side mirror, I watched the shrinking cabin. The sun, just moments below the horizon, still bled mauve light upon the western edge of sky. The desert floor held a Martian red hue in the wake of the passing sun, and I watched the land turn black and lifeless again. Heading east, I looked straight ahead. Night engulfed the Wind River Range.

We sped along a primitive dirt road, a ribbon of dust trailing behind us like the contrail of a jet. Orson hadn't spoken since we'd left the cabin. I rolled my window down, and the evening air cooled my sun-scorched face.

Orson jammed his foot into the brake pedal, and the car slid to a stop. There was an empty highway several hundred feet ahead, the same I'd seen from the bluffs. He reached down to the floorboard at his feet, grabbed a pair of handcuffs, and dropped them in my lap.

"Put one cuff on your right wrist and attach the other cuff to the door."

I put the handcuffs on as instructed. "What are we doing here?" I asked.

He leaned over and tested the security of the handcuffs, and turned off the engine. It became instantly silent, for the wind had died at dusk. I watched Orson as he stared ahead. He wore another blue mechanic's suit and those snakeskin boots. I wore a brown one, identical to his. One of the four closets in the hallway that connected the bedrooms and the living room was filled with them.

Orson's beard had begun to fill in, painting a shadow across his face in the same pattern it spread across mine. Such subtleties create the strongest bond between twins, and as I watched Orson, I felt a glimmer of intimacy in a vessel that had long since died to that sort of love. But this was not the man I had known. *You are a monster.* Losing my brother had been like losing an appendage, but as I looked at him now, I felt like an amputee having a nightmare that the limb had grown back—demonic, independent of my will.

"You see Mom much?" Orson asked, his eyes fixed on the highway.

"I drive up to Winston twice a month. We go to lunch and visit Dad's grave."

"What does she wear?" he asked, still watching the road, his eyes never diverting to mine.

"I don't under—"

"Her clothes. What clothes does she wear?"

"Dresses, mostly. Like she used to."

"She ever wear that blue one with the sunflowers on it?"

"I don't know."

"When I dream about her, that's what she wears. I went to see her once," he said. "Drove up and down Race Street, watching the house, seeing if I could catch a glimpse of her in the front yard or through the windows. Never saw her, though."

"Why didn't you go through with it?"

"What would I say to her?" He paused, swallowing. "She ever ask about me?"

I considered lying but could find no reason to spare his feelings. "No."

"You ever talk to her about me?"

"If I do, it's just about when we were kids. But I don't think she even likes those stories anymore." Down the highway, northbound headlights appeared, so far off, I couldn't distinguish the separate bulbs.

"That car won't pass this spot for ten minutes," he said. "It's still miles away. These roads are so long and straight, the distance is deceiving."

My right hand throbbed in the grip of the metal cuff. Blood wasn't reaching my fingers, but I didn't complain. I massaged them until the tingling went away.

"What do you really want with me?" I asked, but Orson just eyed those approaching headlights like I hadn't said a word. "Orson," I said. "What do you—"

"I told you the first day. I'm giving you an education."

"You think reading boring fucking books all day constitutes an education?"

He looked me dead in the eyes. "The books have nothing to do with it. Surely you realized that by now."

He cranked the engine and we rolled toward the highway. Dark now, the sky completely drained of light, we crossed the pavement and pulled onto the shoulder. I watched the headlights through the windshield, and for the first time, they seemed closer. Confused, I looked at Orson.

"Sit tight," he said. Turning off the car, he opened his door and stepped out. He withdrew a white handkerchief from his pocket and tied it to the antenna. Then he shut the door and stuck his head through the open window. "Andy," he warned, "not a word."

He sat with his arms crossed on the edge of the hood. Rolling my window up, I tried to assuage my apprehension, but I just stared ahead, praying the car would pass. After awhile, I heard its engine. Then the headlights closed in, seconds away.

A minivan rushed by. I watched its brake lights flush in the rearview mirror. The van turned around, glided slowly back toward us, and stopped on the opposite shoulder. The driver's door opened and the interior lights came on. *Children in the backseat.* A man our age climbed out, said something to his wife, and walked confidently toward Orson. His kids watched through the tinted glass.

The man wore khaki shorts, loafers, and a red short-sleeved polo shirt. He looked like a lawyer taking his family on a cross-country vacation.

"Car trouble?" he asked, crossing the dotted yellow line and stopping at the shoulder's edge.

My brother smiled. "Yeah, she's thirsty for oil."

Through the windshield, I noticed another set of northbound headlights.

"Can I give you a lift or let you use my cell phone?" the man offered.

"Actually, we've got someone on the way," Orson said. "Wouldn't want to trouble you."

*Thank you, God.*

"Well, just wanted to make the offer. Bad spot to break down."

"Sure is." Orson extended his hand. "But thank you anyway."

The man smiled and took my brother's hand. "I guess we'll be heading on, then. Hoping to make Yellowstone before midnight. The kids are just wild about that damn geyser."

"Have a safe trip," Orson said. The man crossed the road and climbed back into his van. My brother waved to the kids in the backseat, and they giggled and waved back, delighted. As the van drove away, I watched its taillights begin to fade in the rearview mirror.

The next car was close now. It slowed down before it passed us, then pulled over onto the shoulder on our side of the road, stopping just ten feet from the front bumper of Orson's Buick. From a black

Ford pickup truck, one of the enormous new models with a rack of blinding KC lights mounted above the cab, a large man with a substantial beer gut hopped down from behind the wheel. He left the truck running, and the headlights fried my eyes. A country ballad blared from the speakers, and as the driver walked unsteadily toward Orson, I could tell he was drunk. Two other men climbed down out of the passenger side and approached my brother, too.

"Hello, gentlemen," Orson said as they surrounded him. Each man nursed a pinch of dip crammed between his teeth and bottom lip. The two passengers wore cowboy hats, and the driver held a ragged Redskins cap, his long hair, tangled and greasy, hanging in his face.

"Something wrong with your car?" the driver asked. He spat into the road, wiped his mouth with the back of his hand, and wiped his hand across his black tank top, which had a blue-and-silver Ford emblem across the front. He hadn't shaved recently.

"Don't know," Orson said. "I was hoping someone would stop who had a little mechanical expertise." The two passengers dissolved into a drunken giggle, and the driver glanced over at them and smiled. Their teeth were gray and orange from excessive dipping, but regardless of the men's deficient hygiene, not a one looked older than thirty.

"Where you from, boy?" one of the passengers asked.

Orson assessed the tall, skinny man on the far left and smiled. "Missouri."

"You a long way from home, ain't ye?" he said, then took a sip from his beer can.

"Yes, I am," Orson said, "and I'd appreciate your help."

"It might cost you something," the driver said. "It might cost you a whole lot." He looked at his buddies again, and they all laughed.

"I don't want any trouble, now."

"How much money you got?" asked the heavyset man standing in the middle. With dark, bushy sideburns and a hairy belly poking out between his black jeans and white grease-stained T-shirt, he looked so hideously disheveled, I imagined I could smell him through the windshield.

"I don't know," Orson said. "I'll have to go get my wallet and see."

Orson stepped cautiously by the driver and headed for the trunk, smiling and winking at me as he passed my window. I heard the trunk open, followed by the sound of rustling plastic.

The driver caught me looking at him through the windshield.

"What in the goddamn hell you looking at, boy?" he said. Orson walked by my door again and stopped on the right side of the hood. The three men stared at him suspiciously, though too drunk to notice that he now wore black gloves.

"Your friend's gonna get his ass whupped if he keeps staring at me."

"He's harmless," Orson said. "Look, I could give you twenty dollars. Would that be sufficient?"

The driver glared at him, dumbfounded. "Let me see your wallet," he said finally.

"Why?"

"Motherfucker, I said give me your wallet." Orson hesitated. "You stupid, boy? Wanna get your ass kicked?"

"Look, guys, I said I don't want any trouble." Orson let the fear ooze from his voice.

"Then cough up your wallet, you dumb shit," said the obese middle passenger. "We need more beer."

"Will you fix my car?" The men broke into laughter. "I have more than twenty dollars," Orson pleaded. "At least look under the hood and see if you can tell what's wrong."

Orson moved to the front of the Buick. Reaching through the

grille, he pulled a lever and lifted the massive hood. Then he returned to where he'd been standing, on the right side of the car, near me. I could see nothing now but my brother, still talking to the men.

"Just take a look," Orson prodded. "Now if you guys don't know anything about cars . . ."

"I know cars," a voice said. "Stupid city fuck. Don't know shit about shit, do you?"

The Buick squeaked and sank as if someone had knelt against the bumper.

"Check the radiator," Orson said. "Something's causing the engine to overheat."

The car shifted again. "No, on the inside," Orson said. "I think something melted. You have to get closer to see. Move, guys. You're in his light."

A muffled voice said, "I don't know what in the fuck—"

Orson slammed the hood. The two passengers shrieked and jumped back in horror. Blood speckled the windshield. Orson lifted the hood once more and slammed it home. The driver sprawled momentarily against the hood, squirting the windshield as he sank down into the dirt.

"Get the shotgun!" the fat one yelled, but no one moved.

"Don't worry about it, boys," Orson said in that same timorous voice. "I have a gun." He pointed my .357 at the two men. "I hope you aren't too fucked up to know what this is. You," he told the slender man, "pick up your buddy's head." The man dropped his beer can. "Go on, he won't bite you." The man lifted it off the ground by its long, grimy hair. "Right this way, boys," Orson said. "Walk around the side of the car. That's it." The men walked by the driver's door, and Orson walked by mine. I turned to look through the back window, but the trunk was open. He'd never shut it.

"I'm sorry about the wallet. . . ."

"In you go," Orson said. The car didn't move. "Do I have to shoot you both in the kneecaps and drag you in there myself? I'd rather you not bleed all over my car if it can be helped." When the hammer cocked, the car suddenly shook as the men climbed clumsily into the trunk.

"Stupid, stupid boys," Orson said. "It'd have been better for you if you'd all three looked under that hood." He closed the trunk.

As Orson walked back toward the truck, I heard the boys begin to sob. Then they screamed, pounding and kicking the inside of the trunk. As Orson climbed into the truck and turned off the head-lights and KC lights, I noticed the laboriously slow ballad still pour-ing from the black Ford, the steel guitar solo twanging into the desert. As my eyes readjusted to the darkness, the music stopped. The driver's door of the Buick opened, and Orson reached into the backseat and picked up a two-by-four and a length of rope.

He shut the door and said, "If they keep carrying on, tell them you're gonna kill them."

"Look." I pointed down the road at a pair of headlights just com-ing into view.

Orson untied the handkerchief from the antenna and ran back to the truck. He climbed into the cab again, put the truck in gear, and let it roll forward several feet until it pointed east into the desert. For several minutes, Orson worked on something inside the cab. The men continued to moan, their intoxication intensifying their fear, making their pleadings more desperate. I didn't say a word to them, and still the headlights approached.

The Ford sped off into the desert. I watched it through the wind-shield and then through the windows on the driver's side. In ten sec-onds, it had disappeared into the night. Orson came running up to the car, breathless. He gave me a thumbs-up and dragged the driver to the back of the car. Then he was at my window.

"I need your help," he said, opening the door. He unlocked the handcuffs and handed me the car keys. As we walked to the back of the Buick, I could hear the approaching car in the distance and see the taillights of the minivan, which had yet to fully disappear—a glowing red eye dwindling into darkness. I clung to that happy family. *We let them go. We let them go.* I looked down, but there was still no license plate on the Buick.

Orson pointed at the driver on the ground and said, "When I tell you, unlock the trunk and throw him in there. Can you do it?" I nodded.

"Gentlemen!" Orson yelled: "The trunk is being opened, and I'll be pointing a three-fifty-seven at you. Breathe and I start squeezing."

Orson looked at me and nodded. I opened the trunk without looking inside at the men or the body I had to lift. Heaving the driver from the ground, I shoved his limp, heavy frame on top of the two men. Then I slammed the trunk, and we got back into the car.

Orson started the Buick after the oncoming car passed us. The interior lights came on, and I gasped when I looked down at my brown suit, doused in blood, which had pooled and run down the coarse cloth into my boots. I screamed at Orson to stop the car. Stumbling outside, I fell to my knees and rolled around, scrubbing my hands with dirt until the blood turned granular.

From inside the car, Orson's voice reached me. He was slapping the steering wheel, his great bellows of laughter erupting into the night air.

# 12

HEADING back to the cabin, the men continued to pound against the inside of the trunk. Orson relished their noisy fear. Whenever they screamed, he mocked and mimicked their voices, often surpassing their pleas.

Watching the dirt road illuminated by the headlights, I asked Orson what he'd done to the truck. He grinned. "I secured the steering wheel with that rope so the truck would stay straight, and I shoved that two-by-four between the front seat and the gas pedal." Orson glanced at his luminescent watch. "For the next half hour, it'll roll through twenty-five miles of empty desert. Then it'll run into the mountains, and that's where it'll stop, unless it hits a mule deer along the way. But it'd have to be a big buck to stop that monster truck.

"Eventually, someone will find it. Maybe in a few days, maybe in several weeks. But by then it won't matter, 'cause these boys'll be pushing up sagebrush. Local law enforcement will probably find out where they were coming from and where they were headed. They'll realize something happened on that road back there, but so what? It's gonna rain tomorrow for the first time in weeks and rinse all the blood from the ground. Only two cars saw us, and they both had out-of-state tags, so they were just passing through. This'll be an unsolved disappearance, and judging from the rude dispositions of these young men, I have a hard time believing anyone will give much of a shit."

Upon reaching the cabin, Orson pulled up to the shed. When we got out, he called to me from the front of the Buick, popped the hood, and motioned for me to look inside. Floodlights mounted to the shed illuminated the metallic cavity as I peered in.

"What?" I asked, staring at the corroded engine.

"You'd have fallen for it, too. Look." A few inches in, a piece of metal three feet long had been welded to the underside of the hood. "It's an old lawn mower blade," Orson said. "Razor-sharp. Especially in the middle. If his head had been a little farther to the right, it would've come clean off the first slam." Gingerly, I touched the blade with my index finger. It was scratchy sharp, and there was blood on it, sprayed all over the engine, too.

"Have you done this hood trick before?" I asked.

"On occasion."

One of the men yelled from inside the trunk, "Let me out, motherfucker!"

Orson laughed. "Since he asked politely. Come open it up." He tossed me the keys. "You hear that, boys?" he yelled, moving toward the trunk. "I'm opening it up. No movement."

I raised the trunk while Orson stood with the gun pointed at the men. As I backed away, he whispered, "Go get the handcuffs."

I glanced into the plastic-lined trunk, a gruesome spectacle. The driver had been shoved to the back of the roomy compartment, but not before his blood had soaked his friends. They looked at me as I walked by, their eyes pleading for mercy that wasn't mine to give. I grabbed the handcuffs from the floorboard on the passenger's side and returned to Orson.

"Throw them the handcuffs," he said. "Boys, lock yourselves together."

"Go fuck yourself," said the heavy man. Orson cocked the hammer and shot a hole in his leg. As the man howled and screamed obscenities, Orson turned the gun on the other man.

"Your name, please," he said.

"Jeff." The man trembled, his hands in front of his face, as if they could stop bullets. His friend grunted and squealed through his teeth as he grasped his thigh.

"Jeff," Orson said. "I suggest you take the initiative and handcuff yourself to your pal."

"Yes sir," Jeff said, and as he cuffed his own hand, Orson spoke to the wounded man, who was now grinding his teeth together, trying not to scream.

"What's your name?" Orson said.

Through clenched teeth, the man responded, "Wilbur."

"Wilbur, I know you're in agonizing pain, and I wish I could tell you it's all gonna be over soon. But it's not." Orson patted him tenderly on the shoulder. "I just wanted to assure you that this night has only begun, and the more you buck me, the worse it's gonna be for you."

When Jeff and Wilbur were cuffed together, Orson ordered them to get out. Wilbur had difficulty moving his leg, so Orson directed me to drag him out of the trunk. As he screamed, I pulled him onto the ground, and Jeff fell on him, crushing the injured thigh.

Leaving their cowboy hats in the trunk, the two men came slowly to their feet, and Orson led them toward the back of the shed. As he unlocked the door, he told me to go wrap the driver up in the plastic lining and remove him from the trunk.

"I can't lift him by myself," I said. "The blood'll spill everywhere."

"Just go shut it, then. But we gotta get him out before he starts stinking."

I returned to the car and closed the trunk. Walking back toward the shed, I felt the keys jingle in my pocket. Staring at the brown car, dull beneath the floodlights, I thought, *I could go. Right now. Get in the car, turn the ignition, and drive back to the highway. There's probably a town, maybe thirty or forty miles away. You find a police station, you bring someone here. Maybe you save them.* Sliding my hand into my pocket, I poked a finger through the key ring. Orson's voice passed through the pine structure, taunting the groaning man inside.

*Go.* I started for the driver's seat. *Shit.* The hood was still raised, and I quietly lowered it so that it closed with a soft metallic click, which Orson could not have heard from inside the shed. With the key held firmly between my thumb and forefinger, I opened the car door, my hands shaking now, and sat down in the driver's seat. *Key into the ignition. Check the parking brake. Don't shut the door until you're moving. Turn the key. Turn the key.*

Something tapped on the window, and, flinching, I looked over at Orson, who was standing by the passenger door, pointing the revolver at my head through the glass.

"What in the world are you doing?" he asked.

"I'm coming," I said. "I was coming." I pulled the keys from the ignition and stepped out of the car. "Here." I tossed him the keys and walked toward the shed. *Don't shoot me. Please. Pretend this didn't happen.* At the back door he stopped me.

"I'm considering killing you," he said. "But you've got an opportunity in here to dissuade me. After you."

He followed me into the shed and locked the door behind us,

having already collared the men individually and chained them to the pole. *You've seen this before. It won't be as bad as Shirley. Can't be. We let the family go. We let the family go. Those kids will see Old Faithful tomorrow. Hold on to that.*

Orson retrieved his handcrafted knife and inserted a tape into a video camera that sat on a black tripod in the corner. I didn't recall seeing a video camera on Shirley's night.

When he noticed me looking at the camera, he said, "Hey, I gotta have something to tide me over." Orson walked to the center of the room with his knife as Wilbur moaned on the floor.

"Jeff," Orson said, "you're smarter than your recalcitrant friend here. I've known you only forty minutes, and it's an obvious fact." Orson looked at me and said, "Drag the plastic over here, Andy." I walked to the corner, where at least two dozen neatly folded sheets were stacked. On a nearby shelf, I noticed a cardboard box filled with votive candles, and I wondered to what use Orson put them.

"Look," Jeff said, "please just listen—"

"Zip it, Jeff. It's futile. Normally, I'd have given you two a test, but your roadside manner automatically flunks you both. So with that matter settled, get up, gentlemen."

Jeff stood, but Wilbur struggled. He'd already bled a little pool onto the floor. I spread the sheet near the pole, and the men sat back down, Jeff looking with confusion at the plastic beneath him.

"Jeff," Orson continued, "how long you known Wilbur?"

"All my life."

"Then this might be a difficult decision for you." I was leaning against the double doors, and Orson looked back at me. "Have a seat, Andy. You're making me nervous."

As I sat down in the lawn chair, Orson turned back to Jeff and held up the knife and the revolver. "Jeff, the bad news is you're both going to die tonight. The slightly better news is that you get to decide who gets the easy way and who gets the fun way. Option A. My brother executes you with this three fifty-seven. If you choose the gun, you have to go first. Option B. I take this gorgeous knife and cut your heart out while you watch." Orson smiled. "Take a moment to think it over."

My brother walked to me as the men stared at each other on the plastic—Jeff crying, Wilbur on the verge of losing consciousness. Orson leaned down and whispered into my ear: "Whoever you shoot, you're doing them an act of kindness. They'll feel nothing. I'm not even gonna make you watch what I do with this knife to-night. You can go back to the house and go to bed."

Orson returned to the center of the room and looked down at the men. "Jeff, I'm gonna have to ask—"

Jeff sobbed. "Why are you—"

"If the next words from your mouth aren't 'Shoot me' or 'Shoot him,' I'll take both your hearts out. Decide."

"Shoot me," Jeff cried, his lips pulling back, exposing rotten teeth. Wilbur, still holding his leg, glared at Orson.

My brother walked to the back door and said, "Andy, I thought about it, and I'm only leaving you one bullet in the gun. Wouldn't want you to do them both a favor." Orson emptied the cylinder and reloaded one round.

"Behind the ear, Andy. Anywhere else and you might not kill him. He'd just lay around suffering." Orson set the gun on the floor. "I'd love to stay and watch, but after that incident with Miss Tanner, well . . . I'll come back when I hear the gunshot. Don't do anything heroic like not shoot him or destroy the gun. I have others, and we'd have to play our little game again. I think the stakes are up to sixty percent now against you, and I'm sure you don't want those odds. And if that doesn't encourage you, let me say this. Anything goes wrong, I'll punish our mother. So . . . I'll leave you to your work.

Jeff"—Orson flippantly saluted him—"it's my brother's first time, so take it like a man. Don't beg and plead with him not to shoot you, because you might convince him, and then you'd have to die my way. And I promise you," he said, smiling at Wilbur, "my way's a shitty way to die." Orson stepped out, shut the door, and turned the dead bolt. I was alone with my victim.

Rising, I crossed the floor to the gun, picked it up, and carried it back to the chair. The way Jeff watched me felt unnatural. No one had ever feared me like this.

I sat down to think, my hands sweating onto the metal. Jeff stared at me, and I stared back. Our eyes met, eyes that in another time or place might have been cordial or apathetic, now gravely opposed. *This is preventing his torture.*

When I stood, my legs jellied, like those nightmares when you have to run, but your legs refuse to work. I walked toward Jeff. *It's for his own good. Be professional, calm, and swift.* Even through his pain, Wilbur cursed me under his malodorous breath. *Are you actually going to do this?*

"A joke?" Jeff laughed strangely. "This is a funny joke. Isn't this a funny joke, Wilbur? Let's go now. We have to be at Charlie's before twelve."

Lifting the gun in my right hand, I pointed it at Jeff and tried to aim, but my hands shook. I stepped forward so that, despite my trembling, Jeff's head remained in the sight.

"Don't shoot my face," he begged as tears welled up again in his eyes. Jeff knelt down and leaned forward like a Muslim facing Mecca, his dirty blond hair in his eyes, his right arm stretched out, still connected to Wilbur. He touched the skin behind his ear. "Right here," he said, his voice quaking. "Get close if you have to."

*You aren't going to do this.*

I took a step closer. His face now inches from my boots, he made fists and grunted, preparing to die. With both hands, I steadied the gun, and my finger found the trigger.

I squeezed, but the hammer only clicked.

Jeff gasped.

"I'm sorry," I said, and as his back heaved up and down from hyperventilation, I stepped back. The cylinder of a Smith & Wesson rotates counterclockwise. Orson had loaded the eleven o'clock chamber instead of the two. *You did that on purpose, you bastard.* I dropped the round into the hot chamber, put the barrel behind Jeff's ear, and thumbed back the hammer.

He went limp and rolled onto his left side. I hadn't heard the gunshot or felt my finger move, but a stream of dark blood flowed fast onto the plastic. In five seconds, it had surrounded Jeff above the shoulders, a crimson halo that reflected the lightbulb redly. I could see into his right eye, open but blank, without soul or will. As the pool expanded across the plastic, Wilbur jerked back, dragging Jeff's body with him, and shrieking his name. *Do not analyze this moment. You couldn't bear it.*

The back door opened, and Orson entered, an expression of awe upon his face as he stared at the plastic. He pulled the Polaroid camera from his pocket, and captured me looking down at Jeff.

"This moment . . ." he began, but did not finish the thought. His eyes glistened, joyful. "My God, Andy." He came and took the gun from my hands. Embracing me with tears in his eyes, he rubbed my back. "This is love, Wilbur," he said. "Real as it gets." Orson let go and wiped his eyes. "You can go now if you want, Andy," he said. "You're welcome to stay, but I know you probably don't wanna see this. I won't force you."

As Orson looked at Wilbur, I could see his mind drift from what I'd done. His preoccupation with his next victim took precedence, and his eyes glazed over with predatory concentration. He walked across the room and returned with the sharpening stone. Then he sat down on the concrete and began sliding the knife blade against the stone, returning it to the razor edge it had held before Shirley Tanner. *You killed a human being. No, stop that. Stop thinking.*

"Staying or going?" he asked, looking up at me.

"I'm going," I said, watching Wilbur watch the knife as it scraped across the stone for him. I wondered if Orson would make the knife speech after I left. Orson set the knife on the floor and walked me to the door. When he opened it, I gladly stepped outside. Wilbur strained his neck to see the desert, and Orson noticed.

"You interested in something out here, Wilbur?" he asked, turning around as I stood in the threshold. "Well, take a look," he said. "Take a long, long look at that night sky, and the stars, and the moon, 'cause you'll never see them again. Not ever."

Orson's icy stare returned to me. "I'll see you in the morning, brother."

He slammed the door in my face and locked it. I trudged toward the cabin, the sound of the knife blade on the sharpening stone reaching faintly through the walls.

Ahead the black mass of the cabin pressed against the navy sky. The desert had turned blue again in the moonlight. I thought of my quiet room inside. I would sleep tonight. This staggering numbness was my lifeboat.

As I stepped onto the front porch and reached for the door, the first scream rushed out of the shed and splintered the gentle night. I could not fathom the pain that had inspired it, and as I walked inside and closed the door behind me, I prayed the cabin walls would impede the sound of Orson's handiwork from reaching my ears.

# 13

O N the eleventh day, I didn't leave my room. Orson slipped in during the afternoon. I wasn't sleeping, though. Since first light, I'd been awake. He brought me a ham sandwich and a glass of port and set them on the bedside table. I lay on my side, facing him, staring into nothing. The despondence that always struck him afterward was evident in his cumbrous eyes and hushed voice.

"Andy," he said, but I didn't acknowledge him. "This is part of it. The depression. But you're prepared for it." He squatted down and looked into my eyes. "I can help you through it."

Raindrops ticked on the tin roof. I had yet to get out of bed to look outside, but the light that struggled shyly between the window bars was far from the brilliance of a desert afternoon. Soft and gray, it sulked in the corners. The turpentine fragrance of wet sagebrush perfumed the desert and my room.

"I'm through with you now," he said. "You can go home."

A current of hope flowed through me, and I found his eyes. "When?"

"Pack today, leave tomorrow." I sat up in bed and set the plate on my lap. "Feel better?" I took a bite of the cold smoked-ham sandwich and nodded. "I thought you would," he said, moving to the door. As he opened it, a cool draft swirled into my room. "I'm locking the door. I'll bring you dinner later this evening. The only thing I ask is that you're packed before you fall asleep tonight."

When he was gone, I closed my eyes and saw Lake Norman— mosquitoes humming on the surface, a baby blue sky reflected in the mild water. I could smell the pines again, the rich, living soil. The plagiary of mockingbirds and children's laughter echoing across the lake filled the dead air of the cabin. I could turn this all into a dream. *I'm not home yet.* My eyes opened again to somber reality—the sound of Orson moving about the cabin, and rain flooding a desert.

## Day 11

*I'd estimate the hour to be approaching midnight. It's raining, as it has been all day, and storm clouds have shrouded the moon, so the desert is invisible except when lightning jolts the sky. But it comes without thunder. The heart of the storm is miles away.*

*My duffel bag is packed. I think Orson's waiting for me to fall asleep. I've heard his footsteps approach my door and stop several times in the last hour, as if he's listening for the sound of my movement. This makes me a tad nervous, particularly since he's been so kind today. But strangely enough, I trust him. I can't explain it, but I don't think he'll hurt me, especially after last night. That really touched him.*

*Hopefully, this is the last entry I'll ever make in this cabin. Through writing these pages, I saved some degree of sanity and autonomy, but I haven't written down everything that occurred here. The reason for this is that I intend to forget. Some people find the cravenness to lose entire years of their childhood. They tuck things into their subconscious so that it only eats them away a little at a time, in small, painless bites.*

*This idea of repression is my model. My goal is to forget the unspeakable events of these past eleven days. I'll gladly pay the price in episodes of depression, rage, and denial that are destined to plague my coming years. Nothing can be as devastating as the actual memories of what I've seen and done.*

I signed my name at the bottom of the entry and folded the sheet of notebook paper into thirds. Then I walked to the duffel bag and stuffed it down between the dirty clothes with the other entries I'd saved. Turning out the lantern on the bedside table, I slid under the blanket. Rain on the tin roof was more effective than a bottle of sleeping pills at lulling me to sleep.

.

Lightning broke the darkness, and I saw the whites of Orson's eyes. He stood in my room, dripping onto the floor. When the sky went black again, my pulse raced, and I sat up in bed.

"Orson, you're scaring me." My voice rose above the tinkling roof.

"Don't be afraid," he said. "I came to give you an injection."

"Of what?"

"Something to help you sleep. Like what you had at the motel."

"How long have you been standing there?"

"Awhile. I've been watching you sleep, Andy."

"Will you turn the light on, please?"

"I shut the generator off."

My heart wouldn't decelerate, so I grabbed a book of matches from the bedside table and lighted the kerosene lantern. As I turned up the flame, the walls warmed, and the terror faded from my heart. He wore jeans and a green poncho, soaking wet.

"I need to give this to you," he said, showing me the syringe. "It's time to leave."

"Is it really necessary?" I asked.

"Extremely." He took a step closer. "Lift your sleeve."

Pushing the T-shirt sleeve above my shoulder, I turned my head away as Orson jabbed the needle into my arm. The pain was sharp but brief, and I didn't feel the needle pull out. When I looked back at Orson, the room had already grown fuzzy, and my head fell involuntarily back onto the pillow.

"You don't have much time now," Orson said as my eyelids lowered, his voice as distant as the storm's thunder. "When you wake, you'll be in a motel room in Denver, a plane ticket on the dresser, the three-fifty-seven locked up in your duffel bag. At that point, you can know that Mom is safe, and the evidence I have against you is in a secure place, in my possession. You've upheld your end of the agreement. I'll uphold mine.

"I think we've passed this stage in our relationship, but I'll say it once more. Tell no one what you've done, where you think you've been. Say nothing about me, or Shirley Tanner, or Wilbur and the boys. You were in Aruba the whole time, relaxing. And don't waste your energy coming back out here to look for me. You may have deduced the location of this cabin, but I assure you I'll be leaving this desert with you.

"In the coming months, things may happen that you won't understand, that you may never have dreamed of. But Andy, never forget this: Everything that happens, happens for a reason, and I'll be in control of that reason. Never doubt that.

"You'll see me again, though it won't be for some time. Carry on with your life as before. Guilt will come for you, but you have to beat it back. Write your books, embrace your success, just keep me in the back of your mind."

His face was blurry, but I thought I saw him smile. The sound of the rain had hushed, and even Orson's voice, an eloquent, soft-spoken whisper, I could scarcely understand.

"You're almost gone," he said. "I see it in your slit eyes. I wanna leave you with something as we say good-bye and you fall into that blissful unconsciousness.

"I know you like poetry. You studied Frost our freshman year of college. I hated him then; I love him now. Especially one poem in particular. The thing about this poem is, everyone thinks it applies to them. It's recited at graduations and printed in annuals, so as everyone takes the same path, they can claim uniqueness because they love this poem. I'll shut up now and let Bob put you to sleep."

My eyes closed, and I couldn't have opened them had I wanted to. Orson's voice found my ears, and though I never heard the last line, I couldn't help thinking as I surrendered to the power of the drug that "The Road Not Taken" was undisputedly his.

" 'Two roads diverged in a yellow wood, and sorry I could not travel both and be one traveler, long I stood and looked down one as far as I could to where it bent in the undergrowth;

'Then took . . . as just as fair and having perhaps the better claim because it was grassy and wanted . . . the passing there had worn them really about the same,

'And both . . . in leaves no step had trodden black. . . . ' "

# PART II

# 14

WITH the floor space of a coffeehouse, it surprised me that such a crowd had squeezed into 9th Street Books. One of a dying breed of individually owned bookstores, it felt like the library of a mansion. Though two stories high, the second floor existed only as shelf space, and a walkway, ten feet above the floor, circumnavigated the store, lending access to shelf after shelf of elevated books.

Removing my gold-rimmed glasses, I chewed on the rubbery end of an earpiece, leaned forward with my elbows against the wooden lectern, and read the closing sentence from *The Scorcher:* " 'Sizzle died and went happily to hell.' Thank you."

When I closed the book, the crowd applauded. Adrienne Phelps, the proprietor of 9th Street Books, rose from her seat in the front row. "It's nine o'clock," she mouthed, tapping her watch. I stepped back from the lectern as the small, thin-lipped woman with short jet black hair and a sweetly menacing face pulled the microphone down to her mouth.

"Unfortunately, we're out of time," she told the crowd. "There's a display up front with Mr. Thomas's books, and he's been kind enough to autograph fifty copies of *The Scorcher,* so those are on sale, too. Let's give him a big hand." Turning to me and smiling, she began to clap. The crowd joined in, and for ten seconds the staccato applause filled the old store, the last stop on my twelve-city book tour of the States.

As the crowd dispersed from the store and out onto the street, my literary agent, Cynthia Mathis, left her chair and came across the worn hardwood floor toward me. I dodged an autograph-hungry fan and reached her.

"You outdid yourself tonight, Andy," she said as we embraced. Wearing a perfume that suggested lilac, Cynthia embodied every quality an elegant, successful New York woman might be thought to possess. At fifty, she hardly looked forty. Her hair, frosting into a misty gray, was long, but she wore it wrapped tightly against the nape of her neck in a chignon. A hint of blush glowed beneath her smooth cheeks, in striking contrast to her black suit.

"It's so good to see you," I said as we pulled away. I hadn't seen Cynthia since before I'd started *The Scorcher,* and it felt strange to speak to her in person again.

"I got us reservations at Il Piazza," she said.

"Thank God, I'm starving." But at least fifty people surrounded us, waiting for a personalized autograph and a few seconds of chitchat. The doors of the bookstore, which led to my supper, seemed miles away, but I reminded myself that this was what I loved, what I'd worked so hard for. So I taped a courteous smile to my face, took a breath, and walked into the waiting crowd, hoping their interest would be short-lived.

■

The tall Italian sommelier handed me a ruby-stained cork, and I felt for dampness on the end as he poured a little wine into my glass. I swirled it around, took a sip, and when I nodded again, he filled both glasses with a dark amber Latour that had waited fourteen years for this moment.

When the wine steward left, our waiter came and described several dishes in intricate detail. Then he left us with two burgundy menus. Stumbling through the Italian, I sipped the velvety wine and thought of purple grapes ripening in the French countryside, and then subterranean cellars.

Lights from downtown created the calm, glittering ambience of Il Piazza. On the thirty-fifth floor of the Parker-Lewis Building, the restaurant occupied a corner of the skyscraper, so the best tables were positioned along the two walls of windows that peered out upon the city. We sat at one of these candlelit tables, and I stared down at the waters of the East River far below, gliding beneath the Brooklyn Bridge. My eyes followed the lights of a barge drifting upriver against the black current.

"You look tired," Cynthia said.

I looked up. "I used to love the readings, but they wear on me now. I wanna be home."

"Andy," she said, and I could predict by the gravity in her voice what was coming. I knew Cynthia well, and my disappearance in May had shaken her faith in me. "Look, I've tried to talk with you about what happened, but you always blow it off as—"

"Cynthia—"

"Andy, if you'll let me get this off my chest, we can put it aside." When I didn't speak, she continued. "You understand what bothered me about you just taking off for the South Pacific?"

"Yes," I said, stroking the glass stem with my thumb and fore-finger.

"If you just up and leave without telling me in the midst of writing a book, I don't care. I'm not your mother. But you were gone when your book came out. I don't have to tell you how important it is for you to be around that first week. You're a visible writer, Andy. It's the interviews and readings you do then that help create buzz. Initial sales were down from what *Blue Murder* sold. For a while, it looked like it might flop."

"Cynthia, I—"

"All I'm saying is, don't pull that shit again. Aside from the bookstore appearances your publisher canceled, I had to call a lot of media people and tell them why you weren't coming. I didn't have a clue. Don't put me in that position again." The waiter was walking toward us, but Cynthia waved him off. "God, Andy, you didn't even call to tell me you were leaving," she whispered fiercely, her brow furrowed, arms thrown forward in agitation. "How hard is it to pick up a goddamn phone?"

I leaned forward and said calmly, "I was burned-out. I needed a break, and I didn't feel like calling to ask permission. Now, that was my reasoning then, it was wrong, and I'm sorry. It won't ever happen again." She took a long sip of wine. I finished my glass and felt the glow of warmth in my cheeks. Reaching out, I touched her hand. Her eyes gasped.

"Cynthia. I'm sorry, okay? Will you forgive me?"

"You better smooth things with your editor, too."

"Will *you* forgive me?"

A faint smile overspread her lips. "Yes, Andy."

"Good. Let's order."

■

Cynthia had ordered the braised lamb shank with red-pepper sauce, and as the waiter set her plate down, her glassy eyes lit up. Then I watched with pleasure as my main course—mostaccioli, sun-dried tomatoes, capers, and seared bay scallops—was placed before me. Beneath the bed of pasta shimmered a vodka pink sauce. Before leaving, our waiter uncorked a second bottle of Bordeaux and refilled our wineglasses.

The scallops had taken on the flavor of the sweet tomatoes, and as one melted across my tongue, a grain of sand crunched between my molars. I sipped the wine—glimmers of plum, meat, and tobacco. It went down like silk. Experiencing the perfect balance of hunger and its satisfaction, I wanted to linger there as long as possible.

As the night wore on, I became preoccupied with the city. Drinking exceptional wine in one of New York's finer restaurants, and watching a multitude of lights shining from the skyscrapers and boroughs, is one hell of a way to spend an evening. In the center of the constant twinkling, I knew that millions of people surrounded me, and in this way, the city became inhospitable to the lonely fear that threatened me.

"Andrew?" Cynthia giggled with a feigned English accent. "Too much wine for you."

Turning slowly from the window to Cynthia, the restaurant swayed with my eyes. I was getting drunk. "That's a beautiful city," I said warmly.

"You ought to get a place here."

"Hell no."

"Are you implying there's a problem with my city?"

"I don't have to imply. I'll just tell you. You Yankees are in too much of a damn hurry."

"And that's an inferior state of existence in comparison to the comatose South?"

"We southerners know the value of an easy day's work. Don't fault us for that. I think it's just a little Yankee jealousy—"

"I find the word *Yankee* to be an offensive term."

"That's 'cause you've got a muddled definition in your head."

"Clarify, please."

"All right. *Yankee*: a noun defining anyone who lives north of Virginia, especially rude, anal northerners who talk too damn fast, don't understand the concept of sweet tea and barbecue, and move to Florida in their golden years." Cynthia laughed, her brown eyes glistening. I looked into them.

They hemorrhaged, and I turned toward the window, my heart throbbing beneath my oxford shirt and saffron tie.

"Andy?"

"I'm fine," I said, trying to catch my breath.

"What is it?"

"Nothing." Staring out the window into Queens, I grasped for composure, telling myself the lie again.

"You seem so different lately," she said, bringing the wineglass to her lips.

"How so?"

"I don't know. Since this is the first time we've been together in almost a year, it may be an unfair assessment on my part."

"Please," I said, stabbing a scallop with my fork, "assess away."

"Since your vacation, I've noticed a change in you. Nothing drastic. But I think I've known you long enough to tell when something's wrong."

"What do you think is wrong, Cynthia?"

"Difficult to put into words," she said. "Just a gut feeling. When you called me after you returned this summer, something was different. I assumed you were just dreading the book tour. But I feel the same detached vibe coming from you even now." I finished another glass of wine. "Talk to me, Andy," she said. "You still burned-out?"

"No. I know that really worries you."

"If it's a woman, tell me and I'll drop it. I don't want to pry into your personal—"

"It's not a woman," I said. "Look, I'm fine. There's nothing you can do."

She lifted her wineglass and looked out the window.

Our waiter came for our plates. He described a diabolical raspberry-chocolate soufflé, but it was late, and I had an 8:30 flight out of La Guardia in the morning. So Cynthia paid the bill, and we rode the elevator down to the street. Nearly midnight. I couldn't imagine waking in the morning. I'd drunk far too much.

I hailed a cab for Cynthia and kissed her on the cheek before she climbed in. She told me to call her the following week, and I promised I would. As her cab drove away, she stared through the back window, her earnest eyes penetrating me, gnawing at the root of my restlessness.

*You have no idea.*

When her cab was gone, I started down the sidewalk, and for several blocks, I didn't pass a soul. Though hidden now from view, the filthy East River flowed into the Atlantic. I could smell the stale, polluted water. Four ambulances rushed by, their sirens shrieking between the buildings. With my hotel only ten blocks north, I hoped a stroll in the cool September night would sober me up.

I dreaded going home. Since mid-June, I'd traveled the country, filling my days with appearances and readings that kept me grounded in the present. I never wanted a moment alone. My thoughts horrified me. Now, as I returned to North Carolina, to a slower way of life, I knew the torture would begin. I had no book to write. There was nothing for me to do but inhabit my lake house. To exist. And it was there, I feared, that the two weeks whose existence I'd denied all summer would come for me.

When my mind drifted back to the desert, I'd force-feed myself the jade green sea, ivory sand, sweaty sunlight. Distinctly, I could picture the stuccoed beach house and veranda where I'd watch bloody sunsets fall into the sea. I was aware of the self-deception, but man will do anything to live with himself.

# 15

I filled the beginning of October with crisp, clear days on Lake Norman and unbearable nights in my bed. I fished off my pier for an hour each morning and evening. And in the early afternoons, I'd swim, diving beneath the murky blue water, now holding a cool bite with the approach of winter. Sometimes, I'd swim naked just for the freedom of it, like a child in a cold womb, unborn, unknowing. Nearing the surface after a deep dive, I'd pretend that hideous knowledge buried in the recesses of my mind would vanish when I broke into the golden air. *It's only real underwater,* I'd think, rising from the lake bottom. *The air will cleanse me.*

Dawdling on the end of my pier late one afternoon, nursing a Jack and Sun-Drop, I watched a bobber swaying on the surface of the lake. Early Octobers in North Carolina are perfection, and the sky turned azure as the sun edged toward the horizon. I'd been holding a fishing rod, waiting for the red-and-white bobber to duck beneath the water, when I heard footsteps swishing through the grass.

Setting the rod down, I looked back toward the shore and saw Walter step onto the pier. He wore sunglasses and a wheat-colored suit, his jacket thrown over his left shoulder, tie loosened.

For two weeks, I'd been home. Though he called often, I'd spoken to Walter only twice, and the conversations had been vapid on my part. Each time I'd hung up as soon as possible, revealing nothing of my May disappearance and shying away from his questions. Solitude and self-oblivion had been my sole desire, and as I watched my best friend stroll down the pier, his face sullen, I knew I'd hurt him.

Several feet away, he stopped and tossed a manila envelope onto the sun-bleached wood. Walter looked down at me, and I could see myself in his sunglasses. He sat down beside me on the edge of the pier, and our legs dangled out over the water.

"Your novel's selling well," he said. "I'm happy for you."

"It's a relief."

As I fumbled with the envelope, Walter said, "I never opened it."

"You don't have to tell me that."

"Something's on your line." I grabbed my rod and yanked it back, but the bobber resurfaced without tension in the line. When I reeled it back in, the bobber didn't move.

"Shit, he was big. That was a large-mouth." I tossed the rod onto the pier and picked up my drink. "Come on," I said, standing up. Though the air was mild, the long day of direct sunlight had turned the surface of the pier as hot as summer concrete. It toasted the soles of my feet. "Let's go inside. I'll get you a beer."

In swimming trunks, I ran up the pier toward the shore, leapt into the grass, and waited. Walter came along sluggishly, his usual pace. We walked together up through the yard, a narrow green slope rising from the shore to the house. I hadn't mown the grass in two weeks, so it rose several inches above my ankles, a soft, dense carpet.

As we climbed the steps to the deck, I glanced into the woods on my right. I thought of the corpse buried out there, the one that had flung my life into this disarray. For a moment, I relived finding her— the smell, the fear, the rush of discovery.

Inside, I got Walter a bottle of beer out of the fridge and led him into the living room. Not quite as soused as I wanted to be, I mixed another Jack and Sun-Drop as he lay down on the sofa.

"I'm sorry I haven't been over," I said from the wet bar.

"Book tour wore you out, huh?"

"Just wasn't in the mood to be in front of people constantly. To be *on* all the time." After dropping several shards of ice into the glass and filling it half with citrus soda, half with bourbon, I stirred my drink, walked into the living room, and sat down in the tan leather chair across from Walter.

His eyes caught on *Brown No. 2,* looking down on us from above the fireplace in all its pretentious glory. He smirked, but the tension between us made him withhold comment.

"I know," I said, "A real piece of shit. Loman. I'd like to kick that fucker's ass. Don't know why I leave it up there. It's not like it's growing on me. Fact, I hate it more every day."

"Deep down, he must've known he was a hack. Had to. Should've listened to me, man."

"I know, I know." I yawned. I'd be passing out when Walter left. "How's the fam?"

"Ah. The obligatory inquiry. They're fine. I've been trying to spend more time with them lately. Less at the magazine. I've actually gotta be at a school play in two hours. Thirty six-year-olds on a stage. Can you imagine?"

"What are they doing?"

"Mamet." We laughed. We always laughed when we were together. "Poor thing—Jenna's so nervous about it. She got into bed with Beth and me last night, crying. We fell asleep comforting her. Woke up in a puddle."

"Ooh," I shuddered. "The thrill of parenthood. I'd miss it for the world."

"You serious?" Walter asked, kicking off his wing tips and balancing the bottle on his chest.

"Hell yeah. Everybody feels sorry for me when I tell them I don't wanna get married or have kids. But it's not like pathetic resignation. I just happen to know for a fact that there isn't a single person out there I'd wanna wake up beside day in and day out. Except you, of course. I'd marry you, Walter. Seriously."

He laughed kindly. "Karen did a number on you, but you won't always feel bitter."

"How the hell do you know how I'm always gonna feel?"

" 'Cause it's impossible for someone to go through life without repeatedly falling in love."

*How sad. He really thinks I want his life. He thinks I'm Gatsby to his Daisy. Maybe I am.*

"I was in love with Karen," I said, and a lump swelled in my throat, but I stifled it. "Where did that get me? So I loved her and thought I wanted to spend my life with her. For two years, I felt this way, and suddenly, she didn't, and wanted nothing to do with me. Not even friendship. Said I was a phase. A fucking phase. That's two years of my life wasted. I think about what I could've written during that time—fucking irks me." I shook my head and sipped the soured citrus soda. "I'll tell you—it'll be a genuine miracle if I ever do get married, 'cause I'm not looking for it. I just don't think it'll happen, and after two years of Karen—hell, I'm fine with that. I make a great mate."

"You bit into a bad apple, and now you think all apples taste that way, but they don't," he said with the swagger of someone who knows they're right.

"Maybe some people just like the taste of rotten apples." His face dropped. "I'm sorry. I don't know why I'm being an asshole. I'm just a little shit-faced right now."

"Hey, people go through phases. Be glad you aren't a full-time asshole like Bill York."

"That prick's still your copyeditor?"

"Yep. He's such a dick. He was giving me shit today for leaving early."

"You run the magazine. Fire him."

"If he wasn't such a good editor, I'd have canned his ass a long time ago. But I don't pay him to be a decent human being. Long as he keeps the text grammatically perfect, he can be the Prince of Darkness."

"God, I admire your principle." We laughed again. There was a brief period of silence, but because it followed laughter, it elapsed unstrained. Walter looked up at me from his beer.

"Andy," he said, "wanna tell me what's going on?"

I looked into Walter's eyes, and I wanted to spill everything. The urge to tell another human being where I'd been and what I'd done was overwhelming.

"I just don't know."

"It has to do with that trip you took last May?"

I held my breath, thinking. "I guess you could say that."

"Is it taxes?" he asked. "You in trouble with the IRS? That's no shit."

"Of course not." I laughed.

"What can't you trust me with?" His eyes narrowed, and I shrugged. "So talk to me."

"You willing to chance prison, or your personal safety, to know what happened to me?"

He sat up and set his half-empty bottle on the floor. "I know you'd do it for me."

My stomach contracted at the thought of the desert. I finished my drink and looked into his hazel eyes. His gray hair had grown out considerably since May. "You know I have a twin?"

"You've mentioned it. He disappeared, right?"

"We were twenty. Just walked out of our dorm room one night. Said, 'You won't see me for a while.'"

"Bet that was hard."

"Yeah, it *was* hard. He contacted me last May. Walter, you can't tell anyone. Not Beth, not—"

"Who am I going to tell?"

"You remember that black teacher who went missing last spring?"

"Rita Jones?"

I swallowed. *You say it now, he's involved. Think about it. You're too hammered to make this decision.*

"She's buried in my woods." Walter's face blanched. "My brother, Orson, put her there. He blackmailed me. Told me my blood was all over her and that the knife he killed her with was hidden in my house. Swore he'd call the police if I didn't come see him. Threatened my mother."

"You're drunk."

"Wanna see the body?"

Walter stared at me, eyes laced with doubt. "He killed her?"

"Yes."

"Why?"

"He's a psychopath," I said, steadying my hands.

"What'd he want with you?" Tears welled up in my eyes, and I couldn't stop them. They spilled down my cheeks, and as I wiped them away and looked up at Walter, my eyes filled again.

"Horrible," I said, my lips quivering as tears ran over them and down my chin.

"Where'd you go?"

"The Wyoming desert."

"Why?" I didn't answer him, and Walter allowed me a moment to regain my composure. He didn't ask why again. "Where is he now?"

"I don't know. Could be anywhere in the country."

"You never went to the police?"

"He threatened my mother!" My voice rose into the second floor. "Besides, what would I say? 'My twin brother killed Rita Jones and buried her in my backyard. Oh, by the way, my blood's all over her, she was murdered with my paring knife, and my brother's disappeared, but I swear I didn't do it!'"

"What other choice do you have?" he asked. I shrugged. "Well, if what you're saying is true, people will continue to die until he's caught. It could be Beth or John David next. That doesn't concern you?"

"What concerns me," I said, "is that even if I could find Orson, haul him into a precinct, and tell the detectives what he'd done, Orson would walk out the free man. I have no proof, Walter. It means shit in a court of law that *I* know Orson is a psychopath, that *I've* seen him torture and murder. What matters is that Rita Jones is covered in my blood."

"You've seen him murder?" Walter asked. "Actually watched him kill?" Tears came to my eyes again. "Who did he—"

"I don't wanna talk about it anymore."

"But you're telling me you—"

"I won't talk about it!" Leaving the chair, I walked to the window, which looked across the lawn and, farther down, the lake. On the forest's edge, yellow poplars had begun to turn gold, and scarlet oaks and red maples would soon set the woods ablaze with their dying leaves. My forehead against the window, my tears streaked down the glass, leaving blurry trails in their wake.

"What can I do?" Walter asked, his voice gentle again.

I shook my head. *I murdered, too. Cut out a woman's heart and shot a man in the head, because Orson told me to.* The words ricocheted inside my head, but I couldn't tell Walter what I'd done. Somehow, I thought it'd be enough that he knew about Orson and where I'd been.

"I have nightmares every night. I can't write. The things I saw . . ."

"You have to talk to someone. Something like this could fuck you over for—"

"I'm talking to you," I said, watching a boat drag an inner tube across the lake and wondering what really was coursing through Walter's mind.

He came to the window, and we both leaned against the glass.

"She's right out there," I said, pointing toward the woods. "In a shallow grave."

We stood for ages by the window. I thought he might push for more details, but he kept the silence, and I was grateful.

It was soon time for him to leave. He had his daughter's play to attend. I pictured Jenna onstage, Walter and Beth in the audience, beaming. I swear it only lasted a second, but I was gorged with envy.

# 16

JEANETTE Thomas lived alone in a dying neighborhood in Winston-Salem, North Carolina, in the same ranch-style house where her sons had grown up and her husband had died. It had been a thriving middle-class neighborhood when I was a child, but now as I drove my red CJ-7 slowly along Race Street, I marveled at how the area had changed. Rusted chain-link fences enclosed the yards, and some of the homes were derelict. It seemed as if an elderly person sat in a rocking chair on every front porch, waving at the infrequent cars that passed through. This neighborhood served as the final zone of independence for many of its residents, most only several years from a nursing home existence.

Approaching my mother's house, I couldn't help but ruminate on what this place had once been. In my childhood, kids had filled the streets, and I saw them now, riding bicycles and scrap-wood contraptions, laughing, fighting, chasing the ice-cream truck as it made the rounds on a sweltering summer afternoon. A wonderland, shrouded in shady green trees and electric with youthful energy, it had been mine and Orson's world. We'd climbed its trees, navigated the cool darkness of the drainage ditches, and explored the forbidden woods that bordered the north side of the neighborhood. We'd formed secret clubs, constructed rickety tree houses, and smoked our first cigarette here on a deserted baseball diamond one winter night. Because it was the only home of my childhood, the memories were thick and staggering. They overcame me every time I returned, and now that this neighborhood had become a ghost town, my childhood felt far more spectacular. The present listless decay made my memories rich and resplendent.

My mother always parked her car at the bottom of the driveway so she wouldn't back over the mailbox. When I saw her car edged slightly into the street, I smiled and parked near the curb in front of her house. I cut off the Jeep and opened the door to the grating whine of a leaf blower. Stepping outside, I slammed the door.

Across the street, an old man sat in a chair on his front porch, smoking a pipe and watching a crew of teenagers blow the leaves on his lawn into a brown pile. He waved to me, and I waved back. *Mr. Harrison. We were twelve when we learned about your subscription to* Playboy. *Stole the magazine for three consecutive months. Checked your mailbox every day for its delivery when we got home from school. You caught us the fourth month. Peeped from behind your curtain for a whole week, waiting to identify the thieves. Came tearing out of the house, fully intent on dragging us to our mother, until you realized she'd know you were a dirty old man. "Well, you got three of 'em already!" you shouted, then whispered, "I'll leave 'em on my back porch when I'm through. How about that? At least let me get my money's worth." That was fine by us.*

"Hey!" a man shouted from a gray Honda that had stopped in the middle of the street. I stepped back down off the curb and walked toward the car.

"Can I help you with something?" I asked. I placed him at twenty-six or twenty-seven. His hair was very black, and his razor-thin face was baby ass–smooth and white. The interior of his car reeked of Windex. I didn't like his eyes.

"Are you Andrew Thomas?" he asked.

*Here we go.*

Since the publication of my first novel, I'd kept a running count—excluding conferences, literary festivals, and other publicized appearances, this was the thirty-third time I'd been recognized.

I nodded. "No way! I'm reading your book right now. Um, *The Incinerator*—no, ah, I know what it's called. . . ."

"*The Scorcher.*"

"That's it. I love it. In fact, I've got it with me. Do you think that, um, that . . ."

"Would you like for me to sign it?"

"Would you?"

"Be happy to." He reached onto the floorboard in the back, grabbed my newest hardcover, and handed it to me. *I guess I just look like I have a pen on me.* Sometimes it was disappointing meeting the fans. "You got a pen?" I asked.

"Shit, I don't—oh, wait." He opened the glove compartment and retrieved a short, dull pencil. He'd played miniature golf recently. As I took the pencil, I glanced at the jacket of *The Scorcher*—an evil smiling face, consumed in flames. I hadn't been particularly pleased with this jacket design, but no one cares what the author thinks.

"You want me just to sign it?" I asked.

"Could you do it to . . . sign it to my girlfriend?"

"Sure." *Are you gonna tell me her name, or do I have to ask? . . . I have to ask.* "What's her name?"

"Jenna."

"J-E-N-N-A?"

"Yep." I set my book on the roof of his car and scribbled her name and one of the three dedications I always use: "To Jenna—may your hands tremble and your heart pound. Andrew Z. Thomas." I closed the book and returned it. "She's gonna love this," he said, shifting the car back into drive. "Thank you so much." I shook his cold, thin hand and stepped back over the curb.

As he drove away, I walked through my mother's uncut grass toward the front door. A gusty wind passed through the trees and tickled my spine. The morning sky was overcast, filled with bumpy mattresslike clouds, which in the coming months might be filled with snow. In the center of her lawn, against the ashen late-October sky, a silver maple exploded in burnt orange.

As I continued through the grass, the appearance of her house grew dismal. Beginning to pull away from the roof, the gutters overflowed with leaves, and the siding had peeled and buckled. Even the yard had turned into a jungle, and I didn't doubt Mom had fired the lawn service I'd hired for her. She'd been infuriatingly stubborn in her refusal to accept any degree of financial assistance. I'd tried to buy her a new house after *The Killer and His Weapon* was sold to Hollywood, but she refused. She wouldn't let me pay her bills, buy her a car, or even send her on a cruise. Whether it was her pride or just ignorance concerning how much money I made, I wasn't sure, but it irritated me to no end. She insisted on scraping by with Social Security, her teacher's pension, and the tiny chunk of Dad's life insurance, now almost gone.

I stepped up onto the front porch and rang the doorbell. Bob Barker's voice from *The Price Is Right* escaped through a cracked window. I heard my mother dragging a stool across the floor so she could reach the peephole.

"It's me, Mom," I said through the door.

"Andrew, is that you?"

"Yes, ma'am." Three dead bolts turned, and it opened.

"Darling!" Her face brightened—a cloud unveiling the sun. "Come in," she said, smiling. "Give your mom a hug." I stepped inside and we embraced. At sixty-five, she seemed to grow smaller every time I visited. Her hair was turning white, but she wore it long, as she always had, pulled back in a ponytail. Though too big for her now, a green dress dotted with white flowers hung upon her feeble frame like outdated wallpaper.

"You look good," she said, inspecting my waist. "I see you lost that spare tire." Smiling, she pinched my stomach. She had a paralyzing fear I'd suddenly gain six hundred pounds and become trapped in my house. It was hell being around her if I was the slightest bit overweight. "I told you it wouldn't take much to lose those love handles. They're really not attractive, you know. That's what happens when you spend all your time inside, writing."

"The yard doesn't look good, Mom," I said, walking into the living room and sitting down on the sofa. She walked to the television and turned the volume all the way down. "Is that lawn service not coming anymore?"

"I fired them," she said, blocking the screen, hands on her hips. "They charged too much."

"You weren't paying for it."

"I don't need your help," she said. "And I'm not gonna argue with you about it. I wrote a check to you for the money you gave me. Remind me to give it to you before you leave."

"I won't take it."

"Then the money will go to waste."

"But the yard looks terrible. It needs to be—"

"That grass is gonna turn brown and die anyway. No need to make a fuss about it now."

I sighed and leaned back against the dusty, sunken sofa as my mother disappeared into the kitchen. The house smelled of must, aged wood, and tarnished silverware. Above the brick fireplace hung a family portrait that had been taken the summer after Orson and I graduated from high school. The picture was sixteen years old, and it showed. The background had reddened, and our faces looked more pink than flesh-colored.

I remembered the day distinctly. Orson and I had fought about who would wear Dad's brown suit. We'd both become fixated on it, so Mom had flipped a dime, and I won. Furious, Orson had refused to have his picture taken, so Mom and I went alone to the photographer's studio. I wore my father's brown suit, and she wore a purple dress, black now in the discolored photograph. It was eerie to look at my mother and myself standing there alone, with the plain red background behind us, half a family. *Sixteen years later, nothing has changed.*

She came back into the living room from the kitchen, carrying a glass of sweet tea.

"Here you are, darling," she said, handing me the cold, sweaty glass. I took a sip, savoring her ability to brew the best tea I'd ever tasted. It held the perfect sweetness—not bitter, not weak, and the color was transparent mahogany. She sat down in her rocking chair and pulled a quilt over her skinny legs, the wormy veins hidden by fleshy panty hose.

"Why haven't you come in four months?" she asked.

"I've been busy, Mom," I said, setting the tea down on a glass coffee table in front of the couch. "I had the book tour and other stuff, so I haven't been back in North Carolina that long."

"Well, it hurts my feelings that my son won't take time out of his high-and-mighty schedule to come visit his mother."

"I'm sorry," I said. "I really feel bad."

"You should be more considerate."

"I will. I'm sorry."

"Stop saying that," she snapped. "I forgive you." Then turning back to the television, she said, "I bought your book."

"You didn't have to buy it, Mom. I have thirty copies at home. I could've brought one."

"I didn't know that."

"You read it?"

She frowned, and I knew the answer. "I don't want to hurt your feelings," she said, "but it's just like your other ones. I didn't even reach the end of the first chapter before I put it down. You know I can't stand profanity. And that Sizzle was just horrible. I'm not gonna read about a man going around setting people on fire. I don't know how you write it. People probably think I abused you."

"Mom, I—"

"I know you write what sells, but that doesn't necessarily mean I'm gonna like it. I just wish you'd write something nice for a change."

"Like what? What would you like for me to write?"

"A love story, Andrew. Something with a happy ending. People read love stories, too, you know."

I laughed out loud and lifted up the glass. "So you think I should switch to romance? My fans would love that, let me tell you."

"Now you're just being ugly," she said as I sipped the tea. "You ought to be ashamed of yourself. Mocking your own mother."

"I'm not mocking you, Mom. I think you're hilarious."

She frowned again and looked back at the television. Though strong-willed and feisty, my mother was excruciatingly sensitive beneath her fussy exterior.

"Have you been to Dad's grave yet?" she asked after a moment.

"No. I wanted to go with you."

"There were flowers by the headstone this morning. A beautiful arrangement. It looked fresh. You sure you didn't—"

"Mom, I think I'd know if I laid flowers on Dad's grave this morning."

Her short-term memory was wilting. She'd probably taken the flowers there yesterday.

"Well, I was there this morning," she said. "Before it clouded up. Sat there for about an hour, talking to him. He's got a nice spot under that magnolia."

"Yes, he does."

Staring into the olive shag carpet beneath my feet, at the sloped dining room table next to the kitchen, and that first door in the hallway leading down into the basement, I sensed the four of us moving through this dead space, this antiquated haunt—felt my father and Orson as strongly as I did my mother, sitting in the flesh before me. Strangely enough, it was the smell of burned toast that moved me. My mother loved scorched bread, and though the scent of her singed breakfast was now a few hours old, it made this deteriorating house my home, and me her little boy again, for three inexorable seconds.

"Mom," I began, and I almost said his name. *Orson* was on the tip of my tongue. I wanted her to remind me that we'd been carefree children once, kids who'd played.

She looked up from the muted television.

But I didn't ask. She'd driven him from her mind. When I'd made the mistake of talking about him before, she had instantly shut down. It crushed her that he'd left, that thirteen years ago Orson had severed all ties from our family. Initially, she dealt with that pain by denying he'd ever been her son. Now, years later, that he'd ever been born.

"Never mind," I said, and she turned back to the game show. So I found a memory for myself. *Orson and I are eleven, alone in the woods. It's summertime, the trees laden with leaves. We find a tattered canvas tent, damp and mildewed, but we love it. Brushing out the leaves from inside, we transform it into our secret fort, playing there every day, even in the rain. Since we never tell any of the neighborhood kids, it's ours alone, and we sneak out of the house at night on several occasions and camp there with our flashlights and sleeping bags, hunting fireflies until dawn. Then, running home, we climb into bed before Mom or Dad wakes up. They never catch us, and by summer's end, we have a jelly jar full of prisoners—a luciferin night-light on the toy chest between our beds.*

Mom and I sat watching the greedy contestants until noon. I kept the memory to myself.

"Andrew," she said when the show had ended, "is it still cold outside?"

"It's cool," I said, "and a little breezy."

"Would you take a walk with me? The leaves are just beautiful."

"I'd love to."

While she went to her bedroom for an overcoat, I stood and walked through the dining room to the back door. I opened it and stepped onto the back porch, its green paint flaking off everywhere, the boards slick with paint chips.

My eyes wandered through the overgrown yard, alighting on the fallen swing we'd helped my father build. He would not be proud of how I'd cared for his wife. *But she's stubborn as hell, and you knew it. You knew it better than anyone.* Leaning against the railing, I looked thirty yards beyond, staring into the woods, which started abruptly where the grass ended.

Something inside of me twitched. It was as though I were seeing the world as a negative of a photograph—in black and gray, two boys rambling through the trees toward something I could not see. A fleeting image struck me—a cigarette ember glowing in a tunnel. There was a presence in the forest, in my head, and it bowled me over.

I could not escape the idea that I'd forgotten something.

# 17

I left my mother's house before dusk, and for the forty miles of back roads between Winston-Salem and my lake house near Davidson, I thought of Karen. Normally, I'd banish her from my thoughts at the first flicker of a memory, but tonight I allowed her to remain, and watching the familiar roads wind between stands of forest and breaks of pasture, I imagined she sat beside me in the Jeep.

*We ride home in one of those comfortable stretches of silence, and within an hour, we're walking together through the front door of my house. You throw your coat on the piano bench, and as I head for the kitchen for a bottle of wine, I catch your eyes, and see that you could care less about wine tonight. So without music, or candles, or freshening up, we walk upstairs to my bedroom and make love and fall asleep and wake up and go again and fall back asleep. I wake up once more in the night, feel you breathing beside me, and smile at the thought of making us breakfast. You're excellent company in the morning, over coffee, in our robes, the lake shimmering in early sun. . . .*

I was speaking aloud to an empty seat, with Davidson still fifteen miles away.

Last I heard, Karen was reading manuscripts for a small house in Boston and living with a patent attorney. They were going to be married in Bermuda over Christmas. *Try this, Andy: Around 8:30, you'll unlock the front door, walk into your house, and go straight upstairs to bed. Alone. You won't even feel like a drink.*

•

I awoke to the earsplitting scream of the stereo system in my living room downstairs, the speakers pumping Miles Davis through the house at full volume. It was two o'clock in the morning. I remained motionless under the covers, in utter darkness, thinking, *Someone is in the house. If you turn on the light, you'll see him standing at the end of your bed, and if you move, he'll know you're awake and kill you. Please God, let this be a power surge, or something fucked up in the circuitry. But I don't own a Miles Davis record.*

As the music rattled the windows, I reached my left hand to the bedside table and opened the drawer, expecting at any moment for lights to blind me, followed by the immediate onset of unthinkable pain. My hand touched my new pistol, a subcompact .40-caliber Glock. I couldn't remember if I'd chambered the first round, so I brought the handgun under the sheet and, pulling back on the slide, felt the semijacketed hollow-point poke out of the ejection port, ready to fire.

For two minutes, I lay in bed, letting my eyes adjust to the darkness. Then, squinting so he wouldn't see the whites of my eyes, I scoped out my room: At a glance, I seemed to be the only occupant.

*Unless he's in the closet.* Rolling to the other side of the bed, I lifted the phone to dial 911. Miles blared through the receiver. *Oh Jesus.*

I planted my feet on the carpet and crept toward the door, thinking, *Don't go down there. Orson could be anywhere in this house. I know it's him. Please be dreaming.*

The exposed second-floor hallway ran the length of the living room, with my bedroom at the end. At my door, I stopped and peered down the empty hallway. *Too dark to see anything in the living room below.* I did, however, notice the red and green stereo lights glowing by the staircase. Through the tall living room windows, I could see the woods, the lake, and that remote blue light at the end of Walter's pier. *I might die tonight.*

Finger on the light switch, I couldn't decide whether or not to turn on the track lighting in the hallway. *Maybe he doesn't know I'm up yet. I won't alert him to the fact.*

There were three open doors leading into black rooms along the right side of the hall, the oak banister on the left. My heart clanged like a blacksmith's hammer. *Get to the staircase.* I sprinted down the hall as "So What" masked my footsteps. Crouching at the top of the staircase, freezing sweat burning in my eyes, I stared through the banister at the expansive living room—the couch, the baby grand, the wet bar, the hearth—ambiguous oblique forms in the shadows below. Then there were the places I could not see—the kitchen, the foyer, my study. *He could be anywhere.* Resisting waves of hysterical trembling, so intense that I kept my finger off the trigger, I thought, *He's doing this for the fear. That's what gets him off.*

Anger displaced my terror. I stood up, charged down the staircase, and ran into the living room.

"Orson!" I screamed above the music. "*Do I look scared? COME ON!*"

I moved to the stereo and cut it off. The gaping silence engulfed me, so I turned on a lamp beside the stereo, and the soft, warm light it produced eased my heart. I listened, looked, heard and saw nothing, took five deep breaths, and leaned against the wall to tame my renascent fear. *Go out through the kitchen and onto the deck. Get away from here. Maybe he's just fucking with you. Maybe he's already gone.*

As I started for the back door, something in the bay-windowed alcove between the kitchen and the living room arrested my exit. An unmarked videotape stood atop the glass breakfast table. Picking it up, I again glanced over my shoulder at the hallway above and then into the foyer. Still nothing moved. I wanted to search my study and the three guest rooms on the second floor, but I didn't have the equanimity to roam my house, knowing he skulked in some corner or nook, waiting for me to stumble blindly past.

Returning to the stereo and the entertainment center, I inserted the videotape into my VCR, turned on the television, and sat down on the sofa so I could watch the screen and still see most of the living room.

The screen is blue, then black. The date and time emerge in the bottom right-hand corner: 10/30/96, 11:08 A.M. *That's today. No, yesterday now.*

I hear a voice, then two voices, so low and muffled that I turn up the volume.

"Would you like for me to sign it?" . . . "Would you?" . . . "Be happy to." . . . "You got a pen?" . . . "Shit, I don't— oh, wait" . . . "You want me just to sign it?" . . . "Could you do it to . . . sign it to my girlfriend?" . . . "Sure." . . . "What's her name?" . . . "Jenna." . . . "J-E-N-N-A?" . . . "Yep." . . . "She's gonna love this. Thank you so much."

The screen still dark, the sound of a car engine vibrates the television set, and then the first shot appears—through the back window of a moving car and from a few hundred feet away—me walking up the steps to my mother's house. The screen goes black and silent.

Still 10/30/96, now 11:55 A.M. The picture fades in, and the camera slowly pans a dark room. *Oh God.* Concrete walls and floor. The objects in the room are the giveaway: two red bicycles, a dilapidated exercise trampoline, a fake white Christmas tree, mountains of cardboard boxes, and several stacks of records—the small windowless basement of my mother's house.

The cameraman holds on a shot of the fourteen steps that lead upstairs, and then the picture jerks nauseatingly as he ascends. The first hallway door creaks open, and the camera zooms in on my face as I sit quietly on my mother's couch, watching the muted television. "Such a good son to visit her," he whispers. Then the cameraman closes the door and tiptoes back down the steps.

After placing the camera atop a stack of our father's records, Orson squats down in front of it, the staircase behind him now, and the screen blackens.

The picture returns from the same position in the basement—10/30/96, 7:25 P.M. Orson leans into the lens and whispers, "You just left, Andy." He smiles. He wears a mechanic's suit, though I can't tell its color in the poor basement light. "I don't want you to worry, Andy," he whispers. "This following you around thing is quite temporary. In fact, as you watch this now in your living room around two in the morning, I'll be hundreds of miles away, driving into the capital of this great nation. And when I finish there, I'll be blending back into the faceless masses for a good long while." Orson sneezes twice.

"Because you can't keep your mouth shut, I'm considering having a friend of mine visit Walter and his beautiful family. Would that upset you? I think you've met Luther." He smiles. "He's a fan." Orson pulls a length of wire from his pocket. "In one minute, it'll occur to you that you have this all on tape. Well, you *had* it all on tape. Remember that. Shall we?" Orson lifts the camera and continues to whisper as he climbs the staircase. "The rage you're about to feel will liberate you, Andy. Think of it that way. Oh, one last thing—watch the news tomorrow morning."

He opens the door to the hallway. Somewhere in the house, my mother is singing. Orson slams the door, opens it, and slams it again before rushing back down the steps. Setting the camera back on the stack of records, he moves offscreen, somewhere in the semidarkness, amid the innumerable boxes. I have only a view of the staircase now and a section of the bare concrete wall.

Silence. At the top of the steps, the door opens.

"Andrew, did you come back in?" My mother's voice fills the basement, and I begin to tremble, my head shaking involuntarily back and forth. Descending five steps, she stops, and I can see her legs now. I'm muttering, "No" continuously, as if it will drive her back up those steps.

"Andrew?" she calls out. No answer. After three more steps, she leans down so that she can see into the basement. She inspects the rows of clutter for several seconds, then straightens up and clumps back up the staircase. But her footsteps stop before she reaches the door, and she goes back down again to where she was and looks directly into the camera. I see the confusion on her face, but it's not yet accompanied by fear.

My mother walks carefully to the bottom of the staircase and stops before the camera. She's still wearing that green dress, but her white hair is down now. She stares curiously into the lens, that sharp crease wrinkling up between her eyebrows.

"*HI, MOM!*" Orson screams. She looks behind the camera. The fear in her face destroys me, and as she shrieks and runs for the staircase, the camera crashes to the concrete floor.

■

After the screen turned blue again, I sat for five seconds in unholy shock. *He did not kill our mother. He did . . .* I smelled Windex. A hard metallic object thumped the back of my skull.

■

Lying on my back beside the couch and staring up through the windows, I saw that morning was now just a few hours away—that purple-navy tinge of dawn leeching the darkness from the sky. As I struggled to my feet, the tender knot on the back of my head throbbed on mercilessly.

The television was still on. Kneeling down, I pressed the eject button on the VCR, but the tape had already been removed.

After hanging up the phone in the kitchen, I trudged up the steps to my bedroom. I returned the Glock to the drawer and lay down on top of the covers, bracing myself for the tsunami of despair to consume me. I closed my eyes and tried to cry, but the pain was too intense, too surreal. *Could this have been a new nightmare? Maybe I walked down there in my sleep and banged my head. Dreamed a fucked-up dream. That is a possibility. Hold on to that. She's sleeping. I could call her now and wake her up. She'll answer the phone, peeved at my rudeness. But she'll answer the phone, and that's all that matters.*

In darkness, I reached for the phone and dialed my mother's number.

It rang and rang.

# PART III

# 18

O N  a cold, clear Halloween morning, the world watched Washington, D.C., as city police, FBI, Secret Service, and a myriad of media
swarmed the White House. It had begun before dawn.

At 4:30 A.M., a jogger running down East Street noticed a pile of
cardboard boxes stacked in the frosty grass of the Ellipse, close to
the site of the national Christmas tree. Upon returning home, she
called 911.

By the time the police arrived, the Secret Service was already on
the scene, and suspicion immediately arose that the boxes might
contain explosives. So the president was flown to a safe location, the
White House staff evacuated, and the quarter-mile stretch of East
Street behind the White House occluded.

In Washington, bad news travels fast. By eight o'clock, local and
network news crews were camped along the perimeter that the
police had established two hundred yards from the boxes. The story

broke on every news channel in the country, so by nine o'clock, as a bomb-squad robot rolled toward the portentous heap of cardboard boxes, the world was watching.

For two hours, cameras zoomed in on technicians in bomb-resistant suits as they utilized the robot and X-ray unit to investigate each cardboard box. When a box had been cleared, it was set inside an armored truck. Each was opened, but the cameras were too far away to determine what, if anything, was inside. There were at least a dozen boxes, and the bomb squad treated each one as if it contained a nuclear bomb. Their precision made the task tedious, and eleven o'clock had passed before the last box was cleared and the armored truck drove away.

Speculation began. What was inside the boxes if not a bomb? A hoax? An assassination attempt on the president? Rumors and unconfirmed reports swirled through the coverage until a statement was issued by the FBI at 1:30 as East Street reopened.

Special Agent Harold Trent addressed the nation of reporters, speaking into a cluster of microphones, the back side of the White House visible behind him beneath the late October sky. Twelve boxes, most between one and three cubic feet in volume, had been taken into possession by the FBI. No explosive devices had been found. Inside each box was what appeared to be a human heart and a corresponding name.

The reporters fired questions: Were the names those of real people? Would the names be released? Were there any suspects? Why were the boxes left near the White House? Agent Trent refused to theorize. The investigation had only begun, and a special FBI task force would be assembled to work with state and local police until the person or persons responsible had been taken into custody.

Agent Trent took a deep breath, his exhaustion already evident on the screen that transported his image into my living room. He looked into the cameras and spoke words that would be repeatedly broadcast as sound bites in the coming days.

"There's a long road ahead of us," he said. "It'll take some time to verify if these are actually the hearts of missing persons or known murder victims. I pray it's not the case, but this appears to be the work of a serial murderer. And if it is, he'll continue to kill until he's caught." The sturdy black agent walked away from the microphones as reporters shouted questions that he ignored.

The nation was captivated, and the media fueled its obsession. Rampant speculation ignited as the country fell in love with its own fear. Even before the FBI confirmed that the hearts represented actual murders, the media had conceived and birthed a monster.

To the dismay of doctors, they would call him "the Heart Surgeon," the professional title marred from that day forward. No one could say the words without provoking images of FBI agents and the Washington, D.C., bomb squad loading cardboard boxes, the work of a madman, into an armored truck.

How strange it felt to be the only one who knew.

# 19

**M I S T** whipped my face as my boat crawled toward the middle of the lake. I could hear nothing over the gurgling clatter of the outboard motor mounted to the stern of my leaky rowboat. The evening sky threatened rain as I glided across the leaden chop, scanning the empty lake for Walter's boat.

A half mile out from my pier, I cut the motor. The cold, darkening silence closed in on me, and I wondered if I'd make it home before the rain set in. Though I despised coming out on the lake, I couldn't speak to Walter in my house anymore without fear that Orson was eavesdropping.

I heard the groan of Walter's boat before I saw it. My nerves took over, and I regretted not having knocked back several stiff drinks to facilitate what I had to tell him. Walter pulled his equally powerless rowboat beside mine, tossed over a rope, and I tied us together.

"What's up?" he asked when he'd killed the motor.

"You see the news?"

"Yeah."

He pulled a pack of Marlboro Lights from his brown raincoat and slid a cigarette into his mouth. From a pocket on my blue rain- coat, I tossed him a butane cigar lighter. "Thanks," he said, blowing a puff of smoke out of the corner of his mouth and throwing the lighter back to me. "The media's tickled pink," he said. "You can see it in their ambitious little faces. I'll bet they blew their load when they got the tip."

"Think they were tipped, huh?"

"Oh, whoever planted those boxes knew exactly what they were doing. Probably called a dozen newspapers and TV stations after the drop. I'll bet he told them there was a bomb behind the White House. Then that jogger called nine-one-one, confirming the story, and boom . . . media frenzy." Walter took a long drag from his ciga- rette and spoke as the smoke curled from his mouth. "Yeah, the only person happier about those hearts than the press is the sick fuck who left them there. He's probably sitting in front of a TV right now, jacking off, watching the nation drool over his—"

"It's Orson," I said. Walter took in a mouthful of smoke, attempt- ing to look unfazed.

"How do you know?" he asked, coughing a little as he exhaled.

"He keeps the hearts. In his cabin in Wyoming, there was a freezer full of them. They're his trophies, his little keepsakes."

"Andy . . ."

"Just listen for a minute, Walter."

A gust banged our boats together, and a raindrop hit my face.

*How do you tell a man you've endangered his wife and children?*

"The thing in Washington," I said, "is small potatoes. My mother's dead. Orson strangled her last night. He videotaped it. . . . It's . . ." I stopped to steady myself. "I'm sorry. But I think I've put you in danger." His head tilted questioningly. "I don't know how, but Orson knows or suspects that I told you about the desert."

"Oh Christ." Walter flicked his cigarette into the water, and it hissed as he put his face into his hands.

"I should never have told you anything about—"

"You're goddamn right you shouldn't have."

"Look—"

"What did he say?"

"Walter—"

"*What the fuck did he say?*" His voice rang out across the lake. A fish splashed in the water nearby.

"The exact words aren't—"

"Fuck you." He wiped the tears from his face. "What did he say?" I shook my head. "Did he mention my family?" Tears, the first of the day, streamed from my eyes as I nodded. "He mentioned my family?" Walter hyperventilated.

"I am so—"

"How could you let this happen, Andy?"

"I didn't mean—"

"What did your brother say? I want to know each word, each syllable, verbatim, and I dare you to say exact words aren't important. *Tell me!*"

"He said because I can't keep my mouth shut . . ." I closed my eyes. *I want to die.*

"Finish it!"

"He was considering having a friend of his come visit you. And your 'beautiful family.'"

Walter looked back toward his pier and his house, concealed behind the orange leaves. It was drizzling now, so I pulled up the hood of my rain jacket. An inch of water had collected in my boat.

"Who's his friend?" he asked.

"I have no idea."

"Is this—" He started to hyperventilate again.

"Walter, I'm gonna take care of this."

"How?"

"I'm gonna kill Orson."

"So you do know where he is?"

"I have an idea."

"Tip the FBI."

"No. Orson can still send me to prison. I'm not going to prison."

Our boats rocked on the rough water. I felt queasy.

"If I find Orson," I said, "will you come with me?"

"To help you kill him?"

"Yes."

He guffawed sardonically. "Is this real? I mean, are you off your rocker?"

"Feels that way."

The drizzle had become rain. I shivered.

"I have to get home," he said. "I've gotta take John David and Jenna trick-or-treating."

"Will you come with me?" I asked again.

"Take a wild guess."

"I understand."

"No. No, you don't. You don't understand anything." He started to cry again, but he managed to hold himself together for another moment. "Let's get something straight, all right? Don't call me. Don't come to my house. Don't e-mail me. Don't think about me. Don't do one goddamn thing that would make this monster think we're friends. We clear?"

"Yes, Walter. I want you to—"

"Don't you say another word to me. Give me the rope."

I untied our rowboats and cast the end of the rope to him. He cranked the outboard motor and chugged away, making a wide circle back toward his pier.

It was nearly dark, and the rain fell steadily and hard into the lake. I started the motor and pressed on toward my pier. Were the safety of Walter and his family not in question, I would have been heading home to kill myself.

# 20

**THE** walls of my office consist almost entirely of windows, and because the room juts out from the rest of my house into the trees, I feel as though I spend my hours writing in a piedmont forest. My desk is pushed against the largest wall of glass, facing the forest, so that nothing but an occasional doe or gray fox distracts me from my work. I can't even see the lake from my desk, and this is by design, because the water mesmerizes me and would only steal my time.

Books abound, stacked on disorganized shelves and lying in piles on the floor. In one corner, there's an intimidating stack of manuscripts from fans and blurb-seekers. A mammoth dictionary lounges across a lectern, perennially open. There's even a display case, which holds first editions and translations of my novels, standing on one side of the door; a small gold frame enclosing a mounted photocopy of my first, meager royalty check hangs on the other.

Staring into the black forest as streams of rain meandered down the glass, I sat at my desk, waiting for the Web page to load. This would be the fifth college Web site I'd checked. I was focusing my search on the history departments of schools in New Hampshire and Vermont, but as the doors closed one after another, I'd begun to wonder if that cowboy's memory wasn't askew. Franklin Pierce, Keene State, the University of New Hampshire, and Plymouth had given me nothing. Maybe Dave Parker was Orson bullshit.

When the home page for Woodside College had loaded, I clicked on "Departments," then "History," and finally "Faculty of the History Department (alphabetical listing)."

Waiting on the server, I glanced at the clock on my desk: 7:55 P.M. *She's been dead twenty-four hours. Did you just leave her in that filthy basement?* With his gig in Washington, I couldn't imagine that Orson had gone to the trouble to take our mother with him. Depositing her body outside of the house would have been time-consuming and risky. Besides, my mother was a loner, and she'd sometimes go days without contacting a soul. *My God, she could lie in that basement a week before someone finds her.*

The police would have to notify me. I hadn't even given consideration to reporting her murder, because for all I knew, Orson had framed me again. *Matricide. It seems unnatural even among the animals.* I couldn't begin to wonder why. I was operating on numbness again.

At the top of the Web page listing faculty was a short paragraph that bragged about the sheer brilliance and abundant qualifications of the fourteen professors who constituted the history department. I scanned that, then scrolled down the list.

*Son of a bitch.*

"Dr. David L. Parker," the entry read.

Though his name was hyperlinked, his page wouldn't load when

I clicked on it. *Is that you? Did I just find you because of one short exchange with a stoned Wyoming cowboy?*

The doorbell startled me. I was not expecting company. Picking up my pistol from the desk (I carried it with me everywhere now), I walked through the long hallway that separated my office from the kitchen and the rest of the house. Passing through the living room, I turned right into the foyer, chambered the first round, and stopped at an opaque oval window beside the door.

The doorbell rang again.

"Who is it?" I said.

"Trick-or-treat!" *Children's voices.* Lowering the gun, I shoved it into the waistband at the back of my damp jeans. Because my house stood alone on ten acres of forest, at the end of a long driveway, trick-or-treaters rarely ventured to my door. I hadn't even bought candy for them this year.

I opened the door. A little masked boy dressed up as Zorro pointed a gun at me. His sister was an angel—a small white bathrobe, cardboard wings, and a halo of silver tinsel. A calamitous-faced man in a brown raincoat stood behind them, holding an umbrella—Walter. *Why are you—*

"Give me candy or I'll shootcha," John David said. The four-year-old's blond hair poked out from under the black bandanna. His mask was crooked, so that he could see through only one of the eye-holes, but he maintained the disguise. "I'll shootcha," he warned again, and before I could speak, he pulled the trigger. As the plastic hammer clicked again and again, I cringed with the impact of each bullet. Stumbling back into the foyer, I dropped to my knees.

"Why, John David, why?" I gasped, holding my belly as I crumpled down onto the floor, careful that my Glock didn't fall out. John David giggled.

"Look, Dad, I got him. I'm a go see if he's dead."

"No, J.D.," Walter said as I resurrected. "Don't go in the house."

I walked back to the door, caught Walter's eyes, and looked down at the seven-year-old angel.

"You look beautiful, Jenna," I said. "Did you make your costume?"

"At school today I did," she said. "You like my wand?" She held up a long pixie stick with a glittery cardboard star glued to the end.

"Take a walk with us," Walter said. "I left the car by the mailbox."

"Let me see if I can find some candy for—"

He rustled the trash bag in his right hand. "They've got plenty of candy. Come on." I put on a pair of boots, grabbed a jacket and an umbrella from the coat closet, and locked the door behind me as I stepped outside.

The four of us walked down the sidewalk, and when we reached the driveway, Walter handed his umbrella to Jenna. "Sweetie, I want you and J.D. to walk a little ahead of us, okay?"

"Why, Daddy?"

"I have to talk to Uncle Andy."

She took the umbrella. "You have to come with me, J.D.," she said, bossing her brother.

"Nooooo!"

"Go with her, son. We'll be right behind you." Jenna rushed on ahead, and John David ran after her and ducked under the umbrella. They laughed, their small buoyant voices filling the woods. His toy gun fired three times.

Walter stepped under my umbrella, and we started up the drive, the tall loblollies on either side of us. I waited for him to speak as the rain drummed on the canopy. The night smelled of wet pine.

"Beth's packing," he whispered. "She's taking the kids away."

"Where?"

"I told her not to tell me."

"She knows about—"

"No. She knows the children are in danger. That's all she needs to know."

"Stoppit!" John David yelled at his sister.

"Kids!" Walter shouted gruffly. "Behave."

"Dad, Jenna—"

"I don't wanna hear it, son."

I wondered where Walter's anger toward me had gone.

"Do you really know where he is, Andy?" he whispered.

"I've got a possible alias in New England. Now, I can't be sure until I get there, but I think it's him."

"So you're definitely going?"

"Yeah."

He stopped and faced me. "You're going there to kill him? To put him in a hole somewhere, where no one's ever gonna find him?"

"That's the plan."

"And you have no compunctions about killing your own brother?"

"None."

We started walking again. I had an awful premonition.

"You've called the police, haven't you?" I said.

"What?"

"You told them about Orson."

"No, Andy."

"But you're going to."

He shook his head.

"Why not?" I asked.

"Come here, Jenna!" Walter hollered. His children turned around and ran back to us, their umbrella so low, I couldn't see them. Walter took his umbrella from Jenna and lifted it up.

"Jenna, show Uncle Andy the tattoo you got at school."

"Oh yeah!" she said, remembering. "Look, Andy, isn't it cool?"

Jenna raised the sleeve of her robe and held up the delicate underside of her right forearm. My knees weakened. In pink Magic Marker, scribbled from her elbow to her tiny wrist: *w——shhhh. o*

I looked up at Walter. His eyes flooded.

"All right, kids." He smiled through it. "Here. Go on ahead now. Let us talk." Jenna took the umbrella and she and John David ran ahead as we continued on, the mailbox not far ahead.

"She had it when she came home from school," Walter said. "Beth noticed it when they were putting on her costume. Fuckin' teacher didn't know anything about it. Jenna said a nice man was drawing tattoos on all the kids at their Halloween carnival. She hadn't seen him before."

"Jesus, Walter. I am—"

"I don't want your apologies or your pity," he whispered. "I'm going with you. That's what I came to tell you. We're gonna bury Orson together."

The kids had reached the white Cadillac. We stopped ten feet from the end of the driveway and Walter turned to me. "So when are you leaving?" he asked.

"A day or two. I've gotta go before my mother's discovered."

His eyes softened. "Andy, I want you to know that I am s—"

"And I don't need your pity," I said. "It won't help either of us do what we have to do."

He nodded and looked over his shoulder at Jenna and John David. The umbrella cast aside, they were throwing gravel from the driveway at my mailbox, and coming nowhere close to hitting it.

# 21

THE eve of my departure for Vermont was our thirty-fifth birthday, and Orson mailed me a handmade card. On the front, he'd designed a collage out of photographs, all taken in the sickly orange light of his shed. There was a head shot of Shirley Tanner's boot-bruised face; a full body shot of Jeff in a hole in the desert; Wilbur on red plastic from the waist up—inside out.

Below the colorful collage, scrawled in Orson's unmistakable hand: *What do you get for the guy who has it all?* On the inside he'd written, *Not a goddamn thing. A big happy birthday from Shirley and the gang.*

•

Woodside is a foothill community in midwestern Vermont, isolated from the major cities of the North by the Green Mountains in the east and New York's Adirondacks in the west. On an autumn day, it's quintessential American countryside, breathtaking in its open vistas of rolling hills, endless mountain chains, and a quaint college town tucked into a vale.

According to the gas station attendant, we were three weeks late. Then the forests had been burning with the brightest color in thirty years. Now, the leaves brown and dead, few remained on the trees, and the blue sky gleamed awkwardly against the winter bleakness of the countryside. Vermont in November smacked of the same stiff beauty as dolling up a corpse for its wake.

Beyond the outskirts of Woodside, on the fringe of the Green Mountains, Walter and I approached the inn. Heading up a long, curving driveway, I saw a large white house perched halfway up the mountain. There was movement on its wraparound porch—empty rocking chairs swaying in a raw breeze.

Walter pulled his Cadillac into the gravel parking lot adjacent to the sallow lawn behind the house. There were only seven other cars, and I felt relieved to be outside of Orson's town. We'd almost stayed at a motel in downtown Woodside because of its proximity to the college campus, but the risk of running into Orson was too great.

Hauling our suitcases up the front porch steps, we collapsed into a pair of rockers. The mountainside fell away from where we sat for a thousand feet, and the late-afternoon sun shone on the forest of bare trees in the valley below. Naked branches moved with the breeze, and I imagined that three weeks ago the sound of chattering leaves had filled the air. Across the valley, which extended twenty miles west, I could see into New York State, and the grander mountains of the Adirondacks that stood there.

Wood smoke scented the forest, and sitting in the cold, listening and watching, I sensed Walter's restiveness.

After a moment, he said, "It's too cold to sit out here. I'll check us in." He stood up and lifted his suitcase off the porch. "You just gonna sit there?" he asked, walking toward the door.

"Yep."

•

Our room was at the end of a creaky hallway on the second floor. There were two double beds, placed on opposite sides of the room, a dormer window between them, from which you could view the mountains. The ceiling slanted up on both sides and met in a straight line, which bisected the room. Two paisley love seats faced each other in the center of the hardwood floor, a squat square coffee table between them. For seventy-five dollars a night, it was a lovely room. There were even fresh irises in glass vases on each bedside table. They made the room smell like an arbor.

Walter sat on his bed, unpacking his clothes, and I lay on mine, my suitcase still unopened on the floor. Voices moved through the walls, and I heard the hollow clack of footsteps ascending the staircase. Someone knocked.

Crossing the room, I stopped at the door. There was no peephole, so I asked, "Who is it?"

"Melody Terrence." I opened the door to a striking longhaired brunette, far too young and pretty to be an innkeeper.

"Hi there," I said.

"You guys settling in all right?" she asked.

"We sure are."

"Well, I just came to let you know that we're serving dinner in thirty minutes, if you're interested. Danny forgot to put the sign up again."

"Thanks for the invitation."

"Will you be joining us? There's a cozy dining room downstairs, and Danny's been smoking a bird all day. We'll have fresh vegetables, homemade biscuits—"

"It sounds wonderful," I said. "We'll see you there."

"Excellent." She smiled and walked down the hall to the next room. I closed the door.

Walter had placed a stack of shirts into a drawer, and, slamming it, he looked up at me, smoldering. "You call yourself a crime writer? Think we should go down and meet all the guests? What if someone recognizes you, Andy? If it ever got out that Orson, the Heart Surgeon"—he whispered the infamous title—"was your brother, and lived in Woodside, someone could put two and two together. They might remember that you were here in Vermont around the same time David Parker disappeared. And, you know, that's all it'd take to put the FBI on our ass." Walter moved into the dormer. His back turned, he looked into the woods, dark now that the sun had set. If the moon was up, it had yet to rise above the mountains and spread its meek light.

I moved across the room to my friend.

"Walter," I said, but he didn't turn around. "What? You scared?"

"We can't fuck anything up," he said. "Not one thing."

Staring out into the Vermont night, the foreign darkness lodged a splinter of homesickness in my heart. A child again, I acknowledged the nostalgic pain, and then it passed.

"Thank you for coming," I said, my hand on his shoulder. "You didn't have to do this, Walter. I'm never gonna forget it."

He turned back and faced me. "It has nothing to do with you," he said. "Nothing."

■

On a cold, cloudy Thursday, at eleven o'clock in the morning, I parked Walter's Cadillac in downtown Woodside and set out at a keen pace for the campus. Two- and three-story buildings lined both sides of the street, which was quite busy for a small town. People filled the sidewalks, sitting on benches, gliding along on Roller-blades, on gazing into storefront windows. Most were students, and they vivified the town, easily identifiable by their backpacks and the unbridled, merry apathy in their faces.

I passed a drugstore, the Woodside General Store, the Valley Café, several apparel stores, and a coffee shop called Beans n' Bagels, in front of which, canopied tables cluttered the sidewalk. It was the liveliest store by far, brimming with caffeine junkies and quirky music. The rich smell of roasted coffee beans mingled with the air outside the open vestibule. I would've bought myself a cup had I not downed two at the Woodside Inn, where Walter still slept in our room, drained from the previous day of driving.

The buildings ended, but the sidewalk continued from the down-town toward the wooded campus. I could now see the mountains that surrounded the town, the highest slopes already white with early snow. I wondered how many students had skipped classes for a day of skiing. A steely wind made my eyes water and I zipped my leather jacket all the way up to my chin and dug my hands into the warm pockets.

A brick walkway veered off from the main sidewalk toward a group of brick buildings. Heading up the walkway, I reached a hexag-onal white gazebo within several minutes. It appeared to stand in the exact center of campus, as most of the buildings, each not more than forty yards away, surrounded it. Plaques had been nailed to each side of the gazebo, engraved with WOODSIDE COLLEGE, EST. 1800."

I passed beneath the portico of a stone-columned building, the largest of the ten or so in the vicinity, and walked up the steps. A great clock surmounted the roof, surrounded by scaffolding, its black hands stuck suspiciously on 4:20.

Inside, the building was dim and stale. The floor was constructed of burnished marble, and the walls of the foyer, wooden and intricately carved, were adorned with large portraits of former deans, founders, and dead professors. A life-size statue stood in the center of the circular room, staring vacuously at me. I didn't stop to see who he was.

Glass double doors led into the office of the university registrar. I caught my reflection as I pushed them open—my hair and recent beard now brown, a pair of wire-framed spectacles on the bridge of my nose. In jeans and wearing a faded denim shirt under my jacket, I looked nothing like myself.

In the bright windowless room, there were several open cubicles, each holding a desk and portioned off from the cubicle next to it. I walked to the closest one, where a woman typed fervidly on a computer. She looked up from the screen and smiled as I approached.

"May I help you?" she asked. I sat down in the chair before her desk. The constant pecking of fingers on keyboards would've driven me insane.

"I need a campus map, a class directory for this semester, and a campus phone book."

She opened a filing cabinet and withdrew a booklet and a blue pamphlet.

"Here's a map and here's the phone book," she said, setting the items on her tidy desk. "I'll have to get a class directory from the closet." She walked across the room, mumbling something to another secretary as she passed. I opened the phone book. It was only fifty pages thick, with the faculty listings in the first ten pages and those of the two thousand students in the remaining forty. I thumbed through it to the *P*'s.

I skipped over the entries for Page and Paine, then spotted "Parker, David L." The information given beneath the name was sparse—only an office number—Gerard 209—and a corresponding phone number.

The woman returned and handed me a directory of classes. "Here you are, sir."

"Thanks. Are the students in class today?" I asked, rising.

She shook her head doubtfully. "They're supposed to be," she said, "but this is the first cold snap of the season, so a fair number probably played hooky to go skiing."

I thanked her again, then walked out of the office and into the foyer, where I passed three college girls standing in a circle beside the statue, whispering to each other. Exiting the building, I walked through snow flurries to the gazebo and sat down on the bench that circumnavigated the interior of the structure. First, I unfolded the map and located Gerard Hall. I could see it from where I sat, a two-story building that displayed the same charmingly decrepit brick as the others.

With hot breath, I warmed my hands, then opened the directory of classes, a thick booklet, its first ten pages crammed with mountains of information regarding registering for classes and buying books. I found an alphabetical listing of the classes and their schedules, and flipping through anthropology, biology, communications, English, and French, stopped finally at the roster of history classes for fall '96. There was a full page of history courses, and I skimmed down the list until I saw his name:

| Hist 089 | | History of Rome | | LEC |
|---|---|---|---|---|
| 3.0 | 35 | 26229 | 001 | TR |
| 11:00 A.M.–12:15 P.M. | | HD 107 | | Parker, D. L. |

It appeared to be the only course he taught, and, glancing at my watch, I realized that it was currently in session.

According to the building abbreviation key, HD stood for Howard Hall. I found it on the blue map. Just twenty yards away, it was one of the closest buildings to the gazebo. An apprehensive knocking started in my chest as I looked down the walkway leading to its entrance.

Before I could dissuade myself, I was walking down the steps, away from the gazebo, heading toward Howard Hall. To the left of the registrar's building, it made up the eastern wall of the quasi courtyard surrounding the gazebo. Two students smoked on the steps, and I passed them and touched the door, thinking, *What if this isn't him? Then I'll go to prison, and Walter and his family will die.*

As the door closed behind me, I heard his voice. It haunted the first floor of Howard Hall, its soft-spoken intensity reeling me back to the Wyoming desert. I walked slowly on, leaving the foyer, where political notices, ads for roommates, and a host of other flyers papered the walls. In the darker hall, light spilled from one door. I heard a collection of voices, then an outburst of laughter. Orson's voice rose above the rumblings of his students, and I turned right and walked down the hallway, taking care my steps didn't echo off the floor.

His voice grew louder, and I could soon understand every word. Stopping several feet from the doorway, I leaned against the wall. From the volume of laughter, I approximated the class size at thirty or forty students. Orson spoke again, his voice directly across from me on the other side of the wall. Though I wanted to run, to hide in a closet or a bathroom stall far from that voice, I remained to listen, trusting he'd have no reason to step into the hall.

"I want you to put your pens and pencils down," he said, and the sound of writing implements falling onto wood engulfed the room. "To understand history, you have to see it. It's more than words on a page. It happened. You can't ever forget that. Put your head on your desk," he said. "Everybody. Go on. Now close your eyes." His footsteps approached the door. He flipped a switch, the room went black, and the footsteps trailed away.

"Megalomania," he said. "Somebody tell me what it means."

A male voice sounded in the dark. "Delusions of omnipotence."

"Good," Orson said. "It's a mental disorder, so keep that in mind, too."

The professor kept silent for half a minute, and the room was still. When he spoke again, his voice had a controlled, musical resonance.

"The year is A.D. thirty-nine," he began. "You're a Roman senator, and you and your wife have been invited to watch the gladiatorial games with the young emperor, Gaius Caligula.

"During the lunch interlude, as *humiliores* are executed *ad bestias* before a rejoicing crowd, Caligula stands up, takes your wife by the hand, and leaves with her, escorted by his guards.

"You know exactly what's happening, and it's apparent to the other senators, because the same thing has happened to their wives. But you do nothing. You just sit on the stone steps, under the blue, spring sky, watching the lions chase their prey.

"An hour later, Gaius returns with your wife. When she sits down beside you, you notice a purple bruise on her face. She's rattled, her clothes are torn, and she refuses to look at you. There are six other senators who've been invited along with you, and suddenly you hear Caligula speak to them.

"'Her breasts are quite small,' he says, loudly enough for everyone around to hear. 'She's a sexual bore. I'd rather watch the lions feed than fuck her . . . again.'

"He laughs and pats you on the back, and everyone laughs with him. No one contradicts Gaius. No one challenges the emperor. It's pure sycophancy, and you sit there, boiling, wishing you'd never come. But to speak one word against Caligula would be your family's certain death. It's best just to keep silent and pray you never receive another invitation."

Orson's footsteps approached the doorway. I stepped back, but he'd only come for the lights. The room filled with the sound of students shifting in their seats and reopening notebooks.

"Next Tuesday," he said, "we'll talk about Caligula. I notice some of your classmates aren't with us today, and that may or may not have something to do with the snowstorm in the mountains last night." The class laughed. It was obvious by now that his students adored him.

"There will be a quiz on Caligula next Tuesday. Know the basics. When was he born? When did he become emperor? When and how did he die? Read chapter twenty-one in your text, and you shouldn't have a problem. I think you'll find him to be one of the most complex, intriguing, yet misunderstood rulers in Roman history." He paused. "Have a nice weekend."

I heard notebooks closing and backpacks zipping. Then the class seemed to rise all at once and dash for the door. Orson would be coming, too.

Across the hall, a door was ajar. I pushed my way through the students and slipped unseen into a dark, empty classroom. Then, peering through the cracked door, I waited for him to emerge.

# 22

**ORSON** descended the steps and started down the walkway. I waited inside the foyer of Howard Hall, watching him through the window beside the door. Dressed in a beige wool suit, a red bow tie, and green suspenders, he carried a tan briefcase and wore gold wire-framed glasses. When he was beyond the gazebo, I opened the door and followed him as he strode quickly across campus and disappeared into Gerard Hall.

As I approached his building, the light snow continued. The temperature had dropped as the day progressed, and the sky, only partly overcast this morning, was now completely masked by low gray clouds, which grazed the mountain peaks.

Gerard Hall was one of the smaller buildings on campus—two stories and narrow. Its name was incised into the stone pediment above the door. I felt exposed standing out in front of Orson's building in the cold. His office was on the second floor, but he could be anywhere inside, and while from a distance I felt safe, I knew that in proximity, my brother would instantly know my eyes.

I sat on the steps for five minutes, until I'd worked up the nerve to go inside. But as I stood to reach for the door handle footsteps pounded on a hardwood floor, and looking through the window, I saw a figure appear from the hallway. I turned away and leaned against the black railing just as the door opened.

I smelled her perfume before I saw her. An older woman, still beautiful, cascaded down the steps in high heels and a black over-coat. Her blond hair, streaked with silver, jounced as she walked away on a path leading to the town. I peeked again through the tall, slim window by the door, then, seeing only the empty foyer, pulled the handle and stepped inside.

Without voices, or fingers on keyboards, the fluorescent lights hummed deafeningly overhead as they shone hard light upon the dusty floor. According to a glass-encased magnetic message board, this was the office building of the history department, and the last names of professors and their respective office numbers were displayed in white lettering behind the glass. Looking down the hallway, I saw there were stairwells at both ends. Arbitrarily, I turned left and started walking to the stairs, passing four unmarked doors and a janitor's closet.

Jazz music poured softly from the second floor. I stopped at the top of the stairwell and looked into the hallway. All the flourescent lights were out save one, which flickered sporadically at the other end. The only constant light emanated from two open and opposing doorways, where voices rose in conversation above a moaning trumpet.

In the shadows, I walked toward the first office along the corridor. It was closed, and a brass nameplate affixed to the door read

STCHYKENSKI 206. Across the hall, someone typed inside of 207, where light and classical music escaped in slivers beneath the door.

On the right side, fifteen feet down the hall, Orson's door stood wide open, the wonder of Miles Davis's "Blue in Green" lingering in the doorway. I inched forward until I could see into Orson's empty office, and hear the conversation in the room across from his.

"I'm not sure yet," Orson was saying.

"David, there's no rush. We just need to make the decision before Christmas. I think the deadline's the twenty-first of December."

"That's plenty of time," Orson said. "I just want to finish a thorough reading of his publications. I like what I've seen so far, but I want to be sure, Jack."

"We all do," Jack said, "and right now what I'm hearing from the others is that Dr. Harris would fit in nicely. Those of us who've read his work think he's more than qualified."

Footsteps reverberated in the opposite stairwell, and I backed away.

"Damn," Orson said. "I've got to meet with a student. How about lunch tomorrow?"

"Splendid."

A chair squeaked, and I ran down the hall. There was a men's bathroom on my right that I'd unwittingly passed before, and I slipped inside as Orson stepped from Jack's office into the hall. In the dark bathroom, a faucet dripped into the sink. Cracking the door, I glanced back into the hallway. Orson now stood in the threshold of his office, leaning against the door frame and speaking to a pudgy girl with walnut hair and a pale white face. She wore a backpack on the outside of her yellow rain jacket, and she smiled as Orson invited her into his office and shut the door.

I let the bathroom door close, immersing myself in darkness.

Closing my eyes, I took steady breaths until the banging in my chest subsided.

Suddenly, I remembered—walking up the steps, I'd seen a red box with the word *Fire* on it.

I opened the door. Orson's was still closed, so I ran from the hallway into the stairwell. The fire alarm was mounted on the wall, and I stopped and looked back down the hallway. Now the only light came from Jack's office.

I pulled the white handle and the alarm screamed.

Back inside the bathroom, the darkness now riddled with blinking lights, I found my way into a stall and sat down on the toilet. The door opened, someone shouted, and then it closed again, the darkness assuring whoever had entered that the men's room was vacant. After thirty seconds, I walked to the door.

The floor vacated, most of the doors were open now, brightening the hallway considerably. I ran toward 209 as the alarm rang. Empty. Rushing inside, I shut the door behind me and moved to the window. Outside, a crowd was gathering at the building's entrance, people staring up in wonder, looking for the smoke. It was snowing hard now, sticking to the grass, melting on the brick. I wondered how long it'd take the fire department to arrive.

There were no filing cabinets. I opened the bottom right-hand drawer of the desk and found it stuffed with graded papers and tests. The drawer above it overflowed with supplies—pens, pencils, several legal pads. Two roll books and two packs of note cards filled the drawer in the center, and the left-hand drawers were both empty. No trophies. No photographs. But this did not surprise me. He was too careful to keep them here. I'd known it, but I had to check.

A monitor, processor, and keyboard stood separately on the floor—an old Tandy 1000 with the letters and numbers worn completely off the keys. There was a bookshelf on either side of the window. I glanced at the titles but found nothing peculiar. They were history texts, most on ancient Rome and Greece. A poster of Athens and a framed photograph of Orson standing in the Coliseum hung on the wall in front of his desk.

A stack of unopened envelopes lay on top of his desk, and I picked them up. Of the four, three had been addressed to his school office, the other to 617 Jennings Road, Woodside, Vermont. *Yes.* Grabbing a pen and a sheet of paper from the supply drawer, I copied down the address. Then I looked through the drawers once more to make sure I hadn't disturbed anything. Orson would know.

The fire alarm stopped ringing. Stuffing his address in my pocket, I opened the door. Though still quiet in this hall, there were firemen on the floor below—I could hear their shouting and heavy footsteps. Rushing to the stairwell on the right, I looked down, then, seeing nothing, descended the steps. At the bottom, I saw two firemen in the first-floor hallway disappear into different rooms. There was an exit at the side of the building, and I bolted for the door and sprinted down stone steps into snowy grass. After fifty yards, I slowed to a walk, and glancing over my shoulder, saw the people still waiting in front of the building, Orson among them.

The snow had let up and was now falling in big downy flakes. Exhilarated, I walked through frosted grass back toward the town. Walter and I still had to dig Orson's hole before dark.

# 23

**W** E waited until 6:30, when the cloudy sky darkened into slate. I drove the Cadillac onto 116, a lonely stretch of highway that shot through the wilderness between Woodside and Bristol. Little snow remained in the valley now. The temperature had hovered in the upper thirties throughout the evening, melting the half inch of wet snow that had fallen in the early afternoon.

Pines blitzed by on both sides of the road. I could smell them even from inside the car—a clean, bitter scent. We passed several picnic areas and a campground, all part of the Green Mountain National Forest. But I wanted land where people never walked. The campgrounds were empty now, and their trails offered easy access to the woods. But if the weather turned warm again, which undoubtedly it would do before the ground froze for the winter, people would flock to these trails, some with dogs. I didn't have the time or energy to dig that deep a hole.

I'd been driving for ten minutes when the shoulder widened to two car lengths. Slowing down, I swerved off the road, and the tires slid to a stop in the muddy grass. I turned off the engine and the headlights and looked through the windshield and the rearview mirror. The highway stretched on, dark and empty.

"You think this spot is safe?" Walter asked.

"Safe as any," I said, pulling the keys from the ignition.

I opened the door and stepped down into the cold, wet grass. The sound of our doors slamming resounded through the woods. Opening the trunk, we each took a shovel and a pair of leather gloves to keep our hands from going numb.

I led us back into the trees. We didn't go far, because it'd be difficult to find this place on a moonless night. We'd be carrying Orson, and stumbling through the woods with him would be hard enough. The white pines dripped snowmelt, and within moments, I was shivering and miserable, thinking of the fireplace at the Woodside Inn.

Forty yards in, I stopped. The trees grew so close to one another that the highway was now invisible. I drew an arrow in the pine needles, pointing toward the road. If we somehow became disoriented in the forest, we could wander out here all night looking for the highway.

"Let's dig," I said, motioning to a level space between the trees.

I stabbed my shovel through the pine needles, and it cut into the moist earth below. The work was initially difficult because we were cold, but the exertion soon drew sweat. In no time, I could feel only the biting chill in my ruddy cheeks.

We traced the outline first. Then we began to dig, and with the two of us working, we'd soon gone two feet down. When I thought it was sufficiently deep, I lay in the hole and Walter measured how far an animal would have to dig to reach me: There'd be a foot of earth between Orson and the forest floor.

I climbed out and brushed the dirt from my jeans, now damp and mud-streaked. Walter leaned against the trunk of a red spruce and lit a cigarette. In the blue dusk, there was no detail in his face, but I could tell that he stared at me strangely, the tobacco cinder glowing and fading.

"What?" I asked, but he shook his head. "No, what is it?" I'd begun to shiver again.

"We're actually going to kill a man."

"Not *a* man, Walter. *The* man who's threatened to sic a psychopath on your family."

"You might not be scared, Andy, but I'm shitting my pants. I hardly slept last night. I can't stop thinking that a million things could go wrong tomorrow. He could escape. Kill us. He might even know we're here. You considered that? He's a psychopath, and we're fucking with him."

A twig snapped in the distance.

"Aren't you doing this for your family?" I asked. "Think about them when you're scared. What it'll feel like to see the animal who threatened Jenna bleeding in that hole."

The woods had become unnervingly dark.

"It may get rough tomorrow," I said. "We may have to . . . do things to him if he won't tell us what we need to know. You up for that?"

"I will be."

Walter started in the direction of the highway. I picked up my shovel and followed him, counting the steps from Orson's grave to the edge of the forest. When we emerged from the trees, the highway was silent, and a cold fog was descended from the high country. I could only see a hundred yards down the road now—beyond, an impenetrable black mist.

I left my shovel leaning against the largest pine tree I could find.

We would need some marker to find this place at night. As we climbed back into the car and the interior lights came on and the seat belt warning beeped, something sank inside of me. Walter was wrong. Perhaps the foggy dusk intensified it, but I was afraid. Driving back toward the inn, my hands trembled as they gripped the steering wheel. I wondered in the back of my mind if I could do it. In spite of everything he'd done, Orson was my brother. My twin. There was a bond.

Walter and I didn't speak. I imagined our silence might be analogous to that which develops between soldiers who have a bloody task ahead of them. No place for superficial chatter. Only an intense focus on the coming hours, and mental preparation to do a horrible thing.

# 24

FRIDAY, early afternoon, as the sun reached its apogee and crossed into the western sky, my bed resembled a small arsenal: my subcompact .40 Glock; Walter's full-size .45; two boxes of Remington .40-caliber 180-grain semijacketed hollow-points; two boxes of Remington .45-caliber 185-grain semijacketed hollow-points; two extra magazines for each handgun; a pair of Amherst RS446 walkie-talkies; eighteen vials of benzodiazepines; one vial of antidote; three hypodermic needles; latex gloves; leather gloves; a penlight; handcuffs; and two mechanic's suits I'd purchased from an Army-Navy surplus store in Davidson.

The benzodiazepines had been tricky to come by. Walter's mother-in-law suffered from a panic disorder, and among the sundry medications she stockpiled was a medium-acting sedative called Ativan. He'd helped himself to thirteen 1-mL vials. According to our on-line research, this would be sufficient to keep Orson sedated for a couple of days if need be. The downside, however, was that the onset of Ativan took upward of twenty minutes, and I needed something that could knock Orson down in less than two.

So I'd done a very bad thing.

Horror writers get away with murder in the pursuit of realism, and over the years, I'd befriended attorneys, detectives, and professionals in various fields, all of whom had graciously consulted with me on the accuracy of my novels. The investigative and courtroom procedures in my stories are religiously unerring. I always get the gun right. A coroner friend of mine even let me sit in on an autopsy, just so I could nail the olfactory experience in the opening chapter of my latest book.

There's a vignette in *Blue Murder* where the protagonist steals drugs from a hospital. So in the course of my research for the book, I'd asked my doctor, "If you wanted to steal narcotics from a hospital, how would you do it?" Writers can ask these questions, and no one suspects their motives because "it's for the book," and they show up in the acknowledgments.

He told me exactly what to do, and goddamn if he wasn't right. His advice: "Raid the recovery room. It doesn't matter if the narcotics are locked up, as long as the keys are left in drawers that aren't. Pray for incompetent nurses. Know where the cameras are. Acquire a janitor's uniform, and stay busy long enough to see where the keys to the narcotics cabinet are kept."

Thanks to careless, unobservant nurses in the recovery room, two days before we left for Woodside, I walked out of Mercy Hospital in Charlotte, North Carolina, with five 1-mL vials of the short-acting benzodiazepine, Versed. Used for sedation in surgical procedures, when administered intravenously, it can render someone unconscious inside of ninety seconds. Unfortunately, it also has the potential to induce respiratory depression, so I'd stolen a vial of its antidote, flumazenil, as well.

In addition to my larceny, I'd extensively researched intravenous and intramuscular injection. I knew the dosages and monographs for Ativan and Versed. I'd done my homework, had reliable firearms, and a well-devised plan. As Walter and I sat on opposite love seats, pushing the brass-shelled hollow-points into the magazines, a calmness settled upon me. *We're actually doing it,* I thought. *Who does this kind of thing? Pretty fucking gutsy. It'd make one hell of a book.*

.

While Walter took a catnap, I went downstairs. Dirty dishes and empty wine bottles cluttered the dining room table—casualties of lunch. I walked back into the kitchen and asked the chef if he would make me a turkey sandwich. He didn't want to. Lunch had already been served. But reluctantly, he agreed and said I could wait by the fire.

I sat down in a rocking chair. In the brick hearth, a fire was in the process of burning out. I imagined it had been blazing in the early-morning hours, before the dusting of snow had melted, as other guests planned their day. It still warmed the snug sitting area, though now halfheartedly. As I waited, I stared at the only remaining log. It glowed underneath, the embers slowly eating it away, turning the wood to ash and smoke.

In the nearby lounge, a TV blared. I heard the voice of Agent Trent, discussing recent developments in the search for the Heart Surgeon.

A couple walking by on their way to the front door glanced curiously at my outfit. A gray one-piece mechanic's suit was anomalous attire for this upscale inn.

.

Jennings Road branched left off of Main Street, a mile beyond the college. Leafless sugar maples and birches shielded the road from the sky as it climbed a hillside. There were mounds of leaves along the sides of the road. I pictured them in full, fiery color, littered across the street and through the lawns, turning this small New England neighborhood into a mystical universe all its own.

Near the top of the hill, on a black mailbox in slanted white numbers, I saw 617. Walter slowed the car, but I told him to drive casually by and park a ways up the street. As we continued on, I gazed at Orson's home, disbelieving I'd actually found it. From the outside, it was modestly elegant. A white two-story house, with dormer windows protruding from the second floor, larger bay windows from the first. A split-rail fence enclosed the front lawn, and flowers grew along a brick walkway that curved from the driveway to the front porch. There was no garage, and there were presently no cars in the driveway.

We crested the hill and Walter parked near the curb, scattering a pile of leaves. He turned off the engine and looked warily at me as I reached under my seat and grabbed the walkie-talkies.

"Channel eight, subchannel seventeen," I said, handing one to Walter. We adjusted our frequencies accordingly. "We passed a diner before we turned onto Jennings. Wait there. This car looks conspicuous sitting up here, especially with an out-of-state tag. You'll get the first communication at the diner. I'll say, 'Go, Papa.' That'll mean he's home, so get your ass up here and start circling the neighborhood. The second communication will be 'Bring it home,' and that means come to six seventeen and back into the driveway. I'll want you to open the trunk for me and get back in the car. When you're inside and the trunk's open, I'll bring him out. He'll be unconscious. I'll put him in the trunk, and you'll drive us to his hole on One sixteen. Any questions?"

"No."

"Don't break radio silence unless it's an emergency. If you have to, call me Wilma. I'll call you Fred. You never know who might be listening. Also, don't forget the channels. Eight and seventeen. Write it on your hand." I clipped on my walkie-talkie and lifted the cumbersome fanny pack from the floorboard. Then I strapped it around my waist, opened the door, and stepped out into the cool afternoon.

"It's only four-thirty," I said, "so it may be several hours before you hear from me." I shut the door, and he drove on down the mountain, disappearing around a bend in the road.

I walked back up the hill, and as I passed over the crest, the town of Woodside appeared before me. I wondered if in spring or summer, when leaves fattened the trees, it would be difficult to see the town, hundreds of feet below. But the naked trees revealed the foothill community—Main Street, the college, even glimpses of the downtown a mile and a half north. *A lovely neighborhood.* There might be hundreds like it in the New England countryside, thousands across the country itself. Who'd ever suspect the Heart Surgeon lived here, among these pastoral dwellings in Woodside suburbia?

I walked up Orson's driveway to a chest-high white fence that picketed the backyard. As I scaled and then straddled it, I wondered if he owned a dog. When my feet hit the grass on the other side, I stayed on all fours, scanning the lawn for a doghouse, listening for the jingle of a chain. Nothing moved in the beautiful grass. A northern white cedar overshadowed the backyard, but there was no dog.

I walked around the corner. A stone patio with white plastic lawn chairs extended from the back of the house. I moved across the grass onto the patio, where French doors led into a solarium. Creeping up to the doors, I peeked through the glass. No lights were on, but peering through the shadows, I could see beyond the sunroom into the kitchen. The house seemed empty. I tried the door, but it was locked. There was no dead bolt, though, and I was relieved I would have to break only a single pane of glass.

I withdrew a pair of leather gloves from the fanny pack and grabbed a baseball-size rock lying in a flaccid garden adjacent to the patio. When the gloves were on, I shoved the rock through the pane nearest the doorknob. There was a concussive crack, and splinters of glass spilled across the floor inside. Still holding the rock, I listened for the sound of an alarm, but the house remained silent. I dropped the rock and turned the lock.

The warm breath of central heating caressed my face as the doors swung open. I stepped inside, removed the leather gloves, and put them back in the fanny pack. After wiping my fingerprints off the outside doorknob, I squeezed my hands into a pair of latex gloves and pulled the doors closed behind me.

I distrusted the silence. Standing in a sunroom, I noticed the fading light filtering in through long, curved panels of glass. Wicker chairs had been placed somewhat erratically across the brick-patterned linoleum floor, and potted plants lent the room the earthy bouquet of a greenhouse. I moved cautiously across the floor, my footfalls crunching bits of glass. Taking my Glock from the fanny pack, I chambered the first bullet, praying I wouldn't have to fire the unsilenced weapon in this tranquil neighborhood. Walter and I had been unable to locate black-market silencers.

From the solarium, I proceeded into the kitchen, which was decked out with white appliances on miles of counter space. I examined pictures on the refrigerator of a white-water rafting trip, and of

Orson and a woman I'd never seen before, standing arm in arm on the barren summit of a mountain.

To the right, a doorway led into a dining room, complete with china hutch, chandelier, and a mahogany table set with crystal, silver, and china on a white tablecloth.

But I went through the doorway to the left, leaving the kitchen and entering the living room. Orson had impeccable taste. Over the mantel there hung a print of Odilon Redon's monochromatic *Anthony: What Is the Object of All This? The Devil: There is No Object.* Incidentally, the subject of the black lithograph looked jarringly similar to the man who'd stopped me for an autograph on my mother's street. *Luther.* In the far left corner stood an old Steinway upright piano, and before the gas-log fireplace, a Persian rug spread across the floor, framed by a futon and two burgundy leather chairs. A staircase ascended to my immediate right, and just ahead, at the foot of its steps, loomed the front door.

I walked through the living room, my steps resonating on the hardwood floor. A doorway on the left wall, near the Steinway, opened into a library, and I crossed the threshold into the room of books.

It smelled good in his study, like aged paper and cigars. A lavish desk dominated the center of the room, identical to the one in my office. Even his swivel chair was the same. Sifting through the drawers, I found nothing. Every letter was addressed to Dr. David Parker, and most of the files consisted of research materials on ancient Rome. There weren't even pictures on the desk—just a computer, a cedar humidor filled with Macanudo Robusto cigars, and a decanter of cognac.

The walls were covered by bookcases. The titles indicated the same specific, academic sort of subject matter as the books I'd seen in his office: *Agrarian Society in Rome in the Third Century B.C. Tri-*

*bunal Policy and Imperial Power Before Caesar. Foreign Relations: Rome, Carthage, and the Punic Wars.*

The low shudder of a car engine pulled me to the window. I split the blinds with two fingers and watched a white Lexus sedan turn into Orson's driveway. I waited, my stomach twisting into knots. If Orson came in through the back door, he'd see the broken glass.

He appeared suddenly, walking swiftly up the sidewalk in an olive suit, briefcase in hand. I stepped back from the blinds, dropped to my knees, and crawled under his desk.

A key slid into the dead bolt, and the front door opened. Orson whistled as he strode inside, and I drew back as far as I could into the darkness under the desk. His footsteps moved through the living room, then into the study. A deafening clump shook the desk and set my heart palpitating. He'd dropped his briefcase on the desktop. As he came around the desk toward the chair, I readied the gun.

A phone rang somewhere in the house. He stopped. I could see his legs now, his pointed black wing tips. I smelled him—clean, cologne-sweet, familiar. The scent of our sweat after a long day was identical. The phone rang again, and he rushed out of the study, mumbling something indecipherable under his breath.

He answered from the kitchen after the third ring. "Hello? . . . Hi, Arlene. . . . Yes, of course. . . . Well, why don't you, then? We'll put something on. . . . No, don't do that. And just come on in. . . . All right. Sounds good. See you then."

He hung up the phone and went back into the living room. For a moment, I thought he was returning to the study, and I raised the gun. But his footsteps died away as he ran up the staircase.

Shaking, I climbed out from under the desk. As the shower cut on upstairs, I squatted down, took the walkie-talkie from the fanny pack, and pressed the talk button.

"Wilma," I whispered. "Wilma? Over?"

"Over." Walter's voice crackled back through the speaker. I lowered the volume. "You're Wilma. I'm Fred," he said.

"He's here," I whispered. "Upstairs, taking a shower."

"Did you find—"

"Can't talk now. Go, Papa."

"What?"

"Get up here and wait for the next signal."

I turned off the walkie-talkie and walked into the living room. The staircase was carpeted, so my footsteps fell silently as I ascended to the second floor. Emerging in the center of a dim hallway, I saw there was a bedroom at each end, and a closed door directly ahead, which, because it glowed underneath, I presumed to be the bathroom. Orson's shoes, his navy-speckled brown socks, black belt, and olive suit trailed right up to the door.

He sang the Beatles' "All You Need Is Love" in the shower.

I stepped toward the bathroom. *Open the door, slip inside, and then stick him with the needle through the shower curtain. . . .*

The doorbell rang, and I froze in the hallway, wondering if he'd heard it, too. After five seconds, the shower cut off, and I heard the plop of wet feet on tile and cloth rubbing frantically over skin. I ran down the hallway, then into the bedroom on the right. Because there were clothes strewn all over the floor, I assumed this was his room. To my right, a dormer window overlooked Jennings Road and, beyond it, the snowy Adirondacks. Pillows filled the alcove, and I couldn't help thinking that Orson must spend a great deal of time reading in that dormer nook.

A roomy walk-in closet opened to my left, and I darted inside as the bathroom door opened. The doorbell rang again, and Orson shouted, "I told you to just come in!" as he rushed down the staircase.

I did not hear him answer the door. Jostling my way between hangers of mothball-stinking suits and stiff sweaters, I finally ducked down in the farthest corner of the dark closet.

After a moment, Orson came back up the stairs and entered his room. I saw him briefly through the hangers—naked, stepping into a pair of boxer shorts and blue jeans, still conjoined on the floor, just as he'd left them. He stood shirtless in front of a full-length mirror, combing his wet hair, grown out now from the crew cut he'd sported in the desert. Grinning at himself, he bared his teeth, mouthing words into the mirror, none of which I could understand. It was the first good look I'd had of my brother, and I drank it in.

Still in marvelous physical condition, his appearance was more civilized and handsome than in the desert. He radiated charisma, and his eyes sparkled.

"Pour yourself a glass of wine!" he yelled. "There's a pinot noir in the wine rack!"

Orson opened a dresser drawer and perused it for a moment, finally lifting out a gray box cutter. He exposed the razor, a small blade that obtruded no more than an inch from its metal sheath. Fingering the edge with his thumb, he smiled at himself again in the mirror.

"You behave." He giggled. "You behave tonight."

"Dave?"

Orson spun around. "Arlene. You scared me."

Her voice came from the top of the stairs. "Where's the wine rack?"

"Kitchen counter." He held the box cutter behind his back. From my angle, I could see it in the mirror as he fidgeted with it, pushing the blade in and out. "Oh, Arlene. Put on some music, will you? Miles Davis, if you don't mind."

Retracting the blade, he slipped the box cutter into his back pocket, and continued to primp.

·

Through the dormer window, the last strands of sunlight receded behind the Adirondacks. It was tempting to hide in that closet for the entire night, cloistered safely behind hangers, between smelly old garments. But I steeled myself, pushed my way through the clothes, and stumbled at last out of his closet.

Their voices rose to the second floor. I heard my brother laugh, and the tinkle of silverware on china. It'd taken me an hour to summon the nerve to walk out of the closet. *Thank God they're still eating.* It suddenly occurred to me: *The broken glass. Please don't go into the sunroom.*

Since I had his room temporarily to myself, I took the opportunity to check the dresser, the bookshelves, and the closet for the pictures and videos of the desert. I found nothing, however, to substantiate his hobby, not even a journal. In fact, the only item in his bedroom that reflected in a small way Orson's taste for violence was an enormous William Blake print hanging on the wall across from his bed—*The Simoniac Pope,* a pen and watercolor hellscape of Pope Nicholas III in a vat of flames, the soles of his feet on fire. I knew this work. It was an illustration of *Hell, Canto 19* from Dante's *Divine Comedy.* Those who didn't know him might be perplexed at Orson's morbid choice of wall decor.

I walked down the hallway and entered the guest room. It was impersonal, filled with ill-matched, eclectic furniture. The closet was empty, as were the two drawers of the bedside table. I doubted if anyone had ever slept in the single bed.

Slinking back into the hallway, I turned and went down several steps. Orson spoke softly in the dining room. Chairs moved, and I heard footsteps heading toward the foyer. I retraced my steps, and when their footsteps continued in my direction, I clawed my way up the staircase, raced back down the hallway, and hid again in his closet.

They entered the room and fell together onto his bed. I heard Orson say, "I like you a lot."

"I like you, too."

"Yeah?"

"I wouldn't be here if I didn't." Arlene sounded as if she was about thirty, and though her voice was throaty, it retained a sliver of girlish innocence. I knew why Orson liked her. The lamp on his bed-side table cut off. They kissed for a while in the darkness, and the intimate slurping reminded me of Friday nights, in high school.

"What would you think about me doing this?" he asked.

"Ooooh."

"Yeah?"

"Uh-huh." The room fell silent for a moment, excepting the moist sucking murmurs.

"Can you guess what I have in my back pocket?" Orson said finally.

"Mmm. What?"

"You have to guess, silly."

"Is it round and crinkly?"

"Actually, it's hard."

"Mmm." She shuddered in a good way. I could hear the alcohol thickening up her voice.

"And very sharp."

"Huh?"

"You told any of your friends about me?"

"What do you mean?"

"Does anyone know we've been seeing each other?"

"Why does it matter?"

"Just tell me." I caught a grain of anger in his voice, which I'm sure she didn't register.

"Only the girls at work."

Orson sighed.

"I asked you not to tell *anyone*. You tell them my name?"

"Why?"

"Arlene, did you tell them my name?"

"I don't remember." Her voice mellowed. "What do you think about this, sweetie?" A zipper started to descend.

There was sudden movement in the dark. "Don't you touch me," he hissed.

The bed squeaked, and I wondered if she'd sat up.

"Turn on the light," she said. "Turn it on!" The light did not come on.

"Did you tell your girlfriends my name?"

"Why are you acting so weird?"

"Tell me, so I can show you what's in my pocket."

"Yes, I told them your—"

"Goddamnit."

"What?"

"You can go now."

"Why?"

"Leave."

"What is *wrong* with you? I thought—I mean . . . I like you, and I thought—"

"I had something extraordinarily special planned for us tonight. And you just ruined it. I was going to open you up, Arlene."

"To what?"

"Get out of my house."

The bed moved again, the floor creaked, and it sounded as though clothes were being smoothed.

"I can't believe I—you need help, David."

"Perhaps."

"You can go to—"

"I'd advise you to leave while you're still able."

She stormed from his bedroom into the hallway, screamed "Fucking freak!" and was sobbing by the time she reached the front door.

# 25

**ORSON** sat for a while in the dark after Arlene left. For some reason, I expected him to cry, to come apart in pathetic flinders when no one was around. But this didn't happen. As my eyes grew accustomed to the dark, I began to make out the shapes in his room— the painting on the wall, the bookshelves, his legs stretched out on the bed. I could see barbs of light through the dormer window, on the black slopes across the valley.

After thirty minutes, I thought he'd fallen asleep, and I began to psych myself up to crawl out of the closet and do what I'd come here to do. But when I started to move, he sat up abruptly. Stiffening, I watched his arms reach down under the bed and lift what appeared to be a shoe box up onto the mattress. Orson slipped out of his loafers and kicked them in opposite directions across the room. One hurtled into the closet and nearly struck me in the head.

I heard a mechanical clicking. He settled back onto the mattress and began speaking in a low, monotonous voice: "It is . . . seven forty-three P.M. on Friday, November eighth. Arlene came over this evening. I told you about her. That legal assistant from Bristol. It was going to happen tonight. I thought about it all day. All week. But she'd mentioned me—my name, I mean—to some of her coworkers, so that's the end of that. It was an exercise in self-control. I'd never used a box cutter before, so I'm more than a little disappointed that tonight didn't work out. If I go much longer without any play, I may resort to doing something careless, like that time in Burlington. But you made the rule never to do that in this town, and it's an intelligent rule, so don't fuck things up." He stopped the Dictaphone, but then pushed the record button again.

"Last thing. I was on-line today, and I saw that James Keiller's second appeal was denied. Guess that means they'll be setting an execution date in the near term. That's a beautiful thing, what I did there. It really is. I may have to make the trip out to Nebraska when they juice him. And I do believe they juice 'em in the Cornhusker State."

He returned the Dictaphone to the shoe box and took out something else. Climbing out of bed, he walked toward his dresser, upon which sat a TV/VCR combo. He inserted a videotape and turned on the TV. As it started to play, he lay down on his stomach, his head at the edge of the mattress, propped up on his elbows, chin cupped in his hands.

It was in color. *Oh God. The shed.* I resisted a surge of nausea.

"This is Cindy, and she just failed the test. Say hi, Cindy."

The woman was tied to the pole, with that leather collar around her neck. Orson turned the camera on himself, sweaty-faced, eyes twinkling, beaming, bridelike.

"Cindy has chosen the six-inch boning knife."

"Stop it!" she shrieked.

I plugged my ears and shut my eyes. The fear in her voice sickened me. Even with the volume muffled, I could still hear the most piercing of screams. On the bed, Orson was making noise, too. I squinted and saw that he'd turned over on his back and was watching the screen upside down, jerking off.

The footage of Orson killing her wasn't terribly long, so he watched it over and over. If I hyperfocused on my heartbeat, I found that I could block out the television and Orson's groans almost completely. Counting the beats, I worked my way up to 704.

■

When my eyes opened, the room was silent. I'd nodded off, and it horrified me to think I might've been snoring or lost precious hours asleep in his closet. Checking my watch, I saw that 9:30 had just passed, and I felt relief knowing that Walter and I still had the majority of the night to kill my brother.

From the bed—deep breathing. I recognized the pattern of Orson's long exhalations. Almost certain he was asleep, I withdrew a syringe and a vial of Versed. Flicking off the plastic cap, I stuck the hollow needle through the rubber seal and pulled the plunger back until the bottle was empty. I then aspirated the contents of two more vials. With fifteen milligrams of Versed in the syringe, I secured the caps and placed the three empty vials back into my fanny pack, closing the zipper so slowly, I couldn't even hear the minute teeth biting back together. The needle in my left hand, the Glock in my right, I poked my head through the hangers and proceeded to inch my way out.

As I came to my feet on the hardwood floor of the walk-in closet, it occurred to me that he might not be asleep. Perhaps he was merely resting, breathing patiently in a yogic trance. After three steps, I stood at the threshold of the closet, staring down at Orson on the bed.

His chest rose and fell in an unhurried rhythm indicative of sleep. I went down on my knees, held the plastic syringe with my teeth, and crawled across the dusty floor. At the edge of his bed, I stopped and spurned another wave of nausea and hyperventilation. Sweat trickled down my forehead and smarted in my eyes. Under the latex skin, my hands were wet.

Squatting down on the floor, I took the syringe from my mouth, then, holding it up before my face, squirted a brief stream through the shaft of the needle to remove air bubbles. Orson shifted on the bed. His back had been to me, but he turned over, so that we faced each other. *All he has to do is open his eyes.*

His left arm was beautifully exposed. Withdrawing a penlight and holding it between my teeth, I spotlighted his forearm and could see numerous periwinkle veins under the surface of his skin. With great patience and concentration, I lowered the eye of the needle until it hovered just an inch above his skin. There was a chance this would kill him. Because I was attempting to inject intravenously, the substantial dose of Versed would be tearing through his bloodstream, and when it slammed into his central nervous system, he might stop breathing. *Steady hands.*

As I slipped the needle into the antecubital vein opposite the elbow, his eyes opened. I injected the drug. *Please have hit the vein.* Orson shot up and gasped. I let go of the syringe and jumped back, the needle still dangling in his arm. He pulled it out and held it up before his face, flabbergasted.

"Andy?" he whispered, cotton-mouthed. "*Andy?* How did you . . ." He swallowed several times, as though something was blocking his windpipe. Standing, I pointed the gun at him.

"Lie back, Orson."

"What did you give me?"

"Lie back!"

He leaned back into the pillows. "God," he said. "That's strong."

He sounded medicated already, and I thought his eyes had closed. I turned on the bedside lamp so I could be sure. They were slits.

"What are you doing, Andy?" he asked. "How did you . . ." His words trailed off.

"You killed my mother," I said to him.

"I don't think you . . ." His eyes closed.

"Orson?" I could see the red dot on his arm where the needle had penetrated the skin. "Orson!" He still didn't move, so I reached forward and slapped his face. He groaned, but it was an incoherent response, which only assured me that the drug had taken control of him.

Backpedaling toward the closet, I took the walkie-talkie from my fanny pack.

"Walter?" I said, breathless. "Walt . . . Fred?"

"Over."

"You close?"

"A hundred yards."

"Get up here and come inside."

I leaned against the wall and wiped the sweat from my eyelids.

Orson lunged from the bed and drilled his head into my stomach before I could even think about my gun. As I lost my breath, he drove his knee between my legs and grabbed the back of my neck with both hands. He butted his forehead into my nose, and I felt the cartilage crunch and then the subsequent burn. Cool blood flowed over my lips.

"What are you thinking, Andy? *You can just do this to me?*"

I'd just managed to fill my lungs with air, when he shovel-punched me in the gut, right below my navel. As I hunched over, he kneed my face, and I dropped to the floor.

Instantly, he was on me, his fingers digging under my stomach, where my hands retained an iron grip on the Glock. A sharp, brutal pinch speared through my shirt into my back, and I moaned.

"Yeah, you like that, don't you? I'm gonna do it again and again." He'd stuck me with the needle. I felt it wiggling in me. "You're gonna give it up," he said, "and I'm gonna spend the weekend killing you. *What were you thinking, Andy? What?*"

I kept thinking that I should at least try to fight him, but if I moved, he might wrangle the gun from my hands.

A hard bone pummeled the back of my head, and it hurt like hell. I felt the needle pull out and enter again.

"Ah shit," he muttered. He struck the back of my head again, but it wasn't nearly as powerful a blow. "Ah, fuck you, Andy." He slumped onto the floor, crouching on his hands and knees, trying to preserve his consciousness. "Stay with it," he mumbled. "No. No."

Yanking the needle out of my back, I stood up and moved to the open doorway of his bedroom. My face felt swollen, and I could not see as clearly through my left eye. But the adrenaline masked the pain, even the deep microscopic holes in my back. Beneath the mechanic's suit, lines of blood streamed down my legs. Orson fell over onto his side on the floor.

"No." He sighed sleepily, his speech beginning to slur. "Andy. Don't do things . . ." He shut his eyes and was still.

There was a knock on the front door. I held the gun by the muzzle and hammered Orson across the forehead until I saw blood. Then I ran into the hallway and rushed down the staircase.

"Walter?" I yelled through the door.

"It's me," he said, and I let him inside. The coldness of the night radiated off his clothes. "Where's your broth— Oh God, your face . . ."

"I'm fine. Come on," I said, starting back up the steps. "Put on your latex gloves. He's upstairs."

# 26

**WHILE** Walter dragged Orson down the steps in his boxer shorts and rolled him up in the florid Persian rug, I again searched every crevice of my brother's bedroom. Searching under the bed, I located the shoe box of microcassettes and two more videotapes, but this was the extent of my discovery. Another thorough inspection of the closet produced nothing out of the ordinary. In the guest room, I found nothing, and by the time I'd begun a second perusal of the study, I waxed furious.

"You see this?" I said, exiting the hallway on the first floor and lifting the shoe box above my head. "It's all he keeps in his entire house that would clue anyone in to what he is."

In a mechanic's suit like mine, Walter sat on top of Orson, who was now cocooned inside the rug.

"There are more pictures than this," I said. "Pictures of me doing horrible things to people. In a self-storage unit or a safety-deposit box. You know what happens when this son of a bitch can't pay the bill 'cause he's dead? They clear out his space and find pictures of me digging a heart out of a woman's chest." *Now you know.*

Walter looked at me, but he didn't ask for elaboration. Standing up, he walked across the hardwood floor into Orson's study. He lifted the decanter of cognac and poured himself an immoderately full snifter.

"You want one?" he asked, warming the brandy with a delicate swirling motion of the glass.

"Please." He poured me one, too, and brought it into the living room. We sat down on Orson's futon before the hearth, swirling and sipping our brandies in silence, each waiting for that euphoric calm, though it never fully came.

"Will he tell us?" Walter asked finally.

"Tell us what?"

"About the pictures of you, and the man who wrote on Jenna's arm."

I turned my head and found Walter's eyes, my cheeks candescent with the liquor.

"Absofuckinlutely."

■

We carried him out the front door and down the steps. The moon shone bone white through the leafless, calligraphic trees. The alcohol numbed my face, diminishing the sting of the cold.

The rug wouldn't fit into the trunk, so we unrolled it and let Orson slide into the dark, empty cavity. I checked his breathing, and though it was steady, they were damn shallow breaths. A light cut on in the house across the street. The figure of a man came to a bay window.

"Come on, Walter," I said. "This is just about the worst place we could be right now."

We headed back down the mountain the way we'd come and turned right onto Main Street. I stared out my window as we passed the campus, its brick walkways lighted but empty. Farther on, I caught a glimpse of the white gazebo, where I'd stood in the snow just yesterday, in search of the man who now lay unconscious in the trunk.

"We got him, didn't we?" I said, and the brandy drew a smirk across my face.

"I'll celebrate when he's got a hundred pounds of cold dirt on top of his face, and we know where the man is who threatened my daughter."

Downtown Woodside was hopping for 10:30 at night. In spite of the cold, students filled the sidewalks. I could see a hundred minia-ture clouds of breath vapor, and hear their hollering through the glass. Dueling bars on opposite sides of the street had students milling outside the doors in long, anxious lines, waiting to reach the mirthful warmth inside. It made perfect sense to me. It was too cold in this town to do anything but drink.

Seven point eight miles from Beans n' Bagels, Walter eased off the pavement, pulling onto the soft, wide shoulder of 116. He drove through the grass for a hundred yards and stopped in the shadow of two oaks.

"Your shovel's back there," he said. "I saw it against that tree." He leaned back in his seat and killed the engine. I turned around and looked through the back windshield. Up and down the highway, bathed now in blue frozen moonlight, nothing moved.

"How's your face?" he asked.

"My nose feels broken, but it's not." It was hot to the touch, the skin across the bridge having tightened from swelling. My left eye had nearly closed, but, surprisingly, it didn't hurt.

"You wanna help me get him out?" I asked.

Two door slams echoed through the pine forest and up the slopes. An owl hooted somewhere above us, and I pictured it sitting on the flaking branch of a gnarled pine, wide-eyed, listening. I was tipsy from the brandy, and I staggered a little en route to the rear of the Cadillac.

Walter inserted a key and popped open the trunk. Orson lay on his stomach, his arms splayed out above his head. I reached in without hesitation and, grabbing his arms just above the elbows, dragged him out of the trunk and let him fall into the grass. Though he was shirtless, the cold didn't rouse him. Walter opened the back door and then lifted my brother's feet. We crammed him into the backseat, and Walter climbed on top of him and handcuffed his wrists behind his back. Turning Orson over, he slapped him hard across the face five times. I didn't say anything.

Hurrying back to the door, I hopped inside. "Turn the heat on," I said. "It's cold as shit."

Walter cranked the engine, and it idled noiselessly. I bent down and held my face before the vents, letting the engine-heated air thaw my cheeks.

"Orson," I said, getting up on my knees in the seat and facing the back. He lay unmoving on his stomach, stretched out from door to door. I could see his face—his eyes were closed. Reaching into the backseat, I grabbed his arms and shook him violently, but he made no sound.

I climbed into the backseat and knelt down on the floorboard so we were face-to-face. "Orson," I said, so near to his lips, I could've kissed him. "Wake. Up." I slapped him. It felt good. "Wake. Up!" I shouted, but he didn't flinch. "Fuck it." I crawled back into the front seat. "Guess we'll just wait."

"How much did you give him?" Walter asked.

"Fifteen milligrams."

"Look, I don't want to sit out here all night. Just give him the antidote."

"It might kill him. It's a hell of a shock. We should let him come to on his own if he can."

I stared down the highway and watched a set of headlights suddenly appear and vanish.

"Out in Wyoming," I said, "you can see headlights when they're still twenty or thirty miles away." I angled the seat back and turned onto my right side, facing the door. "Walter?"

"Yeah?"

"I killed a man in Wyoming."

He didn't say anything, and we were quiet for some time.

"You remember that party I threw last May?" I asked finally.

"Yeah."

"I keep thinking about that night. We were sitting out on my pier—"

"Pretty drunk, if I recall."

"Yep. I distinctly remember thinking: You lucky, lucky man. Thirty-four, successful, respected. You have a quality of life most people can't even fathom. . . . One week later, to the day, I received that envelope from Orson. . . . How do we go home after this? I can't imagine ever wanting to write again. Or feeling normal. Like anything's good. Like people are capable of goodness." I motioned to Orson. "When we were in the desert, he told me I had murder in my heart."

"I think it's safe to say he was projecting."

I glanced down at the gun in my lap.

"I think he was right, Walter."

"You are not an evil person."

"No, but I could be. I see that now. We're a lot closer to it than you think." I dropped my Glock into the fanny pack. "Will you stay awake and watch Orson?"

"Yeah."

"Wake me up in an hour, and I'll let you sleep."

"There's no way I'm going to sleep."

"Then wake me when he wakes." I curled up in the seat. To fall asleep, I imagined I was lounging in a beach chair in Aruba. The vents were my tropical breeze, and I could even hear the ocean in the vibration of the idling engine.

.

Hands shook me, and I sat up. My head ached as if a fault had rifted around the perimeter of my skull. Walter stared at me, the .45 in his lap.

"What time is it?" I asked.

"One. He's stirred, but I don't think he's waking up anytime soon. Not coherently at least."

"All right. I'll give him the antidote."

I searched through the fanny pack until I found the 10-mL vial of the benzodiazepine antidote, flumazenil. Aspirating the entire vial, I climbed into the backseat and took hold of Orson's left arm. Locating the same vein I'd hit before, I penetrated the skin, depressed the plunger with my thumb, and injected one milligram of flumazenil. When the syringe was empty, I slid it out and climbed back into the front seat.

"You ready?" I asked. "He's gonna come out of this fast. Bright-eyed and bushy-tailed."

A minute elapsed. Then Orson moved, rubbing his face into the seat and trying to sit up. There was a nasty gash on his forehead where I'd coldcocked him with the butt of the Glock. A trail of dried blood traversed a path from his left eye to the corner of his mouth, like runaway mascara. He mumbled.

"Sit him up," I said, coming to my knees again and facing the backseat.

Walter grabbed him by his hair and jerked him ruthlessly up into the center seat. Orson steadied himself and opened his eyes. When he saw me, he produced an enervate smile.

"Andy," he said clearly, "what in the world—"

"Where are those videotapes you made of the killings? And the pictures you took, like that card you sent me?"

"I had a dream we fought," he said. "I kicked the shit out of you, as I recall." The reversal of the sedation was miraculous. Orson was lucid, pupils dilated, heart racing.

"Hit the cigarette lighter, Walter," I said, and he punched it in.

"Walt?" Orson said. "What are you doing here?"

"Don't talk to him," I said to Walter.

"He can talk to me if he wants to. How's the fam, Walt?"

"Orson," Walter growled. "I'm gonna—" I grabbed Walter's arm and, catching his eyes, shook my head. Flushed, he nodded.

"No, let him talk," Orson said. "He's probably a little pissed at me and wants to get it off his chest."

"No, Orson. Tonight's about you."

Orson smiled, finding Walter's eyes in the rearview mirror. "How's little Jenna?" Hands on the steering wheel, Walter looked down into his lap at the .45. "I hear she's precious. I'll bet you're proud as—"

"Walter isn't moved by your taunts," I said. "You aren't in any position to—"

"If he isn't moved, why'd he just look down at his gun?" Orson smiled at Walter. "Thinking of doing something rash?"

"Orson," I said, "this is between—"

"I think he's upset because one of my other protégés has his eye on the Lancing clan."

Walter's fingers constricted around the Glock. Coming to his knees, he faced my brother.

"His name's Luther," Orson continued. "Would you like to know more about him, Walter? He may become a big part of your life. In fact, he may already be a big part of your life. You see, when I took him out to the desert three years ago, he took an avid interest in—"

"Walter, just ignore—"

"Let him finish."

"Not that it's my inclination," Orson said, "but among his many interests, Luther likes little things. Well, more specifically, he likes to hurt little things, and me not being one to pass judgment, I told him, 'I know two little things named Jenna and John David Lancing who could use a little hurting.'"

"I don't believe you."

"You don't have to believe me, Walter. Luther believes me, and that's all that matters. His visit to Jenna's school was just an introduction. He's met Beth, too, though she didn't realize it. At my urging, he's added your address to his Rolodex, and if he hasn't already, I'm sure he'll come calling at Fifteen eighteen Shortleaf Drive any day now. Oh, that's right, Beth took the kids away. Well, Luther will find them, if he hasn't already. He's very motivated—what the FBI profilers would call a 'hedonic thrill killer,' which means he receives sexual gratification from the agony of others. Believe me when I tell you, he's one macabre motherfucker. He even scares me."

Walter pressed his gun against Orson's chest.

"No," I said calmly. "Just sit back."

"When I pull this trigger," Walter said to Orson, "the force of the bullet impacting your chest will be so intense, your heart might stop. How does it feel, Orson?"

"I imagine I feel like your wife and children are going to feel. And trust me on this, Walter. You could flay me, and I wouldn't call off Luther."

"Put that fucking gun down," I said. "This is *not* the way to do this."

"He's talking about my family."

"He's lying. He will tell us."

"I'm not lying, Walter. Shall I tell you how Luther's planning to do your family, or do you want it to be a surprise?"

Walter ground his teeth together, trembling with explosive rage.

"I'm not telling you again," I said. "Put it down."

"Fuck off, Andy."

I took my Glock from the fanny pack and pointed it at my best friend. "I won't let you shoot him. Not yet. Think about it. If you kill him, we aren't gonna find out where Luther is. You're risking your family now."

"If he's dead, maybe Luther will leave us alone. Orson's just doing this because I know about him." He chambered the first round.

"Walter, you're a little crazy now, so just—" I leaned forward to take the gun from him, but he jerked back and turned his .45 on me.

"*You* put the gun down."

My finger moved onto the trigger.

"You gonna shoot me?"

"You aren't a parent," he said, incensed. "You don't know." He trained the gun back on my brother. "Count to three, you piece of shit."

"Okay. One."

"Walter!"

"Two."

"You kill him, you kill your family!"

Before Walter reached three, Orson drew his knees into his chest and kicked the back of my seat. Jerking forward into the dashboard, I felt my finger slip, and though I didn't hear the gunshot, my Glock recoiled.

Walter fell back onto the steering wheel, and it bleated through the countryside. I lifted him off the horn and he sagged into my lap, spilling all over me.

I wept; Orson laughed.

# 27

I finished burying Walter a few minutes before five o'clock. Through the ceiling of pines, light was coming, and the white Cadillac would be plainly visible from the highway, if it was not already. The sky kindled with each passing second, and I felt the self-possession I'd known just hours ago disintegrating. Walking back through the trees, the mechanic's suit rigid now with Walter's frozen blood, I thought, *I could crumble so easily.*

When I broke out of the trees, I saw three cars speed by, heading into Bristol. It was light enough that I could see the textureless black mountains clearly against the sky, and anyone passing, if they happened to look, would see me stumbling along the shoulder toward the car. On the eastern horizon a trace of day warmed above the Atlantic. The sun was coming. The moon had disappeared hours ago.

I reached the Cadillac. Orson was unconscious in the trunk, an entire 4-mg vial of Ativan coursing through his bloodstream.

The front seat was a mess—pools of blood on both floorboards, the driver's side window smeared red. I managed to scrape enough blood and brain matter off the glass to drive. Exhausted, I started the car and pulled onto the highway, heading south, back into Woodside.

I kept wondering what I'd do if a cop pulled me over. He'd see the bloodstained interior and the purple mass that was my left eye. I'd have to run. There'd be no other choice besides killing him.

Returning to Orson's house, I backed the Cadillac into his driveway and parked beside the white Lexus. I agonized over leaving the car out here when the town would be waking within the hour. But there was no alternative. I needed to get Orson inside, clean myself up, and figure out what the hell I was going to do.

■

Reclining on a floral-print couch in Orson's den, I dialed Cynthia's home number. It was a sunny Saturday morning, eleven o'clock, and the sunbeams angled brilliantly through the blinds into the den, a scantly furnished room with a large television in a pine cabinet and a tower of CDs standing in the corner. Orson lay across from me on a matching couch, his hands still cuffed behind his back, feet bound with a bicycle lock I'd found in his study.

She answered on the third ring. "Hello?"

"Hi, Cynthia."

"Andy." I detected undeniable shock in her voice, and it concerned me. "Where are you?" she asked. "Everyone's looking for you."

"Who's everyone?"

"The Winston-Salem Police Department called my office twice yesterday."

"Why are they looking for me?"

"You know about your mother?"

She was going to regret asking that.

"What about her?"

"Oh, Andy. I'm sorry."

"*What?*"

"A neighbor found her dead in her house three days ago. On Wednesday, I think. Andy . . ."

"What happened?" I let my voice quake. How could an innocent man explain not crying when he learns his mother has been murdered? Even the guilty manage tears.

"They think she was murdered."

I dropped the phone and produced a few sobs. After a moment, I brought the receiver to my ear again. "I'm here," I said, sniffling.

"Are you all right?"

"I don't know."

"Andy, the police want to speak with you."

"Why?"

"I um . . . I think . . ." She sighed. "This is tough, Andy. There's a warrant for your arrest."

"What in the world for?"

"Your mother's murder."

"Oh no, no, no, no—"

"And I know you didn't do it. I believe you. But the best thing to do is just talk to the police and clear this mess up. Where are you? Let me have someone come get you."

"Thank you for everything, Cynthia." I hung up the phone, thinking, *They had to find her eventually. Orson, you fucked me again.* I stared at my brother on the sofa. He'd be waking soon. *Until you fix this, you don't have a home. In fact, you might never go home again.*

■

Orson awoke in the early afternoon, strapped naked to a wooden chair in his den, handcuffs securing his arms behind the chair back, and a length of rope binding his legs to the chair legs. I'd shut the door, closed the blinds, and turned the television up so loud, the set buzzed.

Sitting on the couch, I waited until he'd regained sufficient clarity of mind.

"You with me?" I shouted. He said something, but I couldn't hear over the television. "Speak up!" I could tell he was still disoriented.

"Yes. What's . . ." I saw it all come back to him—the fight, the trunk, Walter. He smiled, and I knew he was with me. Taking the remote control from the couch, I muted the television.

"Orson," I said. "This is how this works. I ask the questions. You answer them. Quickly, concisely—"

"Where's Walt? No. Let me guess. Is he in my hole?"

I cloaked my fury—I had a hunch the torture would be more effective if I remained placid. Composing myself, I asked him, "Do you still have the videotapes and pictures of you and me in the desert?"

"Of course."

"Where are they?" He smiled and shook his head.

I pressed the mute button and the television roared. It was the episode of *The Andy Griffith Show* that chronicles Barney Fife's attempt to join a church choir, despite his glaring inability to sing. *We watched this with our father.*

Coming to my feet, I walked around to the back of the chair. From my pocket, I took a silver Zippo I'd found in Orson's dresser and struck a flame. Regardless of the hell he'd put me through, I found it exceedingly difficult to burn him. But I did.

Orson grunted wrenchingly, and after six seconds, I withdrew the flame and returned to the couch. Sweat had broken out across his forehead, and his face had crimsoned. I silenced the television.

"Whew!" He smiled through the pain. "Man, that's unpleasant! But you know, the back isn't the most sensitive part of the body. You should burn my face. The lips, the eyes. Make 'em boil."

"Orson, are the videotapes and pictures in this house?"

"No."

"Are they in Woodside?"

"Flame on!"

The cacophony of the television again filled the room. Leaning forward, I positioned the lighter against Orson's inner thigh as he watched with rabid interest. This time, I felt less squeamish about applying the pain.

He hollered over the dissonant voice of Barney Fife as the tonguelike flame licked his skin. When the patch of hairy white flesh began to bubble, I extinguished the flame and hit the mute button. He was still yelping, eyes closed, teeth clicking, breathless.

"I think you missed your calling," he said, wincing and sucking through his teeth, stifling the squeals. Glancing down at his thigh, I noticed the afflicted skin had blossomed into a bright blister. I could smell the sweet charred flesh, a pleasantly devious odor, like gasoline.

"All right, Orson," I said. "Take three."

"Maybe it's in a storage unit in some town you'll never find. Maybe—" The television blared, and standing up, I held the lighter beneath Orson's right eye. When the flame leapt out, he shrieked, "In the desert! In the desert!"

Stepping back, I cut the volume. "I think you're lying."

"Andy," he gasped, "my videos, my photographs, everything I used to blackmail you—it's all out there."

"*Where* out there? In the cabin?"

"Take me to Wyoming, and I'll show you."

"I guess you like being burned."

"No. Don't. Just listen. If I told you, Andy, even after you'd tor-tured me, you'd have no way of knowing if it was the truth till you got out there. And trust me, it wouldn't be. Now think about that."

"You think I'm gonna haul you to Wyoming?"

"How are you gonna find the cabin? My dirt road's in the middle of nowhere. You have to watch the mileage from a certain point even to have a chance at finding it, and I'm not telling you where that is. Not here. No fucking way. You need me; I need you. Let's take a trip."

"I can find it on my own."

"How?"

"I found you."

He snorted. "That fucking cowboy."

I considered holding the flame to Orson's eye until he screamed exactly where in the cabin or shed I could find the paraphernalia of his obsession. But he was right: I wouldn't know if he'd told the truth until I got out there.

I wanted to ask him about my mother and how he'd framed me, but I was afraid the rage would undermine me like it had Walter, and there were things I still had to know.

"Where's Luther?" I asked.

"I don't know. Luther drifts." Discomfort strained his voice.

"How do you communicate?"

"E-mail."

"What's your password?" Part of me wanted him to resist. I flipped open the Zippo.

"W-B-A-S-S."

"Pray he hasn't touched them." I got up and opened the door.

"Andy," he said. "Can I please have whatever you've been giving me? This hurts like hell."

"It's supposed to hurt."

I walked through the living room into Orson's study and booted up the computer. His password gave me access to his E-mail account. Six new messages: five spam, one from LK72:

>From: <LK72@aol.com>

>Date: Fr, 8 Nov 1996 20:54:33 -0500 (EST)

>To: David Parker <dparker@email.woodside.edu>

>Subject:

>

>O—

>

>Getting antsy. Need to head north soon. Ask me about that strpt at stlns. Funny stuff! AT is still gone. As is WL. Still? as to the L. whereabouts. I'll wait if you want. Otherwise, there's someone I need to go visit asap up in Sas. Still all over the tube. Wow! Looking forward to OB.

>

>L

I searched Orson's deleted, sent, and received message folders, but he kept nothing saved or archived. When I'd printed out the E-mail, I took it with me into the den.

"Decipher this," I said, setting the cryptic E-mail in Orson's lap. "It is from Luther, right?"

"Yeah, that's from him."

"So read it back to me like it makes some fucking sense."

He looked down at the page and read aloud in a weary, crestfallen voice: "Orson, getting antsy. Need to head north soon. Ask me about that stripper at Stallion's. Funny stuff. Andrew Thomas is still gone. As is Walter Lancing. Still no idea as to the Lancing whereabouts. I'll wait if you want. Otherwise, there's someone I need to go visit asap up in Saskatchewan. Still all over the tube. Wow. Looking forward to the Outer Banks. Luther." He looked up at me. "That's it."

"So he's still in North Carolina, waiting for you to tell him what to do about the Lancings?"

"Yes."

Returning to the desk in his study, I sat for a moment, staring out the window at a woman raking her lawn across the street. As I drafted the message in my head, it occurred to me all at once what I would do—about Luther, the photographs, even Orson. It was a revelation not unlike the epiphanies I'd experienced upon finding my way out of the woods in the plotting of a novel.

As I typed, I worried that my E-mail response to Luther would deviate too conspicuously from Orson's format and style, but I risked it:

>From: <dparker@email.woodside.edu>

>Date: Sat, 9 Nov 1996 13:56:26 -0500 (EST)

>To: <LK72@aol.com>

>Subject:

>

>L,

>

>Head on to Sas. I may take care of the L's later if need be. I'm heading cross-country, too, to you know where. Want to meet somewhere en route late tomorrow or Monday, and tell me about that strpr in person?

>

>O

I walked back into the den and filled a syringe with two vials of Ativan. Then I jabbed the needle deep into the muscle of Orson's bare ass. On my way out the door, he called my name, but I didn't stop. I ascended the staircase and headed for the guest room, unwilling to sleep in his bed. The mattress was cramped and lumpy, but I'd been up for thirty hours and could've slept on broken glass. Through the window, I heard the college bell tower striking two, birds bickering, wind in the trees, and cars in the valley below—the sounds of a New England town on a Saturday afternoon. *I am so, so far from that.*

My thoughts were with Beth Lancing and her children as I floated into sleep. *I'm trying to save your lives, but I robbed you of a husband and a father. Robbed myself of my best friend.* I wondered if she already sensed that he was gone.

# 28

I came down the staircase at 1:30 in the morning, having slept straight for eleven and a half hours. The house was so still. I could hear only the minute mechanical breathing of the kitchen appliances as they cut on and off in the predawn silence.

After starting a pot of coffee, I poked my head into the den. Orson's chair had fallen over. He was unconscious, naked, still awkwardly attached to the toppled chair. He looked feeble, helpless, and for a moment I let myself pity him.

Barefoot, I walked into his study and sat down at the desk. As the monitor revived, crackling with static electricity, I saw that he had one message waiting. Typing in the password, I opened the new E-mail:

>From: <LK72@aol.com>

>Date: Sun, 10 Nov 1996 01:02:09 -0500 (EST)

>To: David Parker <dparker@email.woodside.edu>

>Subject:

>

>O—

>

>Might be in SB Monday evng. Call when you hit Nbrsk and we'll
see about a rendezvous.

>

>L


Shutting down the computer, I walked back into the den and
gave Orson another injection. Then I went upstairs to take a shower.

The hot water felt immaculate. After I'd tidied up the cuts on my
face with a razor blade, I lingered in the stream, leaning against the
wet tile, head down, the water cooling, watching the blood swirl
under my feet into the drain.

It took a while for the steam to settle in the bathroom, and I sat
on the toilet while it did, thumbing through Orson's wallet, yet
another possession of his, identical to mine. Removing his driver's
license, I set it on the sink. I looked nothing like the picture. His hair
was short and brown, his face clean-shaven. Rising, I wiped the con-
densation off the mirror.

My beard had grown out considerably, gray and bristly. My hair
was in shambles, the dye stripped from this last marathon shower. I
shaved first, even my sideburns, and it was an improvement. There
was an attachment on the electric razor for tonsure, so I climbed
back into the shower and sheared my head.

When I finished, I glanced again into the mirror—much, much
better.

"Hi, Orson," I said, smiling.

PART IV

# 29

SUNDAY, before dawn, I loaded Orson into the trunk of his Lexus and pulled out of the driveway of his house in Woodside. I carried his wallet, filled with his cash and credit cards, and I felt reasonably sure that, should the necessity arise, I could pass for my brother. It was comforting to know that because Orson existed, Andrew Thomas could disappear.

I drove to the Woodside Inn and slipped furtively up the noisy staircase into what had been Walter's and my room. Our clothes were still scattered across the beds, and I stuffed everything from the drawers and the floor into our suitcases and lugged them down to the car.

Heading out on Highway 116, I prided myself on my thoroughness. I'd remembered to check out of the inn. I'd removed all traces of my presence in Orson's home (my blood in his room, my hair in his sink and bathtub), along with all signs of his abduction. I'd even taken care of Walter's Cadillac, driving it down the hill to the Champlain Diner at 3:15 in the morning and leaving it parked beside an overflowing Dumpster. The jog back up into Orson's neighborhood had been a bitch, but it was worth it. Nothing could link me to this town now, and though Walter's gory car would more than likely be discovered within the week, I'd be long, long gone by then.

Prior to leaving Orson's house, I'd downed an entire pot of coffee and swallowed a double dose of a sinus medication that always keyed me up. Caffeine raged through me, and with unfettered energy, I drove southwest out of Woodside into New York State. If nothing went awry, Luther would be dead, and I'd be in Wyoming in less than forty-eight hours.

■

I sped westbound on I-80 through eastern Nebraska. It was 11:45 P.M., and the luster of driving without sleep from Vermont to Wyoming had waned. Orson was awake. He'd been kicking the inside of the trunk for the last fifty miles and cursing at me to pull over.

Traffic was light, and because there was nothing but hewn cornfields and distant farmhouse lights as far as I could see, I obliged him. Pulling into the emergency lane somewhere between Lincoln and York, I hopped out into the chilly Nebraska night and popped the trunk. Lying on his back, in his bathrobe, handcuffed, he lifted his head.

"I'm thirsty, you bastard," he croaked. "I've been dying back here."

"Well, there's some ice-cold water up front with your name on it. But you gotta earn it." Taking Luther's E-mail from my pocket and unfolding it, I asked him, "Is SB Scottsbluff, Nebraska?"

"Why?"

I went back to the front seat and grabbed the full squeeze bottle from the passenger side. Returning to Orson, I stood in front of him and squirted a stream into my mouth.

"Wow, that's refreshing!" I could see the pining thirst in his eyes. "This is all the water that's left," I said, "and when it's gone, it may be hundreds and hundreds of miles before I stop again. Now, I'm not very thirsty, but I'll stand here and guzzle it just the same if you aren't a model of cooperation. Is SB Scottsbluff?"

"Yes."

"What's the significance?"

"Of what?" I squirted another long stream into my mouth. "There's this girl there who Luther stays with sometimes. He's always on the road."

"What's her name?"

"Mandy something."

"You don't know her last name?"

"No."

"What's Luther's last name?"

"Kite."

"Like fly a kite?" He nodded. "Open up." I shot him a mouthful of water. "I saw Luther on the phone list in your wallet. Is that number the best way to reach him?"

"It's his cell. What are you trying to do, Andy?"

"You ever met Luther in Scottsbluff?"

"Once."

"Where?"

"Ricki's. Can I—"

"Who's Ricki?"

"It's a bar on Highway Ninety-two. Please, Andy . . ."

I touched the open nozzle to his lips and squeezed cold water down his throat. He sucked frantically, and I pulled it back after three seconds as a transfer truck roared by. I took Orson's cell phone from my pocket. Dialing Luther's number, I held up the half-empty squeeze bottle.

"The rest of it's yours," I said. "Find out if Luther can meet at Ricki's tomorrow night. And be peppy. Don't sound like you've been drugged up in a trunk for twenty hours. Fuck anything up and you'll die slowly of thirst. I mean it. I'll keep you on the brink of madness for days." He nodded. "Brevity," I said. Then I pushed the talk button and held the phone to his ear.

On the first ring, a man answered. I could clearly hear his voice.

"Hello?"

"Luth?"

"Hey." I dribbled water onto Orson's face.

"Where are you?" Orson asked.

"Gateway to the west. Just crossing the Mississippi. I can see the arch right now. Where are you?"

I mouthed, "Eastern Nebraska."

"Eastern Nebraska," Orson said. "You staying with Mandy tomorrow night?"

"Yeah, you wanna hook up at Ricki's?"

"What time?"

"How's nine? I'm staying tonight in St. Louis, so I won't be in Scottsbluff till late tomorrow."

"All right." I moved my finger across my throat. "Hey, Luth, you're breaking up."

I pressed the button to end the call and returned the phone to my pocket. Then I gave Orson the rest of the bottle and watched the desperation finally retreat from his eyes.

"You need something to eat?" I asked.

He shook his head. "I've gotta piss, Andy."

"Can't help you there."

"What do you want me to do, piss in the trunk?"

"It's your car."

I opened the back door and fished out a syringe and a vial of Ativan from the fanny pack. Another car passed us, heading toward Lincoln, and I suddenly felt anxious to get on the road again.

"Turn over, Orson." I stuck him with the needle.

"Andy," he said as I put my hands on the trunk to close it, "you're very good at this."

•

The coffee and sinus medication had worn off hours ago, and on the tediously straight roads of western Nebraska, I now operated solely on the determination not to fall asleep.

I'd been driving for twenty-three hours and thirty-five minutes, and I existed in a limbo between sleep and consciousness. Occasionally, my forehead would touch the steering wheel, and I'd jerk back up and cherish a five-minute oasis of petrified alertness. Then my mind would drift back, and I'd lose consciousness for that split second and scare myself to death all over again.

Heading up Highway 26, fifty miles northwest of Ogallala, the prairie awoke. A peach sunrise was lifting out of the eastern horizon, and as the light strengthened, the land spread and spread and spread, farther than it seemed possible. It had changed overnight, and because I had not witnessed the gradual topographic expansion, this sudden revelation was staggering. For an easterner driving west, the stark vastness of the land and sky is always inconceivable, and I imagined a symphonic aubade to accompany the majesty of the morning.

At 6:30 A.M., I crossed the tree-lined North Platte River into the town of Bridgeport. In the southern distance, the tips of numerous sandstone buttes were catching coral sunbeams. Though several miles away, it looked like I could reach out and touch them.

Highway 26 cut through the sleeping town. On the western fringe, there was a motel called Courthouse View (named after a prominent butte five miles south), and I got a room there. Since I'd given Orson enough Ativan to maintain sedation for the better part of the day, I left him in the trunk, walked inside, and crashed.

I'd be meeting Luther in fourteen hours.

■

I checked out of Courthouse View in the late afternoon, and heading northwest toward Scottsbluff on Highway 92, I started mulling over what I'd gotten myself into with Luther. In all honesty, I'd done a stupid thing. It was already 5:07, and that left me a little under four hours to determine how I would kill him, dispose of him, and leave town unnoticed. Finally, I concluded that I was being hasty and reckless. Besides, I couldn't get past the idea that I was going to get myself killed fucking with this guy. So fifteen miles outside of Scottsbluff, I decided not to go through with it. I'd been methodical up to this point, and while it was tempting to orchestrate a quick, clever way to do in Luther Kite, four hours wasn't an adequate length of time in which to do it.

Ricki's was a true shithole. On the southern outskirts of Scotts-bluff, in the shadow of the eight-hundred-foot bluff from which the town assumed its name, I pulled into its dirt parking lot and turned off the car. Stepping outside into the dry, tingling cold, night was imminent, though the sun still illuminated the prairie and the spire of Chimney Rock, tiny but distinct in the distance. The tourist brochure in the motel claimed that the five-hundred-foot inselberg had been a landmark for pioneers on the Oregon Trail—the first indication of the Rocky Mountains, which lay ahead. Walking toward the trunk with two squeeze bottles of water and three bags of potato chips, I stared at the golden sandstone buttes of the Wildcat Hills, thinking, *I'd like to pick one of those hills and lie down on top and never leave. I'd just sit out there and erode, alone.*

I'd bought the food at Courthouse View, but the motel parking lot had been too crowded to risk opening the trunk. Ricki's parking lot was empty except for Orson's Lexus and a pickup truck.

Orson was awake. Even the sallow evening light burned his eyes, so he closed them. He'd pulled his cuffed hands under his feet, so they were now in front of him.

"Here," I said, placing a squeeze bottle in his hands. As he drank it like a baby, I dropped the bags of chips and the other bottle inside. "It won't be much longer," I said. "We're just thirty-five miles from the Wyoming border."

I had a syringe prepared and I shot another 4-mg vial of Ativan into his ass.

I located a pen in the glove compartment and tore off a piece of the Vermont state map. I'd considered just calling Luther and having Orson cancel our meeting, but I had misgivings about my brother's current ability to mask the atrophy in his voice. So stuffing the pen, paper, and Glock into my jeans pocket and pulling on a gray wool sweater, I locked the car and walked across the dirt parking lot toward the bar.

Above the door, a neon sign displayed RICKI's in blue cursive. I walked under the humming sign and entered the deserted bar, which was smaller than my living room. Its ceiling was obtrusively low, booths lined the walls, and with only two windows, one on either side of the door, I felt as though I were stepping into a smoky closet.

The sole patron, I sat down at a bar stool on the corner. The bar was constructed of unsanded railroad ties that still smelled of tar. Names, oaths, and declarations of love and enmity had been carved into the black wood.

As I pulled out the pen and scrap of paper, a woman emerged from the kitchen.

"We ain't serving yet," she said. She wore tight jeans shorts and a black turtleneck with BEARCATS: '94 STATE CHAMPS across the chest. Her black hair was wiry and stiff, and she'd have benefited from orthodontic care.

"Your door was open," I said.

"Well shit. What do you want?"

"Whatever you have on tap is fine."

While she grabbed a glass out of the freezer and commenced filling it with bronze ale, I started what would be Orson's note to Luther. *L—I made a*

She set the glass down on the railroad tie. "Dollar fifty."

I handed her two of Orson's dollar bills and told her to keep the change. Foam spilled down the sides of the glass. I took a sip, tasted flecks of ice in the draft, and continued scrawling on the scrap: *friend this morning—you know how that goes. In fact, she composed this letter before I . . . Anyhow, I though it prudent to leave town asap. Sorry we couldn't meet tonight. Have fun in Sas. O.*

I folded the torn map into a neat little square, wrote "Luther" across the town of Burlington, and set it on the bar. Then I sat there, drinking my beer, thinking, *So people actually leave notes with bartenders. How many times have I written this scene? It doesn't feel real.*

Sipping the beer, I surveyed the empty bar—unadorned concrete walls, no jukebox or neon beer signs. There weren't even cute cowboy slogans to fake the prairie culture for transient easterners like me. Just a drab, hopeless place for hopeless westerners to get drunk.

I finished the beer, and as though her ears were attuned to the sound of empty glasses clinking the wood, she came back through the door from the kitchen and stood in front of me.

"You want another one?" she asked.

"No thanks. Where is everyone?"

She looked at her watch. "It's only six," she said. "They don't start getting here till seven."

A car pulled up outside. I heard its tires lock up in the dirt.

"Where's Ricki?" I asked.

"That son of a bitch is dead."

She took my empty glass and set it in a brown plastic container.

"Would you do something for me?" I asked.

"What?" she said joylessly. She was possibly the most indifferent person I'd ever met. I wondered why she didn't just go slice her wrists. I pushed the square of paper across the ties.

"I'm supposed to meet a friend here at nine, but I can't. Will you give this to him?"

She looked suspiciously at the square of paper, then picked it up and jammed it in her back pocket.

A car door slammed outside.

"What's he look like?" she asked.

"Shoulder-length black, black hair. Even darker than yours. Very white. Late twenties. Fairly tall. Dark eyes."

At the same instant I heard footsteps approaching the door, she said, "Well hell, ain't that him?"

I glanced over my shoulder and watched Luther Kite walk through the door. Sliding off the stool, I slipped my hand into my pocket and withdrew the Glock. By the time I'd chambered a bullet, he was standing in my face, looking down on me.

I took it in piecemeal. The reek of Windex. His blue windbreaker.

Ebony hair against a smooth cheek. My finger moving once. Luther falling into me, clutching. Screaming behind the railroad ties. Gasping. Blood on nylon. My right hand warm and wet. Running through the dirt to the car. Cold. The spire of Chimney Rock now dark. The rushing prairie and the maroon hills as I sped toward Wyoming.

# 30

I pulled over after midnight onto the shoulder of I-80, halfway through Wyoming, outside the town of Wamsutter. There was no moon, so I had no sense of the land, except that it was even more expansive and forsaken than Nebraska. Pushing the suitcases onto the floor and curling up in the backseat, I closed my eyes. When cars passed on the interstate, the Lexus shuddered. I fell asleep wondering if Ricki's had really happened.

.

I awoke at 3:30 A.M. to the sound of Orson moaning. When I climbed out and opened the trunk, he was flailing around inside, though his eyes were closed. I stirred him from the nightmare, and as he opened his eyes and regained cognizance of his surroundings, he sat up.

"Where are we?" he asked.

"Middle of Wyoming."

"I'm so thirsty."

"You'll have to wait till tomorrow." He stretched out his arms and yawned.

"I heard a gunshot," he said.

"Orson, how do I find the cabin?"

He lay back down. "Will you give me another shot?"

I sat on the bumper. "Of course."

"This is I-Eighty, right?"

"Yeah."

"Stay on Eighty till you hit Rock Springs. It's in the southwest corner of the state. From Rock Springs, take One ninety-one north and start watching the odometer. When you've gone seventy miles, you're gonna have to pull over and bring me up. I'll take you the rest of the way."

"All right."

"Are we heading for it tonight?"

"Nah, I'm wiped. I'm gonna sleep till morning."

"Andy, did you kill Luther?"

"I chickened out," I said, standing up. "So you left him a note."

"I know I—"

"You're fucked up. I'll go get your shot."

■

Over the course of two thousand miles, it was bound to happen.

Tuesday morning, I'd passed the exits for Red Desert, Table Rock, Bitter Creek, and Point of Rocks, when thirty miles east of Rock Springs, I heard the whine of a siren—a Highway Patrol SUV crowded my bumper. With my Glock wedged into the pouch behind the passenger seat, I pulled over into the emergency lane, reassuring myself, *Why would he want to search the car? Orson's unconscious. I've got the proper license and registration. Ricki's may not have even happened. I'm golden.*

The officer tapped on my window. I lowered it.

"License and registration," he said in that austere, authoritative tone, and removing the papers from the glove compartment, I smiled and handed them through the window.

He walked bowlegged back to his hunter green Bronco and climbed inside.

The clock in the dashboard read 10:15, but it felt later. The prairie had turned arid. Across the northwestern horizon, a chain of tan hills rose out of the flatland. Gray clouds massed beyond.

I noticed the sweater and jeans I'd worn into Ricki's lying on the floorboard on the passenger side. *It happened.* They were stained with Luther's blood, and I regretted not having thrown them out last night at the gas station in Cheyenne. I started to scoop them up, but the gravelly crunch of the officer's footsteps stopped me.

I righted myself and looked back through the open window into his face. The officer was my age. He reminded me of a lawman in a movie, though I couldn't recall which one.

"Know why I stopped you, Mr. Parker?" he asked, handing back Orson's license and registration. I placed them on the passenger seat.

"No sir, officer."

He removed his reflective sunglasses and stared down at me through hard, pale eyes.

"You were swerving all over the goddamn road."

"I was?"

"Are you drunk?" A gust of wind lifted his hat, which he caught and shelved under his arm. He had unruly blond hair, the variety that, if allowed to grow out, might bush into an Afro. The image of the officer with a blond Afro lightened my heart, and I chortled.

"What's funny?"

"Nothing, sir. I'm not drunk. I'm tired. I've been driving for the past two days."

"From Vermont?"

"Yes, sir."

He glanced at the suitcases in the backseat. "Traveling alone?"

"Yes, sir."

"Which one of them suitcases is yours?"

*How sly.*

"Both of them."

He nodded. "And you only been on the road since Sunday?"

"Yes, sir."

"Must be in some kind of hurry."

"No, not really. I just wanted to see how fast I could cross the country."

I thought he might grin at my ambition, but he remained as stolid as ever.

"Where you headed?" he asked.

"California."

"Whereabouts in California?"

"L.A."

"Eighty don't go to L.A. Eighty goes to San Francisco."

"I know, but I wanted to drive through Wyoming, seeing as how I've never seen this part of the country. It's beautiful."

"It's fuckin' shitland." I gazed into the gold badge above his green breast pocket, filled with the presentiment that he was on the verge of ordering me out of the vehicle.

"Well, you ought to know that you're heading into one hell of a storm," he said.

"Snowstorm?"

"Yep. Forecast says it's supposed to get real bad."

"Thanks for the warning. I hadn't heard."

"Might want to find a motel to hole up in. Maybe in Rock Springs, or Salt Lake, if you make it that far."

"I'll consider that."

He looked askance at my face; he'd noticed my fading bruises. "Someone hit you?"

"Yes, sir."

"When did that happen?"

"At a bar this past weekend."

"Must've been one hell of a fight."

Everything was one hell of a something with this guy. I was definitely putting him in a book.

"Looks like you took a few knocks there," he said.

"Yeah, but you should see the other guy." That threadbare cliché got him. He cracked a smile and, looking off across the wasteland, reckoned that he'd better get going. Peering into the rearview mirror, I watched him saunter back to the Bronco.

*Cool fucking cucumber.* And I meant me.

■

Rock Springs was an ugly brown town, dedicated to the extraction of coal, oil, and a mineral called trona from deep beneath the surrounding hills. It was larger and more industrial than I'd anticipated, and I wondered what twenty thousand people did for fun in this northeast boundary of the Great Basin Desert.

I pulled into the congested parking lot of a supermarket. It had been raining and snowing for the last half hour, the flakes sticking to the desert but melting on the sun-warmed pavement. Jogging through the windblown snow toward the entrance, I feared that at any moment the roads would accept the ice, and then we'd never reach the cabin.

The supermarket was an entropic battlefield—frenzied shoppers compulsively stripping the shelves of bread, milk, and eggs. Because I didn't know what Orson had stocked at the cabin, I grabbed a bit of everything—canned food, fruit, cereal, loaves of white bread, even several bottles of the best wines they had (though they were quite unexceptional). The checkout lines stretched halfway down the aisles, and I'd started to roll my shopping cart to the back of one, when I realized I'd have to wait for an hour just to pay. *Fuck this. You've done a hell of a lot worse than steal.*

So I pushed the cart right on through the automatic doors, back out into the storm. The parking lot was frosted now, blanching as the snow swept down in torrents. Behind the strip mall, red cliffs stood out sharply against the white, and it occurred to me that I'd never seen a desert snowfall.

Upon reaching the Lexus, I opened the back door and began shoveling groceries on top of my suitcase and Walter's. Orson was making a racket. I told him to shut up, said we were almost home. The parking space beside mine was empty, so I left the cart there and opened the driver's door.

"Excuse me, sir?" An obese woman bundled up in a puffy pink parka, which did not flatter her proportions, stared at me quizzically from the trunk of the Lexus.

"What?"

"What's that sound?" She tapped on the trunk.

"I don't know what you're talking about."

"I think there's someone in your trunk."

I heard it, too, Orson shouting again, his voice muffled but audible. He was saying something about killing me if I didn't give him a drink of water.

"There's nothing in there," I said. "Excuse me."

"Is it a dog?"

I sighed. "No. Actually, I'm a hit man. There's someone in my trunk, and I'm taking them out into the desert to shoot them in the head and bury them. Wanna come along?"

She laughed, her face rumpling. "Oh my, that's rich! Very rich!" she said, chuckling maniacally.

She walked away, and I climbed into the Lexus and backed out of the parking space. The pavement was becoming icy, so I drove tentatively out of the parking lot and back onto Highway 191, as nervous as a southerner on wheels in a snowstorm.

# 31

**W I N D** blasted the car. The road had disappeared.

I'd been following a single set of tire tracks for the last forty miles. Leaving Rock Springs, almost four hours ago, they'd cut down to the pavement. But as I plowed north up the mind-numbingly straight trajectory of Highway 191, the contrast between the blacktop and the snow had dissipated. Now, looking through the furious windshield wipers, I strained to see the faintest indentation in the snow. It would soon be too deep to negotiate. Even now, I felt the tires slide at the slightest pressure on the accelerator or the brake. Aside from a hurricane that came inland into the Piedmont of North Carolina seven years ago, this was the worst weather I'd ever seen.

Precisely seventy miles north of Rock Springs, I stopped the car in the middle of the abandoned highway. Sitting for a moment in the warm leather seat, I stared through the glass at snow that fell as hard and fast as rain. Beyond one hundred feet, the white was inscrutable, and still the visibility continued to diminish. A violent downdraft joggled the car and whisked the fallen snow off the road. With the pavement revealed, I saw that the tires straddled the dotted line.

I turned off the engine and, grasping the keys, opened the door and stepped into the storm. Driving snow filled my eyes, and, shielding my face against the side of my arm, I struggled toward the trunk. Three inches had already accumulated on the road, more upon the desert. Once the snow depth exceeded all shrubbery except the tallest sagebrush and greasewood, we would have no point of reference by which to follow the road. *But we have time,* I thought, unlocking the trunk and bracing against another icy gust. *This storm is just beginning.*

Orson was conscious, and his dark, swollen eyes widened when he saw the snow. It collected in his hair. There were red lines across his face from hours of sleeping on the carpet, and his lips were parched and split.

"We might be in trouble," I said. "I want you to put your hands behind your back, 'cause I'm gonna undo your feet. Put 'em up here." He hung his legs out of the trunk, and I removed the bicycle lock from his ankles. Tossing it back into a corner of the trunk, I helped my brother climb out and told him to go around to the passenger door. By the time I'd returned to my seat and adjusted the vents to their maximum output, my clothes were soaked from the snow. I opened the passenger door and Orson got in. Leaving his hands cuffed behind his back, I reached across his lap and shut the door.

We sat there for a moment without speaking. I turned off the windshield wipers. The snow fell and melted on the heated glass. The grayness darkened.

"We're exactly seventy miles north of Rock Springs," I said. Orson stared out the windshield. "We near the dirt road?"

"Probably within a half mile. But when it's like this, it might as well be a hundred."

"The cabin's on that side, right?" I pointed out my window.

"Yeah. Somewhere out there."

"What do you mean? You can't find it?"

"Not in this." Concern had tensed his jaw and reduced the gleam in his blue eyes.

"Let's try," I said. "It's better than—"

"Look. About five miles that way into the desert"—he nodded at the swirling grayness out my window—"there's a ridge. You probably remember it."

"Yeah. So?"

"If I can't see that ridge, I have no way of knowing where we are in relation to the cabin. Hell, we could drive that way, but it'd be a shot in the dark, and we'd probably get stuck."

"Shit." I turned off the engine. "I should've stopped in Rock Springs for the night."

"Probably so. But you didn't know it'd be like this."

"No, I didn't." I wiped the snowmelt from my sleek bald head.

"You look like me," Orson said. "What's that about?"

"You thirsty?"

"Yeah."

I fed him a full bottle of tepid water.

"Orson," I said. "You try anything. One thing. I'll kill you."

"I believe it."

The dashboard clock read 4:07. I watched it turn to 4:08, then 4:09.

"It'll be dark out there soon," I said. Sweat trilled down my chest and my legs. Orson leaned back in the seat and closed his eyes. He smelled of urine. His robe was soiled, and I felt ashamed I hadn't let him use the bathroom properly since Vermont.

The seconds ticked on: 4:10. 4:11. 4:12.

"I can't stand this," I said, and I started the car.

"What are you doing?"

"I'm gonna find that dirt road."

"Andy. Andy!" I'd shifted the car into drive, and with my foot on the accelerator, I looked over at Orson. "Quit being stupid," he said calmly. "You aren't gonna find the road. You aren't gonna find the cabin. This is a full-fledged blizzard, and if you get us stuck off this highway, we are fucked. Now, we aren't leaving this car anytime soon. That's a given. So let's wait it out here, in the middle of a highway, where we at least know where we are. If you try to find that dirt road, you're gonna put us in the middle of a desert in a whiteout."

"All we have to do is go straight. The cabin's that way. We'll go straight for—"

"*Which way's straight*? That way? That way? That way? It all looks straight to me!"

I punched the gas, and the tail end of the Lexus fishtailed. Letting off, I pressed more gently, and the tires found the pavement and gave us solid forward momentum. At forty miles an hour, I turned into the desert. The tires sank into the powder, and our speed slowed to thirty. The snow was twice as deep as on the road, and though I felt we might lose traction at any second, I maintained control. Steering between sagebrush, I squinted through the windshield, looking for that long, straight swath of white that would be unmarred by vegetation. It would extend westward, a thin white ribbon in the snow, and we'd follow it and find the cabin.

Orson gaped at me.

"You see anything?" I asked. "You looking?" The engine labored to keep the wheels turning, and the speedometer needle jigged between twenty and twenty-five. I watched it uneasily.

"Circle back," he said. "Do it now and we might reach the highway. But if you let this car stop out here, we don't have a prayer."

"Look for the dirt road," I said.

"Andy—"

"Look for the fucking road!"

Four minutes passed before I realized he was right. I couldn't see farther than fifty feet beyond the hood of the car, and with the needle hovering at ten, I doubted if we had had the velocity to return to the highway.

"We'll go back," I said, easing the steering wheel to the right.

The back end jinked left and the tires instantly lost traction. Panicking, I stomped the gas, and the car spun 360 degrees. By the time I'd backed off the accelerator, our speed had dropped under five miles an hour, and there was nothing I could do to regain it. The Lexus came to rest against a shrub of sagebrush.

"It's fine," I said. "Don't say anything."

Touching the gas gingerly, the tires spun, but they didn't achieve traction. I clenched the steering wheel and pushed the pedal into the floor. The engine roared and the tires spewed up a load of snow, and, for a second, dirt. The Lexus surged forward into fresh snow, and I shoved my foot harder into the pedal until the rpm indicator redlined, and I could smell the engine cooking. But the tires never met the ground again, and after I'd overheated the engine, I turned off the car and jerked the keys from the ignition.

I opened my door and ran out into the storm. At fifty miles an hour, snowflakes become cold needles, and they relentlessly pricked my face. I bent down and scraped through six inches of powder, thinking, *Maybe I'm standing on the dirt road.* My hands ached as I clawed through the snow, and I reached the dirt finally, but it was too loose to be a road.

Staring up into the raging white fog, I screamed until my throat burned. My face stung from the cold, and the snow seeped through my sneakers. *This isn't happening,* I thought, the dread of being stranded out here with him beginning to suffocate me. *This cannot be real.*

# 32

I climbed back into the Lexus and shed my wet clothes. Throwing them onto the floorboard of the backseat, I opened my suitcase and put on a clean pair of underwear, a sweatsuit I'd packed to sleep in, and two pairs of socks.

"Should I turn the car on?" I asked. "Will that run down the battery?"

"It shouldn't. But leave it off for now, at least till it's pitch-black out there. We'll need it to run all night for the heat." He leaned against the window, still haggard and sluggish from the drug. "How are we on gas?"

"Half a tank."

Orson brought his legs up into the seat and turned over on his side, his back to me.

"You cold?" I asked.

"A little."

From Walter's suitcase, I grabbed a pair of sweatpants, wool socks, and a gray sweatshirt featuring the UNC insignia in Carolina blue. Placing them across Orson's lap, I picked up the Glock, which had been at my feet, and took the handcuff key from my pocket.

"I'm gonna uncuff you so you can get out of that nasty robe," I said. "Then they're going right back on." I unlocked the handcuffs and removed them from his wrists. Disrobing, he dropped the bathrobe at his feet and bundled up in Walter's clothes. I moved to put the cuffs back on him, but he said, "Hold on a second," and lowered his sweatpants so he could inspect the burn on his inner thigh. "It itches," he said, and after he'd scratched around the perimeter of the peppermint patty–size blister, he pulled his sweatpants back up, placed his hands behind his back, and allowed me to cuff him.

I tilted my seat back and listened to the wind ravish the car. Lightning blinked against the snowy dusk; thunder promptly followed.

"Orson," I said, "I want you to tell me why you killed our mother."

"You know."

He was right.

"I want you to say it. I'd have come after you for Walter's family. Maybe just for me."

"I'm sure you would have."

"You're an abomination. I've got another theory. Want to hear it?"

"Sure," he said, staring into the storm.

"Because she brought you into this world."

He looked at me like I'd caught him sniffing panties.

■

The temperature inside the car had already begun to plummet when I selected a box of Ritz crackers, a cylinder of provolone cheese, and a bottle of cabernet sauvignon from the stash of groceries.

"We aren't gonna be able to drink this," I said. "No corkscrew."

"There's a pocketknife with one on it in the glove compartment," Orson said.

Finding the Swiss army knife under a stack of road maps, I uncorked the bottle and swilled the spicy wine. Then I tore open the box of crackers and lined them up on my legs.

"You hungry?" I asked, slicing into the smoked cheese with the dull blade. "Here." Sandwiching a disk of provolone between two crackers, I placed it in his mouth. Then I lay back in my seat and watched the night come.

Once the windshield froze, the snow stuck to the glass. The wind blew so savagely that the flakes clung to every window, and within fifteen minutes, we could see nothing of the blizzard all around us. Only the constant shrieking and the cold, voracious energy confirmed its presence.

Orson noticed the bloody clothes beneath his feet.

"Andy," he said, "is that Luther's blood?" I nodded. "Wow. Where'd you do it? Ricki's?"

"We were supposed to meet at nine. I went at six to leave a note with the barkeep that you couldn't make it. Luther walked in as I was getting ready to leave. If he hadn't come early—"

"He came early because he knew something wasn't right."

"How do you know?"

"He's smart. But you were, too. You had your gun. Otherwise, you'd be dying right now."

"Are you sad he's gone?"

"No. And that's nothing against him. We did a lot together."

"Well, I'm delighted he's dead."

Orson smiled. "He's wasn't all that different from you, Andy."

"Sure."

"I happened to him like I happened to you. He just took to it a little faster."

I stared at Orson, astounded.

"You know, you've done worse than kill me," I said. "You've wrecked me. You've taken my mother, my best friend. I can't go home. I can't return from this."

"No, I saved you, Andy. Your home was a sham. You no longer flit around like everyone else, blind to that black hole you call a heart. Be grateful. You now know what you're capable of. Most people never do. But we live honestly, you and I. Truth, Andy. What did Keats say? It's beauty. Not just pretty truth. We have black hearts, but they're beautiful."

We devoured the entire box of crackers and most of the cheese. The wine was diluting my chary vigilance, so I slowed my consumption.

When we'd finished eating, I unzipped my fanny pack. There were two vials of Ativan remaining and two vials of Versed, but because it was the safer drug, I took the last of the Ativan.

"Andy," he said as I poked the needle into the first vial and began drawing the solution up through its hollow shaft.

"What?"

"You remember the summer they found that man under the interstate behind our house?"

"Yeah, I remember that."

Orson sat up straight and stared at me, his head cocked to one side, as though he were buried in thought. I drained the second vial and thumped the syringe. It was steadily darkening in the car—beyond twilight now.

"What do you remember?" he asked.

"Come on, man, I'm tired."

"Just tell me what you remember."

"We were twelve. It was June."

"July."

"Okay. July. Oh, yeah. Around the Fourth. In fact, it was on the Fourth when they found him. I remember that night, sitting in the backyard, holding a sparkler and seeing three police cars pull up on the curb. The officers came running through our backyard with two German shepherds. Dad was grilling hamburgers, and we watched the men disappear into the woods. A few minutes later, the dogs started going crazy and Dad said, 'Sounds like they found whatever it is they're looking for.'"

Orson smiled. "Willard Bass."

"Huh?"

"That's who they found in the tunnel."

"I can't believe you remember his name."

"I can't believe you don't."

"Why would I?"

Orson swallowed, eyes asquint. "He raped me, Andy."

Thunder vibrated the glass. I stared into the half-empty bottle of wine between my legs. My fingers wrapped around the cool neck. I lifted the cabernet to my lips and let it run down my throat.

"That didn't happen," I said. "I can look at you and—"

"And I can look at your face right now and see that you know it did."

"You're lying."

"Then why do you have a funny feeling in your guts? Like something you haven't touched in years is waking up in the lining of your stomach."

I took another jammy sip and set the bottle between my feet.

"Let me tell you a story," he said. "See if—"

"No. I'm giving you this so I can sleep. I'm not gonna sit here and listen to—"

"Do you have a cigarette burn on the end of your dick?"

It felt as though ants were traversing the back of my neck.

"Me, too," he said.

"That didn't happen. I remember now. It was a story you made up after those kids found him."

"Andy."

I didn't want to know, but I did. I sensed it had always been there, tucked away in an alley of my memory, where I could walk by and know that something awful lurked there, without ever wandering down the corridor to behold it with clarity.

"It happened late one afternoon during a thunderstorm," he said. "In a drainage tunnel that ran beneath the interstate. The water was only a couple inches deep and the tunnel was high enough for a man to walk upright in. We played there all the time.

"We'd been exploring the woods since lunch, when a line of storms blew in. To escape the squall, we ran down to the creek and followed it up to the tunnel. Thought we'd be safe from lightning under the concrete, but we were standing in running water."

*I see you in the dank tunnel darkness.*

"I was telling you," he continued, "that Mom was gonna whip our asses for staying out in the storm."

I turned away from Orson and set the syringe on the floorboard. Night was full-blown, and darkness pervaded the car, so Orson was imperceptible beside me. I only saw his words, scarcely audible over the moan of the storm, as they dragged me into that alley.

■

*Our laughter reverberates through the tunnel. Orson splashes me with water, and I splash it back onto his skinny prepubescent legs. We stand at the mouth of the tunnel, where the runoff drops two feet into a waist-deep muddy pool that we think is filled with snakes.*

Two hundred feet away, at the opposite end of the tunnel, we hear the noise of careless footsteps in shallow water. Orson and I turn and see that the dot of light at the other end is blocked now by a moving figure.

"Who is it?" Orson whispers.

"I don't know."

Through the darkness, I detect the microscopic glow of a cigarette.

"Come on," he whines. "Let's go. We're gonna get in trouble."

Thunder shakes the concrete, and I step across the dirty current and stand by my brother.

He tells me he's afraid. I am, too. It begins to hail, chunks of ice the size of Ping-Pong balls pelting the forest floor and flopping fatly into the orange pool. More scared of the storm than the approaching foot-steps, we wait, apprehensive. The tobacco cherry waxes, and we soon catch the first waft of smoke.

The man who emerges from the shadow is stocky and bald, older than our father, with an undomesticated gray beard and forearms thick as four-by-fours. He wears filthy army fatigues, and though hardly taller, he outweighs us by a hundred pounds. Staggering right up between us, he looks us up and down in a utilitarian fashion, which does not unnerve me like it should. I still don't know about some things.

"I been watching you all afternoon," he says. "Never had twins." I'm not sure what he means. He has a northern accent, and a deep voice that rumbles when he speaks, like a growling animal. His breath is rancid, smoky, and sated with alcohol. "Eenie, meanie, minie, moe. Catch a tiger by her toe. If she hollers, let her go. Eenie, meanie, minie, moe." He points a thick grease-stained index finger into Orson's chest. I'm getting ready to ask what he's doing, when a fist I never see coming catches me clean across the jaw.

I come to consciousness with the side of my face in the water, my vision blurred, and Orson moaning.

"*Keep crying like that, boy,*" the man says, winded. "*That's nice. Real nice.*"

*My sight clears, but I don't understand why Orson is on his knees in the water, with the man draped over him, his enormous villous legs pressed up against the back of Orson's hairless thighs. His olive pants and underwear pulled down around his black boots, the man hugs him tightly as they rock back and forth.*

"*Hot damn,*" the man whispers. "*Oh, good God.*" Orson screeches. *He sounds like our cocker spaniel puppy, and still I don't understand.*

*The man and Orson look at me at the same instant and see that I'm conscious and curious. Orson shakes his head and sobs harder. I cry, too.*

"*Boy,*" the man says to me, his face slick with sweat. "*Don't you move. I'll twist your brother's little neck off and roll it like a bowling ball.*"

*So I lie there with my face in the water, watching the man moan. He closes his eyes and starts hugging Orson faster and faster. As he comes, he bites Orson's shoulder through a blue T-shirt, and my brother howls.*

*The man looks so happy.* "*Ah! Ahh! Ahhh! Ahhh! Ahhhhhh!*"

*Willard pulls out and Orson collapses into the water. There's blood all over my brother's ass. It runs down the backs of his legs. He lies in the water, half-naked, too stunned to cry or even pull up his pants. Willard takes a cigarette from his breast pocket and lights it.*

"*You're a sweet piece,*" he says, reaching down toward my brother, who's still curled up in the water. Orson screams.

*I sit up against the concrete wall. It's no longer hailing, and Willard stumbles through the water toward me, his pants still down around his ankles. I've never seen a man's erection before, and though beginning to fade, it's ungodly huge. He stops in front of me.*

"*I can't love you like I did him,*" he says, dragging on the cigarette. "*Ever sucked on a dick?*" I shake my head, and he steps into me. My

*jaw is swollen, but I forget the pain when I smell him. He holds himself
in his hand and brushes it against my cheek.*

*"You put that in your mouth, boy, or I'll twist your head off."*

*Tears slide down my cheeks. "I can't. I can't do it."*

*"Boy, you take that now. And you do me good. Like you mean it.
And mind those braces."*

*The moist bulbous head of his cock touches my lips, and I take it for
a full minute.*

*A grapefruit-size rock drops beside me into the water, and Willard
staggers back into the opposite wall and sinks down into a sitting position in the water. He's dazed, and I don't understand what's happened
until I see Orson's hand lift the rock back out of the water.*

*Because Willard is holding his left temple, he never sees Orson wind
up again. The rock strikes him dead in the face this time, and I hear the
fracture of bone. The man's face is purple now, rearranged. On his
hands and knees, he struggles toward the mouth of the tunnel. Taking
the rock again, Orson mounts him, like we used to ride on our father's
back, and brings the granite down into the man's skull. Willard sus-
tains four blows before his arms give out.*

*With both hands, Orson lifts the rock up high and dashes the man's
head out like a piece of soft fruit. When he's finished, he turns to me,
still astride Willard, his face speckled with blood and pulp.*

*"Wanna hit him some?" he asks, though there isn't much left to hit.*

*"No."*

*He lobs the rock into the pool and comes over and sits down beside
me. I lean over and vomit. When I sit back up, I ask him, "What'd he
do to you?"*

*"Put his thing in my butt."*

*"Why?"*

*"I don't know. Look at what else." Orson shows me his tiny penis.
There's a blister on the end, and it makes me cry to see it.*

*I walk over to Willard and roll him over. He doesn't have a face. His skull reminds me of a cracked watermelon shell. I find the soggy pack of cigarettes in his breast pocket. The lighter's inside the pack, so I take it, along with one cigarette, and sit back down beside my brother. Lighting the cigarette, I pull down my pants and brand myself.*

"We're still the same," *I say, whimpering as the pain comes on.*

Willard Bass was a fly buffet when the dogs found him. Though our parents forbade us from playing in the woods for the remainder of the summer, they never seemed to notice that their sons had been hollowed.

It's funny. I don't remember forgetting.

■

Silence reigned for a long time after Orson finished. The darkness inside the car became complete, and the storm raged on.

"Guess you think that explains a lot," I said.

"No. You want to know what I think? I think if you and I had never gone into that tunnel, we'd still be in this desert. I am not who I am because I was raped when I was twelve. Willard Bass was just gas on my fire. When will you see it?"

"What?"

"What's really in you."

"I do see it, Orson."

"And?"

"And I hate it. I fear it. I respect it. And if I thought for a moment it could ever control me, I'd put a gun in my mouth. Time for your injection."

# 33

**W H E N** I woke up, I didn't hear the wind. The clock read 10:00 A.M. Orson was breathing heavily, and though I shook him, he wouldn't stir.

It had grown uncomfortably hot inside the car, so I shut the vents. I turned the windshield wipers on, and they knocked off a wedge of snow. The sun shone into the front seat with eye-splitting brilliance.

The snow depth had risen above the hood, and as I stared out across the white desert, I saw only an occasional tangle of mature sagebrush poking up through the snow. The sky was orchid blue.

I saw a white ridge several miles ahead, and I wondered if it was the same one that rose behind the cabin and the shed.

Watching my brother sleep in the passenger seat, I felt a knot swell in my stomach. *Bastard.* I'd dreamed about Willard Bass making me take it. The rage lingered, festering in my gut, and the more

I shunned it, the more it swelled. *He should not have done that to me.*

"Orson, wake up!" I slapped his face, and his eyes opened.

"Oh my," he mumbled, sitting up. "There's three feet on the ground." Orson cracked his neck. "Roll down my window." A clump of snow fell onto Orson's lap as the glass lowered into the door. "I see the cabin," he said.

"Where?"

"Two black specks on the horizon."

I squinted through the passenger window. "Are you sure that's it?"

"There isn't another structure within fifteen miles."

"How far is it?"

"A mile or two."

I reached into the backseat, grabbed an armful of clothes from the suitcases, and dropped them on the console between Orson and me. "I'm gonna let you out of the cuffs till we reach the cabin."

"We're going now?" he asked, incredulous. "There's no way we'll make it."

"Orson, we can see it. We got less than a quarter of a tank of gas left. That's not enough for another night of heat, and what if there's another storm coming? We're going."

"Any of these clothes waterproof?"

"No."

"Then forget it. That ice will saturate cotton, and it'll take us several hours at least to reach the cabin in snow this deep. Ever heard of frostbite?"

"I'll risk it. I'm not staying in this car another night with you."

I dug the handcuff key out of my pocket.

"I'm sorry I told you about Willard," he said. "Andy?"

"What?"

"You gonna forget again?"

"Don't say another fucking word to me."

•

The snow came up just shy of my waist. I'd never walked in snow so deep that each step required you to expend the energy of a toddler climbing a staircase. I made Orson walk several yards ahead of me, and, just as he'd predicted, we hadn't taken fifty awkward steps before the ice began to soak through the layers of my khakis and sweatpants. We'd gone a quarter of a mile when the initial icy burn set in above my knees, like a swarm of needles poking in and out of my raw red skin. It hurt to walk. It hurt to stand still, and by the time we'd hiked a mile through the snow, even my eyes burned from the sunny crystal glare. I wondered how I could possibly reach that minuscule black dot, which still seemed a fixture on the horizon.

Orson trudged on at his tireless gait, showing no sign of pain or fatigue. The burning in my legs had grown so unendurable that my forehead broke out into a cold sweat.

"Hold up!" I shouted, and Orson stopped. He was twenty feet ahead, bundled up in two T-shirts, a sweater, a sweatshirt, and a black leather jacket. His legs appeared bulky beneath the long johns, sweatpants, and jeans I'd given him from Walter's suitcase.

"What's wrong?" he asked.

"I just need a breather."

After a moment, I lifted my grocery-filled suitcase up over my head, and we continued on. My legs and feet turned numb shortly thereafter, so I battled only the stinging in my eyes. The sole relief came from closing my eyes, but I couldn't shut them long enough to quell the pain while Orson walked uncuffed ahead of me.

■

With the cabin three football fields away, my legs were spectacularly numb. I kept thinking of that medical definition I'd found for snow blindness while doing research for *Blue Murder*—a sunburn directly on the cornea. It watered my eyes just to think of it, and I fixated on locking Orson into that spare bedroom and falling asleep under his fleece blanket in the soothing darkness of the cabin.

Orson glanced back at me, and I couldn't believe I hadn't noticed it before. He wore my sunglasses. *Did you swipe them from the top of the dashboard while we dressed for this snow trek?* I was going to scream at him to stop, but I thought, *Fuck it, we're almost there.*

Even when squinting, I couldn't adequately shield my eyes from the glare, so I let them close entirely, and it felt wonderful. *I'm just going to shut them for a moment,* I thought, moving clumsily and blindly now through the snow.

After six gargantuan steps, I opened my eyes to check on Orson. He was gone.

Dropping the suitcase, I took the Glock out of my waistband and looked in every direction—nothing but smooth unending snow, which drifted randomly in gentle mounds.

"Orson!" I screamed. My voice cracked and echoed across the blinding white expanse. "Orson!" No sound, not even wind. Trying to follow his tracks through the snow, my eyes watered, and the salt in the tears exacerbated the sting.

I sensed suddenly that someone was running up behind me, and I spun around and pointed the gun back in the direction of the car. The snow sparkled, pristine and empty. Fear tickled my loins. The white Lexus, half-buried and camouflaged in snow, existed now only as a silver glimmer in the distance. Sunlight struck the speck of its windshield like a flake of mica.

*He's out there,* I thought, turning back toward the cabin. *He's lying in the snow, and all I have to do is follow his footprints.* I saw where they ended less than fifty feet ahead.

"Stand up!" I shouted. "I won't shoot you, Orson! Come on! Don't do this!"

Nothing moved. I grabbed up the suitcase, and I had taken three steps, when something occurred to me. Kneeling down in the snow, I hollowed out a sufficient space to sit. With my leather-gloved hands, I attempted to tunnel into the thirty-six-inch wall of snow, and, to my horror, succeeded. During the storm, the wind had compressed the snowpack, so now I could shovel out a passageway, which barely exceeded one foot in height and two feet in width, while keeping the surface above intact. In essence, a man could tunnel unseen under the snow.

I stood up, becoming colder now through my torso. The footprints ahead of me meant nothing. Even as I reached the end of Orson's tracks and saw the suitcase he'd left behind, I knew that he could be anywhere in the immediate vicinity, hiding, waiting just two feet below the surface.

Dropping the suitcase again, I sprinted off into the snow, running in slowly expanding circles and screaming at my brother to show himself. I ran myself dizzy and finally collapsed on top of our suitcases, back again where Orson's tracks had terminated.

On the cusp of blindness, I feared that the numbness in my legs masked tremendous pain, which warmth would soon unthaw. The Glock in my hands was useless, and conceding that for the moment he held the advantage, I came to my feet and bounded on through virgin powder toward the cabin.

# 34

**REACHING** into the side pocket of my frozen khakis, I took the key that Orson had promised me would unlock the front door. Punching it through the icebound keyhole, I turned the key. The door opened; hauling the suitcases behind me, I entered the cabin.

I wagered that no one had been here in months. There was an unpalatable scent in the air, as if I'd climbed into an attic or a crawl space. My effete vision made the interior of the cabin dusky. I staggered across the stone floor so I could look out the window that faced south, the direction from which we'd come. Though late in the afternoon, the sun blazed as it descended over the bluff. Nothing moved in the sprawl of dazzling white, and I took comfort in knowing that were he to approach the cabin now, I would undoubtedly see him.

My attention turned from my brother to the morbid condition of my legs. I could feel nothing below the knees, and I imagined this was the sensation an amputee might endure when first walking on a prosthetic appendage. *I need heat,* I thought, limping toward the kitchen.

My snow blindness caused me to see everything in crimson. Nothing had changed. Orson's cornucopia of books still lined the walls, and on the northern edge of the living room, the perfectly organized kitchen stood against the wall, minus a functional sink. The doors to the back bedrooms were closed, and when I saw them, and that small Monet between the doors, my stomach dropped.

I noticed Orson's record player on the stool by the front door, along with the stack of jazz records he'd left behind. I would've put on a record, but there was no power, and it dawned on me that I should find the fuel supply and crank the generator before nightfall.

Beside the stove, I found what I was looking for—the white kerosene heater. I couldn't find a corresponding can of kerosene, but when I lifted the heater, I heard a plentiful sloshing of fuel inside its tank. After dragging it into the living room and setting it before the black leather couch, I pressed the electric starter, and, to my surprise, the heater ignited on the first attempt. Warmth flooded the subfreezing cabin, and as the drafts of heat splashed at my face, I began removing the sweaters and sweatshirts that had kept me alive on that hike from the car to this cabin.

Leaving the pile of clothes on the floor, I sank down into the couch, unlaced my boots, and pulled the ice-encrusted shoes off my feet. I stripped the stiff socks, the khakis, sweats, and finally the wet long underwear that stuck to my legs. Below my knees, my skin had turned waxy white. I touched my pallid calves, and though they felt cold and hard like a corpse's, the tissue underneath was still malleable. My feet looked much worse. The ends of my toes were tinged with blue, and when I pinched the soles of my feet, there was no sensation of pain or pressure.

I glanced out the window and then, still seeing nothing on the desert, walked into the kitchen. There was a large silver basin on the counter, its interior frosted with the remnants of unbleached flour. I took it out onto the front porch and filled it with snow. The top of the kerosene heater was a level metal plate, exposed directly to the glowing orange coils underneath. I set the bowl of snow on the plate and lay back on the couch to watch it melt.

As the pile of snow disappeared into the basin, I couldn't shake the pavid feeling that being in this cabin fomented inside of me. I felt as if I'd come to my own wake and was standing before the casket, looking down into my lifeless face, unnatural beneath the false warm color of my skin. No sound, no wind, no movement in the back bedrooms—my hands trembled.

*I should not be here. This is very wrong.*

The snow had been melted for some time when steam began to roll off the surface of the water. Reaching forward, I dipped my finger into the bowl. The water was warm, so I used my socks to lift the hot bowl and set it on the floor. Then I slid my blue feet into the basin, unable to feel the temperature or even the wetness of the water. Lying back on the couch, I closed my eyes as my legs came back to life, their resurrection announced by the tingling between my ankles and knees.

After five minutes, I still couldn't feel my toes. Reaching down, I plunged my hand into the water and found that my feet had cooled it more effectively than two blocks of ice. I set the bowl back on top of the kerosene heater, let the water reheat, and once again submersed my feet.

It took two more rounds of cooling and reheating the snowmelt before I felt something awaken in the bones of my toes—the beginning of a deep, freezing burn. I tried to relax, visualizing my lake house in spring and imagining myself sitting out on my back porch beneath the pines, in the presence of the virid forest and the lake-chilled wind.

The lukewarm water bit like acid, and I grunted, sweat running into my tender eyes, my feet burning, as though I held them over an open flame. The pain reduced me to whimpering, and though the impulse to withdraw them from the water was enticing, I knew it wouldn't obviate the burn. I was paying for the cold now, for walking four hours through the snow in leaky boots. I could do nothing but sit on the couch and endure what was perhaps the most virulent pain I'd ever known.

■

By 6:00 P.M. the pain was sufferable, though I still saw the world in red. It was futile staring out the window for Orson. The sun had set, and the desert was blacker than the space between stars.

Retracting my feet from the cold water, I stood up, wobbly, but relieved to have the feeling returned to my ankles. The ends of my toes were blackening, but there was nothing more I could do. At the very least, I might have saved my feet. Who the hell needs pinkie toes?

Rummaging through the kitchen drawers, I located a candle and a book of matches. With the flame throwing soft yellow light against the log walls, I checked the dead bolt for the third time and secured the four living room windows. Then, clutching the tarnished brass candlestick, I walked through the narrow hallway into the back of the cabin.

The key to the dead bolt also unlocked the room that had been my prison. It appeared just as I had left it, meager and confining.

Though the window in the back wall was still barred, I reached through and tested the latch. Then I opened the dresser drawers, which were empty, and peeked under the bed. There was nothing significant in this room, a holding cell, nothing more.

I walked back into the hallway and stopped at Orson's door. Touching the doorknob, I hesitated. *You're alone. Fuck the fear.* I stepped inside.

The freezer chest stood unlocked beneath the window. I opened it. Empty. I locked the window. Now he'd have to break glass to get inside.

Setting the candle atop Orson's pine dresser, I started opening drawers. The top three were empty, but when I tried the last, it was stuck. Yanking on it again, it still wouldn't open, so I kicked it. The wood squeaked, and jerking back once more on the handles, I pulled the drawer entirely out of the dresser and onto the floor.

*Thank you, God.*

I inventoried five videotapes, a stack of manila folders, a box of microcassettes, and three Mead notebooks. Bringing the candle down onto the floor, I held it over the drawer and removed a videotape. I read the label on the tape, written in his straight, microscopic penmanship: "Jessica Horowitz: 5-29-92; Jim Yountz: 6-20-92; Trevor Kistling: 6-25-92; Mandy Sommers: 7-06-92"—all on one label, and there were five tapes here, not counting the three I'd destroyed in Woodside. I noticed that each tape, without exception, had been recorded during the months of May, June, July, and August: his hunting season.

The microcassettes were labeled only by date, and I assumed they contained the same self-absorbed drivel I'd heard Orson dictating in his bed in Vermont. Lifting a green wire-bound notebook from the drawer, I lay on my stomach and thumbed through the pages by candlelight. This one was full of poetry, every page, front and back. I read a short untitled poem aloud to explore the rhythm of his verse, his direct, protean voice flowing through mine:

> *You are always with me*
> *When I lie in bed in the dark*
> *When I walk a crowded street*
> *When I watch the night sky*
> *When I shit*
> *When I laugh*
> *When I possess them, as you possess me*
> *You are omnipotent, but you aren't my god*
> *You raised me but did not make me*
> *You are gas but not the fire*
> *I am deeper*
> *I am incalculable*
> *I am*

The two other notebooks contained short stories, brainstorms, and the fragmented thoughts of someone aspiring to write. Orson wouldn't make it as a writer. He could turn a nifty phrase, but there was a general ungainliness and ambiguity in his verse and prose, which would've doomed him to fail had he ever tried to publish. I wanted to tell him this, and that his poetry was prosaic. I wanted him to watch me burn the notebooks and the tapes.

There were three manila folders. The first, titled "In the News," was filled with newspaper clippings regarding the discovery or lack thereof of Orson's victims. The second folder, "Memory Lane," bulged with photographs, and I studied all of them. I saw myself in half a dozen pictures, but they didn't unglue me like I'd feared, even the one of me staring down at Jeff seconds after his execution.

A handful of photographs featured Luther doing grisly things to people. In one photo, he stared truculently into the camera with dead, soulless eyes, fingernail marks running down each cheek.

In the third folder, "The Minutes," Orson had chronicled six summers of killing on unlined loose-leaf paper. Flipping to the end, I skimmed the synopsis of our time together, until I reached the final paragraph:

## Wyoming: June 2, 1996

*He hasn't been as easy or productive as Luther, but I see in him potential that transcends my other pupil. So I'm letting him go. Another week here and he'd lose his mind, when what I want is for his rage to ferment so he becomes drunk on the hate. He is my brother. He is me in so many ways. I love him, and the least I can do is introduce him to himself. Though I anticipate bringing him out here again, let me make a prediction: I won't have to. He'll come for me, and there won't be anything I can do to prevent it. Andy's smart and remarkably cruel when he needs to be. If he does come for me, I'll give him the gift, because he'll be ready. It's funny—the selflessness he inspires in me.*

# 35

**T H E** moon came up over the Winds, lighting the snowpack like a field of blue diamonds. I simmered a can of pork and beans on top of the kerosene heater, and as they filled the cabin with their sweet, smoky aroma, I surveyed the desert for Orson.

We'd left the car at noon, and it was nearly 8:30. He couldn't have stayed alive on the desert this long. The temperature hadn't surpassed ten degrees all day, and tramping through the snow in deficient clothing would've resulted in his freezing to death by now. So he was either dead out there or he'd found refuge, the only viable shelters being the Lexus, the shed, or this cabin. I knew he wasn't in the cabin. I'd checked the four closets, under the two beds, and I knew with certainty that I was the sole occupant. The shed glowed in the moonlight. I could see it through the window beside the front door. If I'd mustered the nerve, I might've walked outside and searched for tracks leading to the shed. But I didn't have the temerity to go back out into the cold to look for him, especially since my legs were beginning to blister. *Where are you?* I thought. *And what are you going to do?*

When I finished my supper, I sat on the floor beside the heater and pulled a shoe box down from the couch. I'd found it under the defunct kitchen sink, and it contained all sorts of goodies, including Indiana, Oregon, California, and Louisiana state driver's licenses. In addition to Orson Thomas and David Parker, he was also Roger Garrison, Brad Harping, Patrick Mulligan, and Vincent Carmichael. He had passports for every name except Roger Garrison, and flipping through them, I saw that he'd traveled extensively in Europe and South America.

The find that pleased me most, however, was the rubber-banded stack of hundred-dollar bills. I counted $52,800—plenty to disappear.

Closing the shoe box, I tossed it into the drawer of videotapes and folders that I'd carried into the living room. Having scoured the cabin, every incriminating piece of evidence was contained in that single drawer, and it gave me great comfort to have it in my possession now. I stood up and walked to the window beside the door. The bluffs soared above the desert a mile behind the shed, like colossal dunes of white sand. *Orson,* I thought. *Just you now. The only thing left to destroy.*

If he came for me, it would be at night, but exhaustion wasted my mind and body. *I'll sleep until midnight,* I thought. *I'm worthless now anyway.* For all I knew, he might never come. He could be lying out there right now, statuesque under the snow.

I extinguished the heater and went into his bedroom. Wrapped in the fleece blanket, I curled up with the gun beside my pillow, and the handcuffs in my pocket. In the absence of wind and the humming generator, my breathing and my heartbeat produced the only perceptible sound.

•

*I dreamed a memory: Orson and I are ten years old. The church service has just concluded at Third Creek Baptist Church, a chapel in the countryside north of Winston-Salem where Grandmom attends. Because it's the last Sunday of the month, the congregation surges through the front doors outside for a covered-dish picnic. Beside the small brick building, the epitome of homely Baptist churches, a half a dozen picnic tables exhibit a smorgasbord of country cooking. Three grills have been going since midmorning, and the smell of hot dogs and hamburgers and a whole smoked pig floods the August afternoon.*

*When we finish eating, Orson and I sit under a walnut tree and watch a regiment of ants feast on a discarded watermelon rind. It's clear and hot, and we sweat copiously under our matching baby blue suits with yellow bow ties.*

*I see her walking toward us, stepping daintily between families, who are gorged and lounging on blankets in the grass. New to the congregation, her knee-length sleeveless dress is the same premature yellow as the sun-scorched poplar leaves. She stops and stands by the watermelon rind. I watch an ant crawl across her unpainted big toe.*

*When she speaks, she makes the most peculiar sound, something akin to a knife blade sliding across a sharpening stone: "Schick. Aren't you two just the most precious little things I ever saw!"*

*Orson and I look up from the ground into her heavily powdered face. Her curly platinum hair is rigid, and she smells like a concoction of cheap perfumes.*

*"Darlings!" she exclaims, grinning, and we see her false teeth, where broccoli florets still cling. Here it comes—that question everyone*

*feels compelled to ask, though Orson and I are mirror images of each other. "Are y'all twins?"*

*God, we hate that. I open my mouth to explain how we're just fraternal twins, but Orson stops me with a look. He peers up into her eyes and makes his bottom lip quiver.*

*"We are now," he says.*

*"What do you mean, young man?"*

*"Our triplet brother Timmy—he got burned up in the fire three days ago."*

*Through the powder, her face colors, and she covers her mouth with her hand. "Schick. Oh, I am so sorry. I didn't mean to . . ." She squats down, and I'm pinching the back sides of my calves, trying not to laugh. "Well, he's with Jesus now," she says softly, "so—"*

*"No, he wasn't saved," Orson says. "He was gonna do it this Sunday. You think he's in hell with Satan? I mean, if you aren't saved, that's where you go, right? That's what Preacher Rob said."*

*She stands back up. "You'd better talk with your parents about that. Schick." Her feigned giddiness vaporized, she looks off into the bordering wood. With all her makeup, she reminds me of a sad clown. "Schick. Well, I'm terribly sorry," she says, and we watch her walk back into the crowd. Then we run behind the walnut tree and laugh until tears glisten on our cheeks.*

·

I woke and found myself sitting up in Orson's bed, pressing the Glock against my temple. Nothing surprised me anymore. Sliding out from under the fleece blanket, I walked into the living room, the gun at my side. Without the warmth of the kerosene heater, the cabin had cooled again, and I bent down to punch the electric starter, when something curdled my blood: I recalled the dream and the woman's queer nervous tic: *schick, schick, schick.* Instead of lighting the heater as I'd intended, I unlocked the dead bolt and cracked the front door. Subzero night air deluged the cabin.

I hadn't ventured outside again since arriving at the cabin in the late afternoon, and my tracks ran south toward the car. A surge of adrenaline straightened each hair on my neck—another set of tracks, which I had not made, came directly from the shed, up the steps, to the front door, where I now stood. *He's in the cabin.* Closing the door, I turned around and chambered a bullet, regretting I'd not left the votive candles burning in every room. I stepped forward into the red darkness, squinting at the corners in the kitchen and the living room, straining to detect the slightest pin drop of sound—a noisy breath or a clamorous heart that pounded like mine.

*Are you watching me now?* I thought, creeping from the living room back through the hallway. The door to the spare bedroom was cracked, and I couldn't remember leaving it that way. Approaching the door, I kicked it open and rushed inside, spinning around in the darkness, my finger on the trigger, waiting for him to spring at me. But the room was empty, just as I'd left it.

I returned to the hallway. *Your room. You were watching me sleep.* Disregarding my fear, I stepped over the threshold. The only place in the room obstructed from view was the other side of his dresser. The Glock raised, ready to fire, I lunged across the room, beginning to squeeze the trigger as the blind spot between the dresser and the freezer came into view. He wasn't there.

The four closets were the only places I'd yet to comb, but I couldn't imagine he'd squeezed himself into one. They were filled with supplies—one a pantry, another a storage space for gas, bottled water, and a substantial coil of rope. Besides, I'd have heard him banging around in the dark.

I walked out of his bedroom. There were two closets on each side of the twelve-foot hallway connecting the bedrooms to the living room. *You're waiting for me to walk by again, so you can swing a door into my face.* I bolted through the hall back into the living room.

Standing by the cold heater, I'd begun to devise a plan to flush him out, when a bead of water slapped the crown of my bald head. Snowmelt. Wood creaked above me, and I looked up into the rafters. A shadow swung down from a beam, and something blunt and hard smote the back of my head.

·

I came to on the floor, and the Glock was gone. I struggled to my feet. The red darkness twirled, pierced by bursts of light. *Am I dreaming?*

The point of a knife slipped between my right arm and my torso and touched my solar plexus. I saw the ivory handle, and when I felt his breath against the back of my ear, piss flowed down the side of my leg and pooled under my bare feet. When I tried to pull away, the blade pressed against my throat.

"This knife'll cut through your windpipe like it was Jell-O."

"Don't kill me."

"What's that jangle?" Reaching down, he felt the pockets of my sweatpants. "Oh goodie." He removed the handcuffs, with the key still in the lock, and cuffed my left hand. "Give me the other one." I put my right hand behind my back, and he cuffed that one, too. "Now lead the way," he whispered, the blade still at my throat. "There's a surprise for you in the shed."

# 36

**THOUGH** barefoot, I couldn't feel the ice between my toes. I imagined that the sliver of moon lit our faces blue and baleful. The night was surreal, and I thought, *I am not here. I am not walking with him to that shed.* Orson kept close, grunting with each breath, as though it were a struggle for him to stay with me. *Withdrawal or frostbite, or both.* I reached the back door of the shed, stopped, and turned. He shuffled toward me, pointing the Glock waveringly at my head. In the moonlight, I saw his face—the tips of his ears blackened, his cheeks, lips, and forehead corpse-white from the cold.

"You've been guzzling your buttermilk," he said, grinning. "Go on in. It's unlocked."

I pushed my shoulder into the door and it opened. Terror weakened me when I saw what he'd done. The interior of the shed was filled with candles—dozens of them placed on the floor and the shelves. Innumerable shadows jitterbugged along the concrete, up the walls, into the rafters. I saw the pole, the leather collar, the sheet of plastic spread out on the floor to catch my blood.

"All for you," he whispered. "A candlelight death."

"Orson, please. . . ." The tip of the knife pricked my back, urging me through the doorway. As I walked across the concrete, I stared at the hole in the far corner of the wall, presuming he'd crawled in out of the snow sometime after dark. The missing panel of pine lay on the floor.

"On the plastic," he said. When I hesitated, he took three steps in my direction and pointed the Glock at my left knee. Immediately, I moved to the plastic and knelt down. "On your stomach," he said, and I prostrated myself as instructed. I smelled the leather collar as he slipped it over my head and cinched it around my neck—the scent of misfortunate strangers' sweat and blood and tears and spit. I felt a terrible, intimate kinship with those doomed souls who'd worn this putrid collar before me. We were blood now—Orson's hideous children. Papa dragged the stool out from the corner and perched on it, just out of reach.

Shoving the Glock into the waistband of Walter's jeans, he took the sharpening stone from his pocket and began drawing the blade across it: *schick, schick, schick.* Watching him work in the dim, jaundiced light, candles surrounding the plastic, I grew sensitive to the cuffs that dug into my wrists.

They were mine. I'd owned them since a Halloween party in 1987, when a friend presented them as a gag gift to me and this woman I was seeing, Sophie. It embarrassed us at first, but I cuffed her to my bedpost that night. I'd tied up other women with these cuffs and allowed them to shackle me. I'd bound Orson. Now he bound me. Fucking durable metal.

I sat up, facing him. Desperately and discreetly, I tried to pull the cuffs apart, and when my hands turned numb, I strained even harder. A man-burner named Sizzle in *The Scorcher* breaks the chain between a pair of cuffs while sitting in the back of a police car, and goes on to slay the arresting officer. Still pulling my hands apart, I recalled that deft little sentence: "The chain popped, O'Malley's neck popped, and Sizzle climbed behind the wheel and shoved the officer into the wet street." *It's that easy. So break.*

"You're wasting precious energy," Orson said offhandedly as he studied a ding in the blade. "I couldn't break them when you held the flame under my eyeball." He resumed stroking the blade, and his eyes fixed now on me. "A guy does favor after favor for you, and this is how you repay him. This betrayal."

My mouth ran dry; I had no spit.

"I don't know what your definition of favor en—"

"It was all for you," he said. "Washington. Mom. We could've been amazing, brother. I could've freed you. Like Luther. I held the mirror up for him, too, you see. Showed him the demon. He didn't spit in my face." Orson began pinching his cheeks and scraping the skin off his face with the knife, as if amused with the lack of feeling in his brittle epidermis. He bled in several places. "You came in my house," he continued. "While I slept in my bed. Tortured me." He stared into my eyes. "You scare me, Andy. And that should not happen."

"I swear—"

"I know—you'll never come after me again. Andy, when a person knows their death is imminent, they'll say anything. I was carving this guy up once, and he told me his grandfather had molested him. Just blurted it out between screams, like it might change something." He laughed sadly. "You gonna talk to me while I open you? Nah, I'll bet you're just a screamer."

Orson stepped down off the stool. The largest candle in the shed was a red cinnamon-scented cylinder of wax with the girth of a soup can. It sat on the shelf beside the back door, and he laid the knife blade over its flame and pulled the Glock from his waistband.

"Pick a knee," he said.

"Why?"

"Disablement. Torture. Death. In that order. It begins now. Pick a knee."

An extraordinary calm enveloped me. *You will not hurt me.* I came to my feet and found his eyes, invoking that irrevocable love that was our entitlement.

"Orson. Let's talk—"

The hollow-point bored into the meat of my left shoulder. On my knees, I watched blood drizzle across the plastic. I smelled gunpowder. I smelled blood. I blacked out.

•

I stared up into the rafters, flat on my back on the plastic, hands still cuffed behind my back. I attempted to move my feet, but they were tied crudely with thick, coarse rope. One hundred and eighty-five pounds crushed into my ribs, and I moaned.

Straddling me, Orson took the knife off the red candle, which now oozed wax onto the plastic. The carbon blade glowed lava orange, and the metal secreted smoke.

I wore a T-shirt, a sweatshirt, and a shabby burgundy sweater. Starting at my waist, the blade cleaved easily through the layers of scorching fabric, all the way up to the collars at my throat. Then splitting the garments, he exposed my bare torso, the chest hair swaying in the tiny drafts effected by candles in this icy shed. Above the thudding of my heart, I thought I heard something on the desert, a distant whine, like mosquitoes behind my ear.

"Wow. Look how fast your heart's palpitating," he said, placing his hand on my shuddering chest. He tapped my breastbone. "I'm gonna saw through that now. Anxious?"

When the knife point met my left nipple, I chomped my teeth and flexed every muscle, as though the tension might thwart the penetration of the fiery blade.

"Easy," he said. "I want you to relax. It'll hurt more." Orson moved the knife two inches to the left of my nipple and inserted the blade an eighth of an inch. The metal was brutally cold, and I shivered as I watched him slit a sloppy circle, four inches in diameter. Blood pooled in my navel, and Orson spoke to me while he carved, his voice flowing psychotic peace.

"Two-thirds of your heart lies to the left of your sternum. So I'm giving myself an outline to work with." He sighed. "I'd have taught you this, you know. On someone else. Look at that." He held the tip of the knife under my eye so I could see my blood sizzling on the amber blade. "I know you don't feel anything yet," he said. "That's the power of adrenaline. Your pain receptors are blocked." He smiled. "But that won't last much longer. They can only mask so much pain."

"Orson," I pleaded, on the brink of tears now. "What about the gift?"

He looked down at me, puzzled; then, remembering, he said, "Ah, the gift. You nosy bastard." He put his lips to my ear. "Willard was the gift."

He braced his left hand against my forehead and gripped the knife in his other. "Sometimes I wonder, Andy, what if he'd picked you?"

Someone knocked on the back door. Orson stiffened. "I *want* you to say something," he whispered as he stood up. "Swear to God, I'll keep you alive for days." Setting the knife on the stool, he walked to the door and drew the Glock.

Percy Madding's voice came through the door: "Dave, you in there? You all right?"

I strained to sit up on the plastic.

Orson fired eight shots through the wood at waist level. Looking back at me, he smiled. "That, Andy, is what you call—"

A shotgun report blasted through the door, and Orson's chest caught the full load of double-aught buckshot. It knocked him off his feet and slammed him on his back as if a man had thrown him. Orson struggled to his hands and knees, stunned, staring at me as sanguine globs dropped out of his chest onto the concrete. Percy burst through the door and kicked the gun out of his hands. My brother crawled toward me, then eased back down onto the concrete, hissing shoal, sputtering breaths.

Leaning his double-barreled shotgun beside the door, Percy approached the plastic and squatted beside me. From the shallowness of his breathing, I could tell he'd been hit. He looked strangely at the pole, the leash, the sheet of plastic, the ragged bloody circle in my chest.

"He got the key to these cuffs on him?" he asked gruffly, twisting his snowy mustache. His voice was strong, but his hands shook. When I nodded, he walked over to Orson and dug through his pockets until he found the key. He told me to roll over, and then, after unlocking the handcuffs, he unsheathed a bowie knife from his belt and cut the rope that bound my feet.

"You hit?" I asked. He touched his side. Down mushroomed out of a hole in his camouflage vest.

"Just a graze, though," he said as I unbuckled the collar. "I see you took one in the shoulder. Them hollow-points, ain't they?"

"Yes sir."

"Then it's still in there." Percy walked over to Orson and pressed two fingers into the side of his neck. "This your brother?" he asked, waiting on a pulse. I nodded. "What in holy hell was he doing to you?" I didn't answer. "Reckon we better get us to a doctor."

I came to my feet and, starting for the back door, said, "I have to get some things from the cabin first. Would you mind helping me?"

"You bet."

Leaving Orson's vacant eyes open, Percy took his shotgun as he followed me through the obliterated door, back out into the snow. He yelled something about my friend, but my panting drowned his voice, and I didn't stop to ask what he'd said. My shoulder burned now.

A snowmobile idled in front of the cabin. When I reached the front porch, I glanced back and saw that Percy lagged fifteen feet behind, holding his side with his left hand, the shotgun in his right.

Upon entering the cabin, I closed the door behind me. In the perfect gloom, I could see nothing. *Neither will Percy.* I peered out the window, watched Percy wading through the snow, his body illuminated by the snowmobile's single headlight. Receding into the shadows so he wouldn't see me, I thought, *I'll just knock him unconscious. There's food here, and he isn't badly injured. Someone will come for him. There's no other way.* His boots thumped up the steps.

I inched back toward the hinges of the door so I'd be behind him when he entered.

"Dave!" he yelled as the front door swung open. "What was you saying about—"

Ammonia.

Warm breath misted the nape of my neck.

I turned and faced Luther, smiling in the darkness.

# EPILOGUE

**LUTHER** greets the morning with a smile.

Climbing out of bed, he dons jeans and two sweaters and walks into the living room, smiling at Percy's frozen burgundy puddle on the stone.

While the coffee brews, he steps out onto the front porch. Large snowflakes drift lackadaisically down from the overcast sky.

"Howdy, boys."

Orson and Percy don't answer. They sit in their rocking chairs on opposite sides of the door, still as sculptures, their open, unblinking eyes staring into the desert, into nothing. They're upset with him because he made them stay out all night in the cold.

Sitting down on the steps, he listens but doesn't hear it yet. That's all right, though. It's only 10:45. He is not anxious. Beyond the shed, a brown speck darts through the snow—a coyote, foraging. It woke him last night, crooning to the moon.

He hears an infinitesimal drone. Standing up leisurely, he stretches his arms above his head and fetches Percy's twelve-gauge from the breakfast table. Setting it beside him on the front porch, he sits back down on the steps to wait.

The snowmobile streaks across the desert, a black dot skimming the snow.

Percy's wife pulls up on her SnowKat and parks beside her late husband's snowmobile. In her umber bib and black parka, she removes her helmet and dismounts, the snow rising above her waist. Her face is robust and wizened like Percy's, and her hair sweeps long and gray behind her shoulders. She smiles at Luther and leans against the SnowKat to catch her breath. He can see two cabins in her sunglasses.

"Hi, there," he says, chipper. "Pam, is it?"

"Yep."

"It was kind of Percy to bring me over here last night. I was very worried about my friends getting stranded in the storm."

"Well, I appreciate you boys keeping him company last night. I brought your toolbox, Percy, so maybe we can fix your Kat good enough to get home. I always told him I'd kick the shit out of him if he left without a cell. What do you say there, Perce?" She glances at her husband, on Luther's left.

"You report him missing to anyone?" Luther asks, staving off another wave of light-headedness. Pam steps forward, her head curiously tilted at her husband. Luther takes two shells of double-aught buckshot from his pocket.

"Not since I got you on the horn," she says, but she's not looking at him. "Hey, Percy!" She removes her sunglasses, squints at her husband, then at Luther, befuddled. Blood runs over the tip of Luther's left boot into the snow. "The hell's wrong with him?"

"Oh, he's dead."

She smiles, as though Luther'd made a joke, and comes a step closer. When she sees Percy's throat, she looks at Luther, then at Orson, and screams. A raven launches out of the snow beside the shed, croaking bitterly. Pam turns and bounds back toward the SnowKat.

Luther breaks the breech of the shotgun and slides the shells home.

■

Three hours later, he unwinds on the front porch, sipping from a mug of black coffee. He is not void of kindness. He has allowed Pam and Percy to sit side by side, and even arranged Pam's hand to rest in her husband's lap. They will freeze together. That is not altogether unromantic.

"I'm going to bring you guys a new friend," he says. "How would you like that?" He looks over at Orson and slaps him on the back, an arctic slab of stone. "Don't talk much, do you?" Luther guffaws.

He believes now that he is the perfection of Orson, and he burns with ecstasy.

A new thread of warm blood runs down his inner thigh. . . .

■

Luther revives on his back, staring up into the ceiling of the covered porch, the spilt coffee already iced into the wool of his sweater. He sits up. The clouds are gone, the sun low in the sky, half-obscured behind that distant white bluff. Tingling specks of black have infiltrated his vision—particles of dying that will soon overtake him. A small blood puddle has frozen on the wood beneath his feet, rosy in the petering sun. He is blisteringly cold. The pain is back, but he does not respond to discomfort in the whimpering, human fashion.

He is indomitable, though he should depart soon if he intends to survive the bullet Andrew Thomas put inside him.

He stands, takes up the shotgun, and staggers back into the cabin. At the end of the hallway, he unlocks the door of the guest room and kicks it open.

Andrew Thomas lies motionless on the bed.

"Get up," Luther says. He hasn't entered the room since the previous night, when he dragged Andrew inside. With a pained exhalation, Andrew struggles to sit up against the logs. The quilt still wrapped around his shoulders, he shivers, his breath steaming.

"Come with me," Luther says.

Andrew looks up at him, vanquished. "I heard the shotgun. Are they all dead?"

"Come with me."

Orson's brother looks down at the floor, tears filling his eyes. "Just kill me."

Luther falters. Lurching into the wall, blood dripping from the hem of his blue jeans, he tries to take aim. But the shotgun slips from his hands and he slumps down upon the stone.

.

I lift the shotgun from the floor and touch my finger to one of the triggers. When I place the barrel against Luther's chest, I can taste the madness, and my God it's sweet. I want to squeeze the trigger, feel the shotgun buck against my shoulder, and watch him bleed out on the stone. In short, I *ache* to kill him, which is precisely why I don't.

.

I drag Luther, alive but fading, onto the porch and bind him with seventy feet of rope to the last available rocking chair. Then I lift the red fleece blanket I took from Orson's bed and wrap it around Percy

Madding and the woman beside him, who I assume was his wife. I want to bury them, but the ground is frozen beneath the snowpack. This is all I can do for the man who saved my life.

When I've managed to close Percy's frosted eyelids, I wade out into the snow and turn and behold the dying and the dead.

The parting rays of a cold sun gild the spectacle of the front porch, a sight I will never be rid of: Percy Madding, his wife, Orson, and Luther Kite, each in a rocking chair, three dead, one not far behind.

It startles me when Luther speaks. He shivers now, his teeth clicking uncontrollably. I cannot imagine him surviving the night. I wonder whether he'll bleed to death, or if the cold will claim him first.

"You stand there appalled," he says. "At what, Andrew?"

"At all this blood, Luther."

"We all want blood. We *are* war. That's the code. War and regression and more and more blood. Tell me it doesn't speak to you." Luther's black hair whips across a pale, bloodless face. He awaits my reply, but I have none.

At last, I approach my brother. Our faces are inches apart. Orson's eyes remain open, his mouth frozen into the slightest grin. The abject violation of the Maddings and every other human being he butchered consumes me, and I scream at him, raging, my voice filling the desert: "Is this beauty, Orson? Is this truth?"

Then, like a fever breaking, finally I start to cry.

■

Eastward, I glide across the snow toward 191 under the purple immensity of the Wyoming sky, and the madness diminishes as the cabin falls farther behind. I wonder if Luther is dead yet. I wonder many things.

The skis scrape across the pavement, and I bring the snowmobile to a halt on the other side of the road. Alighting, I unfasten the two suitcases filled with clothes and the contents of Orson's drawer. I sit down on the shoulder. The highway has been plowed—the only snow on the road is windblown powder. All is still. My left arm throbs, but luckily, Percy was wrong. The bullet tore through—I extracted the mushroom of lead from the back of my shoulder this morning.

The sun is gone. Ancient images of stars and planets commence filling the night sky.

The moon crawls above the Winds at my back, and I cast a lunar shadow across the road. The empty, pruinose highway stretches on, north and south, as far as I can see.

I'm so cold. I stand and stamp my feet on the road. Instead of sitting back down on the shoulder, I walk out into a thigh-deep drift and make a snow angel. Lying flat on my back, a wall of white enclosing me, all I can see now is the cosmos, and all I can feel is the steady infusion of cold.

My thoughts become electric.

I think of Orson's poem. Defiant. Courageous perhaps.

*If we'd never stepped into your tunnel, we'd still be in this desert.*

*Mom . . .*

*Walter . . .*

*I will not be returning to North Carolina.*

As the cold strengthens, the madness seems to ebb, and my mind clears.

Peace overruns me.

■

I'm nearly asleep when the distant mumble of a car engine reaches me. For a moment, I consider whether I should lie here and die. I've stopped shivering, and false warmth flows through me.

I struggle to sit up. Headlights appear, heading northbound out of Rock Springs. I rise, brush the snow from my clothes, and trudge stiffly into the road. *A transfer truck,* I predict, and standing on the dotted line, I wave my arms when the beam strikes me.

Much to my surprise, the bumper of a long white suburban stops ten feet from my waist.

The driver's window lowers at my approach, and a man several years my junior smiles until he sees the bruises that blacken my face. Elbows on the console, his pretty wife looks warily at me, the side of her face lit blue by the lucent dashboard clock. Three children sleep in the backseat, spread across one another in a tangle of small sibling appendages.

"Are you all right?" the husband asks.

"I don't know. I just . . . I need a ride to the next town. Wherever you're going. Please." The man glances at his wife. Her lips purse.

"Where's your car?"

"I don't have one."

"Well, how'd you get here?"

"Will you please take me to the next town? You're the only car that's passed all night."

The man turns once more to his wife, their eyes consulting.

"Look, we're going to visit family in Montana," he says. "But Pinedale is about fifty miles up the road. We'll take you that far. You can hop in through the back."

"Thank you. I'll grab my things."

"Richard," his wife mutters.

I lift my suitcases from the snow and walk to the back of the suburban. Opening the cargo doors, I stow my luggage on the floor and climb inside.

"Please keep it down back there," the wife whispers. "We want them to sleep through the night." She motions to her children as though she were displaying jewels.

The rear bench seat has been removed, so I find a place on the floor amid the family's luggage: a red cooler, canvas bags, suitcases, a laundry basket filled with toys. With my suitcases at my feet, I curl up against the cooler and draw my knees into my chest. We begin to move, and I stare out the back window, watching the linear moonlit strip of highway spooling out beneath the tires with increasing speed.

We climb subtly for a half hour. Then we're cruising along a plateau, and I'm looking back across the desolate flatland, scanning for two black specks in the sea of snow.

In the front seat, the woman whispers to her husband, "You're a sweet man, Rich." She strokes the back of his neck.

The vents channel warmth into my face, and the speakers emit a solacing oceanic ambience: sparse piano, waves and seagulls, the calming voice of a man reading Scripture.

And as Orson, Luther, and the Maddings harden on the cabin porch, in the massive desertic silence, I bask in the breathing of the children.